The Yogi of Cockroach Court

BOOKS BY FRANK WATERS

Midas of the Rockies (1937)
People of the Valley (1941)
The Man Who Killed the Deer (1942)
The Colorado (1946)
The Yogi of Cockroach Court (1947, 1972)
Masked Gods: Navajo and Pueblo Ceremonialism (1950)
The Earp Brothers of Tombstone (1960)
Book of the Hopi (1963)
Leon Gaspard (1964)
The Woman at Otowi Crossing (1966)
Pumpkin Seed Point (1969)
Pike's Peak (1971)

THE Yogi of Cockroach Court

FRANK WATERS

SWALLOW PRESS/OHIO UNIVERSITY PRESS
ATHENS

First Swallow Press / Ohio University Press edition 1987
00 99 98 97 96 95 94   7 6 5 4 3 2

Swallow Press/Ohio University Press books
are printed on acid-free paper ∞

ISBN 0-8040-0613-X (pbk)
Library of Congress Catalog Card Number 72-91922

The Yogi of Cockroach Court was first published by
Rinehart & Company, Inc., New York, 1947

The line quoted from *Hindustan* on page 65 is reprinted by
permission of The Forster Music Publisher, Inc.
Copyright 1918 and 1946 by Forster Music Publisher, Inc., Chicago

Nos infaman y nos menoscaban, porque somos plebeyos.
Solo nostros que lo hemos sentidos sabemos lo que
son penas, lo que son congojas, como es notorio!

Hexotziquense

The Yogi of Cockroach Court

PROLOGUE

SO BRIGHTLY blazed the sun upon the dunes and down
the curving beach, so tranquilly dozed the village under
its ragged palms, that only the rising wind marked September's
ominous departure. Under its steady drive the village waited.
Men sat and mended nets, backs to the stinging sand. On the
fifteenth day of the wind they began to shake their heads and
mutter.

"Sí, hace quince dias."

"True, my friend. For fifteen days now. The storm will
come soon."

The nights became colder. The wind off the sierras cut
sharper with sand from the dunes. The deep blue of the water
changed to a drab steel grey. And still the village waited in the
steady, growing wind.

Now in the wet grey mist of early evening the wormy
boat, *El Pez-Gallo—The Flying Fish,* rode in on a seventh
wave. A dozen hands were waiting to tie her fast to the creaking pier.

"Hola! El Yanqui!"

"Cómo está, Señor?"

The white man strode down the planks in wet dungarees and a ragged sweater. He waved his hand contemptuously, but made no other answer. The men fell back. For years they had known the Yanqui and the old boat in which he carried their fish to Guaymas and other ports across the gulf, and sometimes their sharkskins as far south as La Paz. In the wake of his broad back he left trailing the discreet eponym, "El Borracho"—the drunkard. For in the square black bottle that was his sole companion, he found his only peace outside drunken oblivion. Two, four weeks later, he returned to the water-stained shack close to the rotting pier.

Here Jesús and the Romeros ate and slept in two rooms stained with the smell of fish. Blue totoabas from the muddy mouth of the Colorado, sometimes a hundredweight or bigger, from whose "buche" bladder Jesús might obtain two needed pesos per kilogram from the Yanqui who sold it for six; the tunny fish known as "atun"; the bonito and corbina, both mackerel; the golden "dorado" finch, enemy of the flying fish; the bagre, white-bellied tarpon with two mustaches long as those on any human lips; the red snapper, huachinago; the green spotted rock bass, cabrilla; large vaya kelp-bass; shell turtles; water hogs; rooster fish; and sometimes a swordfish or a shark.

Jesús was an easy patrón whose swart brown features and fierce mustaches belied his tolerant fat. Each evening he sat on the pier, his broad back against the creaking wall of his shack, smoking the cigarros his calloused hands were always rolling. The Señora was a small wiry skeleton hung with a black cotton rebozo and two ragged petticoats. She seemed forever kneeling; beating out corn meal and patting it into tortillas, or telling off the wooden beads around her throat to insure Jesús a big catch and a safe return.

With them and their five children also waited the result of one of the Yanqui's previous stumblings ashore—a quivering, fear-struck little bastard of this drunken white stray from the States and a Mexican mother the boy never knew. It was a life and family whose uneventful peace was interrupted only by the Yanqui's return.

Now, seeing him enter the door with Jesús at his heels, the boy crowded farther into the corner. The Señora kneeling before the fire raised her head. Her black currant eyes divined instantly the temper of the man, unshaven and hollow-eyed, who stood waiting in the dim flicker of the candle. She dropped her glance immediately.

"Well," demanded El Borracho, "where are yeh?"

The boy stood up, frightened by the harsh twang that had none of the softness of Jesús' voice.

"Come here. Christ! Don't yeh know enough English yet to say howdado?"

The boy crept forth and stared steadily at the man who had cuffed him against the wall too often to be ignored. And as the Yanqui's eyes swept over him and took in the big brown eyes, the splotches of smooth brown torso and bare dirty legs, something of the futility of his own life filled him with sudden resentment. His hand reached out and flung the boy back into the corner.

"Jesus! Think of havin' to be a daddy to that! And every time I come back I think you'll be gettin' different. Why, you ain't nothin' but a dirty little greaser."

He slumped down upon a chair. From a breast pocket he drew out a canvas sack. "Jesús!" he spoke to Romeros giving the Spanish sound to the proper name, "He-soos!"

Romeros at the table held out his hand and the white man

filled it with silver from the sack. "The fish pay you well this time." Then he called to the woman. "Señora! La cena. You got something to eat tonight?"

In the dim smelly room all were silent while he ate. Every eye fastened upon the big bearded man of whom so many tales were told along that dreary strip of coast. The Yanqui whose little boat was known in every port along the Gulf of Cortez; to whom they entrusted precious cargoes of sharkskins and loads of fish, and who always returned some money; the white man afraid of none of the bitter storms that raged the Gulf; El Borracho, the drunken one, of whom they were afraid.

He ate slowly. Finished at last, he let out his belt. From a pants pocket he drew out a pipe. When it was going he turned to Romeros.

"Well. You got anything to drink?"

Jesús glanced quickly at his wife. Followed by the eyes of the children silent in the corner, the old woman rose from her knees and placed an earthen jug on the table. "Sí Señor. Agua dulce, Señor."

"Hell no!" The man's heavy voice filled the room. "Two days out floatin' in that damned tub in the rain and now you give me a jug of water! Damn yeh, I want something to drink. Tequila, whiskey you old fool, sabe?"

The woman averted her eyes and again sank to her knees on the floor. Romeros spread his hands. "No, my friend. Siento mucho. I am so so-rry but there is nothing. No hay wheesky, no hay nada."

The big body of the white man twisted about in his chair. "Hell and Maria!" He wet his lips and leaned across the table. "Got any skins to go or want anything? Get 'em ready by tomorrow morning if you do. I'm goin'."

"No-no, Señor, no!" Jesús' face glowed fiercely eager in the dim light. "You do not go! It is time for the storm. Listen, my frien'." He cocked his head to one side. Above the faint, intermittent patter of drops against the plank walls rose a steady recurring blow of wood against wood. "Listen to your good boat *El Pez-Gallo* which the waves bump against the wharf. The wind an' the rain already come. For fifteen days she blow, Señor, and now listen to the rain. No boat can go out in el Golfo now. You stay here with us, amigo."

The white man rose and kicked his chair against the bare wall. "Pagh. Stay here with yer leaky teapots and two oars. What in hell's a little wind to me if I can get offshore? Lemme get her headed against the wind and I'll make *The Flying Fish* think she is flyin'!"

In two strides he reached the door and yanked it open. A driving burst of wind filled the room. In the splutter of the candle the Señora threw herself before the tiny stove to protect the flames. The boy and the children drew into a closer mass of brown faces and bare legs. The Yanqui slammed the door, reached down and pulled the Señora from the stove. "Here, old woman. Sure you ain't got a bottle ditched around here somewhere?"

She quietly slumped back down again without raising her head. The white man straightened and brought out the little sack from his shirt pocket. Watching the boy, he drew out some coins. "Here, you little brat. Go out and ask around till you find me a drink. No playin' now."

Romeros spoke quickly. At the low command his eldest son, a lad of some sixteen years, rose with the boy and took the money. The two of them went out into the night.

El Borracho caught up his chair and flopped down, extending his long legs before the tiny fire. "Lookin' for a storm, now, eh?" he turned to ask the Mexican at the table.

Romeros looked up from the cigarette he was rolling between his meaty brown fingers.

"I said what you all so damned scared about? 'Fraid of a bit of wind. Trade winds, He-soos; have 'em every year, that's all."

The Mexican laid down his brown-paper cigarette on the table top. Swiftly, with that odd quick motion of the hand which repetition throughout the years makes almost indistinguishable to the unobserving eye, Jesús crossed himself and made the mark on his forehead.

"No Señor. It is the 'Cordonaza de San Francisco'. Always on the birthday of San Francisco comes the storm. Señor, you keep this boat here with me!"

"You an' yer Santos!" sneered the white man. "Think there's always a storm fer a birthday party, eh? Well let the old woman tell it to her beads. Tomorrow I'm goin'." He turned to the door "And if that ain't that damn kid . . ."

Cold wet, the boy and his companion walked in. The boy laid down a bottle, almost full, and retreated to the far corner, his eyes upon his father. The man seized upon it instantly and held it to the light. "Tequila! Fish oil! Is that all there is around this place?" Still muttering, he clutched at the bottle and crawled up a ladder to a small loft. "Don't you fergit," his bearded face leered down into the light. "Git yer stuff ready. Tomorrow, rain or shine, I'm goin'." Scowling like a dog with a bone, he vanished aloft. . . .

2

It was not yet dawn when the boy awoke. A cold darkness filled the room. Recurrent gusts blew through the cracks, and about his legs wrapped a chill he could not kick off. Above the clatter of the loose door could be heard the rising scream of the wind and an angry hiss of waves breaking into a froth about the piles outside. Through it all came the low

monotonous sound of *The Flying Fish* hurling herself against
the pier. The boy buried himself deeper into the cuddle of entwined children.

Already the Señora was up. Between gusts he could hear
the scuff of her bare feet upon the floor. Soon a fire was lit
and by light of the tiny flames she could be seen kneeling over
the morning tortillas and the remains of last night's fish.
Jesús stood listening at the door. He opened it an inch. A
violent burst drove it back upon its hinges and with Jesús to
the wall. A wedge of water swirled in the door, leaving behind a momentary vista of grey cloud and grey sea before
Romeros hurled it shut. From the corner came the whimper
of a child crying with cold from the sudden deluge. The
Señora arose from her knees. With a quick hand she lifted
the child, a chubby girl of four, and deposited her beside one
of the sleeping dogs. The brown fingers of the child twisted
into the hair of the beast as she squirmed between its legs and
then lay quiet. The boy rose and crept to the fire. Shaking
with cold, he crouched down beside the Señora and stretched
out his bare legs.

There was no dawn save the growing grey gloom that
rolled in from the sea. Slowly the lines of table and chair and
keg emerged from wall and shadow. Without movement other
than the ceaseless, repetitive twitch of his fingers as he made
cigarettes, Jesús sat quiet in his chair listening to the bray
of the storm. On the floor beside the boy the Señora told her
beads, her low voice subdued by the monotonous spatter of
the rain.

At midmorning the wind veered. In an hour the rain had
stopped. A quick knock raised Romeros from his chair. He
let in two men, then crawled up the ladder. When he came
back down he shook his head at the two men. For several

minutes they talked among themselves. Then Jesús put on his big coat and with the two men went out into the wind.

Steadily the wooden shack had been growing colder. Breezy drafts cut the room like the chill strokes of blades. With instinctive perception, the boy and the five children sensed a wordless fear in the face the Señora raised from her beads. One of the dogs had risen and stood alert, ears forward. A sudden change, ominous and quiet, seemed to have gripped the room before the boy realized the wind had stopped. Slowly the dog shook its head from side to side. Then with a whine the animal lay down with its nose between its feet, eyes open and cowering. The voice of the Señora had stopped. Her hands were quiet, unmoving, and she crouched as though expecting the shack to collapse under the sudden cold silence that held the room.

A little after noon El Borracho appeared at the loft. His heavy-booted feet swung over the opening and felt for the ladder rungs. Half way down he slipped and fell heavily. Then he clumped across the floor and lifted the water jug to his mouth. A thin trickle crawled down his front. "Qué hora es?" he demanded the time. "Why didn't you wake me like I told you?" His eyes flitted about the room. "Where's Jesús? Don't he know I want to get away?"

He opened the door and without a word stamped out. The boy, the old Señora, and the three eldest children followed him out the door. Other villagers were crossing the beach, trailing him to the pier.

A cold calm held the world in a silent grip. There was now no wind. Even the palms rose motionless into the sky like jagged rents through a grey curtain of mist. At the end of the short pier Jesús Romeros was standing with a group of men. Earlier that morning they had gone out to make fast *The Flying Fish*. She was lashed to the piles and lay heaving with the rise and fall of the waves. The men were watching the breakers.

The fog had lifted, yet there was no horizon. Somewhere, farther than even the sharp eyes of the Mexican fisherfolk could see, the grey expanse of water merged into the grey expanse of sky. One had the feeling that the line where water met the sky was higher than they knew—the unspoken feeling that all that water so quiet beyond the surf would at any movement of the wind be released to seek its level up the sides of the hills behind the beach.

Without wind, with no movement of surface swells or breakers, the whole sea seemed to be rising and falling as with the slow beat of a mighty pulse. Higher than they could believe, the water rose without a ripple, smooth as silk, into swells unequaled in the sight of any man. Suddenly, with a faint coruscant sparkle of water-jewels upon their crests, the great swells broke with a ferocity whose thunder roared miles down the beach. The swirling waters churned as from a mill-race into a ripping foam which had torn into shreds the few boats left out during the night. Higher than any mark of tide the water swirled up the sand. And then again the whole sea seemed lifted from far below, tilted in a smooth incline, and thunderously slid in upon the beach.

All morning these great swells had been rolling in. And still the sea seemed to be rising steadily even as the men watched. They were aroused by the appearance of the Yanqui.

"Loo-k Señor!"

"See how high is the water today!"

They pointed to the swells and the surf along the beach. "See how we have tie El Pez-Gallo for you. Carlos he lose his boat last night. It will be a big storm, Señor. You do not go, no?"

For a moment the white man stood still. In that one mo-

ment as he stood facing the darkening sky, with the roar of
the breakers incongruous in the dreary calm, he glimpsed the
face of his inevitable fate. Then his whiskey-soaked mind,
inflamed to a greater hunger by last night's bottle, awoke him
to his folly.

"Hell yes I'm goin'! What'd I tell yeh last night? Get her
untied and we'll put her past the breakers at low tide. We'll
have to move fast."

The men stood quiet. With an experience born of long
years along the Gulf and innumerable encounters with those
tempests of wind and sea first recorded when Cortez himself
crossed the waters that hold his name in the Spanish tongue,
they sensed better than any falling barometer the ominous
silence. But too, they knew the Yanqui whose bearded frown
brooked no other power than his own foolish will. Obediently
they moved towards *The Flying Fish*.

In an hour the lashings of the boat were removed. Held
only by a dozen lines half-hitched around all available posts,
she awaited low tide.

Four o'clock came. The sky was steadily growing darker.
A black smudge as though from a far off conflagration swept
over the strip of beach. Now and again a puff of wind swept
spume from the surface of the water, and passing through the
village took with it every loose board from the roofs of the
shacks. And still the breakers churned into an impenetrable
milky froth. It was soon apparent there was to be no low tide;
the water was higher along the beach than though the tide
were full.

El Borracho could wait no longer. The men began their
efforts to launch the boat.

Three times, its smoking exhaust making a cloud of
white steam at the stern and the muffled staccato of the old
engine puny in the roar of the surf, *The Flying Fish* made a

clumsy leap into the swirling froth and was hurled back before she could make a start. Three times all the men along the beach heaved at the spreading tangents of ropes that made a dripping web of lines from the old boat, and again had to maneuver the launch to the end of the pier.

At the fourth attempt the boat shook herself free.

Catching the frothy end of a breaker, the white man kicked open the throttle. The boat shook violently, weathered the twist of the ebb, and nosed into the lift of the coming roll. High on the tide she poised, streaming long wet ropes from her exposed stern. Luckily she caught hold. The boat settled and El Borracho held his own. In the next moment he churned into a smooth swell. Past the line of breakers *The Flying Fish* headed for the open sea. Rolling but slightly, her one high stick like a match upthrust against the dark sky, the small boat swiftly receded.

There was no sound along the beach. The people watched without comment the still visible figure of the Yanqui busy at the stern. In five minutes he was lost in the thickening gloom. As though suddenly released from something they would never see again and would soon forget, the villagers ran for their shacks without talk.

Already wet drops had begun to fall.

In less than an hour the wind began. Even now it was dark as midnight. With the wind came first a driving burst of rain. Inside the shack, the boy crouched with the Romeros in the middle of the floor. Impending disaster withheld all speech. Only the Señora on her knees mumbled in a monotonous voice snatches of old litanies. Jesús sat stupefied as the peasant animal that he was. His hands clutched each other in his lap, forgetting to roll their usual cigarettes.

That evening the storm struck: the periodical gale known throughout the Sea of Cortez as the "Cordonaza de San Francisco." Without warning, as though the very walls of sky enclosing that silent breathless beach had collapsed, the wind drove down upon the waiting land. Its hollow, resounding blow boomed for miles. With the rebound the gale lifted roofs from the huddle of shacks. Farther inland even thatched ramadas collapsed. In every direction the knives of the gale whirled and cut at everything that stood upright in its path.

From its shriek, the boy heard it coming. Hand in hand with the eldest Romeros, he ran for the door. Jesús threw himself across the bodies of the children. The roof of the shack flung back as though on hinges. As it fell the small loft collapsed.

Looking back, the boy saw the little girl on the floor before the falling timbers obscured her face from sight. He glimpsed the horrible contortion of the Señora's face as she screamed, heard her voice in the shriek of the wind. Jesús with small Carlos in one arm was crawling toward a split in the wall. Then the wind whipped the boy flat on the sand.

Seaward behind him, distinguishable even in darkness, rose a black wall of water so solid that it did not seem to move. Again he felt himself on his feet and running up the lift of dunes.

"La altura! Jesú y María! Dónde vamos?"

The shriek was lost in the roar. The floor of the pier crumpled like paper. There was a crash as the water struck the shack. The walls collapsed and instantly vanished from sight. One great mass, upended on the crest, turned lazily about and then borne by the swift rush of water swept down upon the boy.

Pulled by his companion, he began to run forward. Almost instantly the water was upon them. His companion's clutching hand relaxed upon his arm as a huge timber struck him and washed away. Then the boy himself was submerged.

The wave swept him up the beach. Gasping, half choked, the boy felt himself clawing at the sand as the water receded. Blinded, in all the pain of a terrible dream, he lay vomiting water. Then without thought, too stunned to direct his bruised little body, he began to crawl with the wind and rain toward the shelter of an old adobe that once had stood far back from the line of beach.

In this only building whose walls were left standing, crowded the villagers who had escaped the storm. The roofless room was full. The boy crawled inside. No one gave him a glance. A pathetic huddle, they lay or sat immobile upon the floor waiting for the next manipulation of San Francisco's mighty hand.

All night the storm swept up and down the two enclosing coasts and ravaged both land and sea. And all night the boy crouched shivering in the room with the roar of the gale in his ears, oppressed by the vacuous silence of those beside him. Towards morning the whole sea lifted with the inundation. Like the last wet vomit of a great sea monster dying from internal convulsions, the wreckage-laden water swirled to their feet and swiftly subsided.

The storm was spent.

In the first light of day the survivors scattered to their tasks. There was no need for words. Each was alone with his own loss. The sun came out, languidly bathing the wreckage of the village. Already the night and the storm began to yawn like a great black chasm between the boy and his childhood.

A wagon was being prepared to go after aid; somewhere a horse was caught. Wrapped in an old coat four sizes large which he pulled out of the sand, the boy crawled into the wagon bed. Within an hour they were deep in the hills above the bay.

Near noon the wagon reached the road crossing over the

sierras. A truck was standing at the junction in front of a store and several thatched ramadas. Unseen by the driver, the boy crawled under the heavy tarpaulin. Here he crouched sleeping while the truck jolted onward. The rain was beginning again; the storm, swirling northward over the mountains, was bringing rain to a desert that had not known a full inch of water in five years.

It was dark when he awoke and peeped out under the dripping canvas. A scatter of small, twinkling lights grew to a large yellow cluster as the truck rumbled into town. The boy slipped out and crossed the slimy adobe road.

Shrouded in the darkness, he crouched down against the wall of the little corner bar. Water filled the pockets of the coat drooping to his bare heels, and tiny rivulets from his hair and clothes joined those which ran across the walk and down into the gutter. A sudden pennant of sheet lightning flung across the sky, revealing a long row of squat adobes. Through the opening a new torrent poured down upon the Borderfront cabarets, bars and cantinas that yet remained unquenched.

Upholding the tail of his coat, the boy moved out into the street. At every slap of the swing doors he caught apprehensive glimpses of brown and scarlet-slashed faces swirling lip to lip through the smoke, heard the sound of drunken laughter and the whine of strings. Then a quick twist of the street left all this behind. Against the gloom of the railroad right-of-way only a few dim, blue-lit windows glowed.

The last door was open. The boy peeked inside, then entered. Down one side of the long room extended a counter on which sat a smoking kerosene lamp. The shadow of his figure kept him pace along the opposite wall, creeping past kegs, boxes and bales, a stack of sugar cane. Toward the back was a pile of burlap sacking. The boy looked about furtively, then flopped down. Immediately he fell asleep.

For moments the cluttered shop remained silent and motionless. Then from the shadows behind the counter a yellow, wrinkled hand reached out to turn down the smoking lamp. After a time a stool squeaked; an old Chinese eased down. In black felt slippers he scuffed across the dusty plank floor and stared down at the sleeping waif. Stooping, he gathered him up and staggered off to the back room.

CHAPTER ONE

THERE IS something in rain and night that becomes a powerful mesmer. The slanting silver rain unravels the curtain of years. The night reveals its components hidden, mysterious and unreal. To one rooted on a corner, the soggy and sullen Border-street before him takes on then its true character.

Everything seems timeless and indestructible, as if he had always known it and would forever—its shrieking cantinas and casinos, the sinister fronts of bar and bagnio, its open lottery stalls, the cluttered windows of Chinese stores. They are no longer faces of buildings; they are faces of moods. And the figures slouching by are inscrutable and enigmatic words written in an unknown tongue.

The deeper meaning of all these makes itself felt in rain and night as at no other time. Yet it is is still unintelligible. What holds a watcher mesmerized he does not know. But if it does have a focus it may well be no more than a single light at the dark end of that dwindling street where ever gleams, though faintly, The Lamp Awake. . . .

Unsteady on his feet, Barby heaved away from the wall of the corner bar. Wide-shouldered, lean-hipped in muddy dungarees, and with the broad, brutal face of a half-breed, he stared drunkenly down the street. Something had first drawn him there years before when he was a ragged little chamaco. It still held a summons he could not ignore. And lurching forward he cursed in a voice thick with mezcal the fate that had kept them both unchanged.

It was the storm which tonight made the street seem familiarly strange, as though he had not known it every night in all the years. The same alcoholic stench and glittering signs. The same heavy laughter and scratch of feet oozing out from the slits of the swing doors past which he reeled. But all impregnated with the same strange wonder and incalculable mystery which marked another significant turn in his life.

For now, as he slumped in another drunken stupor against the window of the last bright-lit cabaret, it happened. Inside, a young girl on the dance floor turned and looked straight into his eyes.

Before him swam the blurred and nebulous faces of a dozen others. Only hers leapt out in perfect focus. For months Barby was to remember the shock of her steady black eyes first meeting his own, the outline of her creamy oval face, the wings of her smooth black hair. Now it whispered to him he would never be without something fresh and tragic, unlooked for and forever permanent, which had come to him at sight of her face.

God damn it! Clawing at the window, he regained his footing in the slippery adobe. But when he looked inside again the girl had vanished. He staggered on.

By now he was quite ill. At the turn of the street he stopped, putting up an arm to steady himself against the wall. In the darkness he retched violently. Warm and weak with sudden sweat, he slipped to his knees and wiped off his face. Then he struggled erect again.

He felt better. For an instant he hesitated, wondering if he wanted a woman, if he wanted to go back. Barby shrugged it off and turned into the quarter. Here the river of mud gave way to a narrow, cobbled lane, Callejon de los Chinos, ill-lit with windows of greasy blue. With the curious blending of the Mexican-Chinese, the names of the shops reflected their character: "Juan Kee y Cia"; "Jose Quong"; "Chino Juan, Abarrotes Mas Baratos." Soon even these signs gave out, and there were only vertical strips of ideographs hung panellike down the doorways.

Then darkness, and at the end of the alley, The Lamp Awake. Outwardly Mexican with its adobe walls peeling from heat and rain, its weathered sign still retained the letters La Lampara though the rest long since had faded. And deep within, ever shining through the greasy window, gleamed the light that gave the Lamp its name and life.

Barby hesitated in front of the shop, then entered. A sanctuary now as on that night when first he had crept in and curled down on a pile of sacks, the room's dusty plank floor echoed his familiar steps. At the back he turned, stumbled up the rickety stairs and flung himself upon the creaking bed.

But even in sleep the face came back to haunt him. He dreamed he was drowning in a vast and powerful flood. Then suddenly it floated by on the surface above him, palely out-lined like the reflection of an oval moon on water. He gave a great gasp, heaved up to clutch and hold it fast. It slipped out of his grasp; the current caught him again; and he rolled over in bed vomiting once more.

2

It was still there before him when he came to, gutted
with sleep, next morning. A dark oval face with smooth black
wings of hair and steady blacker eyes; without background
or meaning, clear and purposeless as the residue of a dream.
He could not remember where, when or if he had seen it
before.

Half blinded and scowling, Barby reared up and struck
at the shaft of sunlight thrust through the window into his
eyes. For a moment he sat still while the passing of a freight
shook him awake. Mechanically he groped about to locate his
crumpled shirt, drew out a cigarette from the pocket and
lit it.

The devil! With a snarl at his impotent memory, he got
up and drank deeply from a jar in the corner. Then, with a
breath like a buzzard and a bursting head, he clumped downstairs.

The old Chinese was sitting at his counter. Before him lay
an abacus, its parallel wires strung with round wood discs.
In his right hand was a writing brush which he dipped into
a can of black ink paste before adding another ideograph to
a strip of yellow paper. Barby watched him a moment. Like a
pool player marking another pocket, Tai Ling slid a disc along
a wire. Then again he scribbled with his brush.

"What's goin' on?"

Tai Ling looked up with a bland smile. "You write book
no make mully. Me kleep book make mully. Me Chinese book
bessy book, hey?" He had never forgotten the boy's ludicrous
attempts to keep his books years ago. It was his favorite jest.

Barby scowled. "Oh, cut it out!" This make-believe pidgin-
English that Tai Ling sometimes affected to American visitors

when he did not want to be disturbed always made him angry.
The old man could talk as good Spanish or English as any
body! "What's all the rumpus?"

Tai Ling kept smiling. "Noise? Ho no. You dlunk?"

"The hell! There was. It woke me up."

"Ho! Yeh. All same tluck bling fish. You catch him, yeh.
Plenty quick move on now."

Fish. Tuesday. The goddamned fish! He had forgotten.

"I'm sorry," Tai Ling said quietly now with a gentler
smile. "You'd better eat something first. I have already sent
to Chan Foo's for a tray. . . . Here." He slid a paper of
crushed herbs over the counter. "Maybe these will help clear
your head. As last time," he added with a sigh.

Late that afternoon, the barrel of fish cleaned and carried
to the stalls, Barby slouched up the street. He entered an empty
storeroom now used by one Bud Cross, boxing manager and
promoter, and slumped down on the floor to wait for Young
Fuera.

Before him two young Mexican lads were at it hammer
and tongs for all the smelly closeness of the room. In one
corner a great Negro, the Deuce of Spades, was jumping rope
with footwork lighter than a child's, while along the wall two
white toughs were punching bag and dummy. Barby watchced
them with little interest, although Young Fuera had promised
him some easy money for Saturday night.

It would not be the first time that he had fought in the
open ring behind the Nuevo Mundo bar—dull, short prelimi-
naries that grew fewer and fewer. He was not a fighter. He
had a natural strength, a deceptive quickness in his listless
carriage, and for three or four rounds he fought crouching
and lashing out suddenly with a smooth twist of his hips in
a disinterested savagery and with an impassive face which
made his opponent believe him better than he was. Then with

his bruises he slunk out to spend his handful of silver pesos. That was all. It was neither sport nor business. If anything it was like cleaning fish or irrigation ditches—but quicker. So that he sat half-asleep until roused by Young Fuera.

"I been looking for you. I fix it with Bud for you to make twenty pesos Saturday night. Listen to him!" He nodded toward Bud Cross, still watching the Negro. "You know he don' like you because you don' train or come around."

Barby yawned.

"Well I fix it anyway. What is one preliminary? The first! The Deuce he take the Bruiser hands down. Bud don' worry about nothin' more. And I tell him if he don' do me something once in a while"—Young Fuera spread his hands. He knew he was getting good. "So he say all right for you. Easy and very fast the first roun' to wake up the crowd. Then you fight, eh? Understan'? Jesú Cristo!—what is the matter, you asleep? Don' I tell you you need a woman! You come with me. I show you what I have fix up for us after the fight. Baby, how nice!"

If there was one thing Barby did not want it was a woman. It seemed to him as he walked down the street with Young Fuera that there had been far too many already. Nevertheless he listened without reply to Young Fuera.

"This Kid Mike is a dub you will take to home easy. You don' have much on boxing, all right, but you got a left very fine. Carajo! But this is not what I have to say. Now, I show you."

With a nudge Young Fuera led the way into Las Quince Letras. Over his beer he lowered his voice. "These two girls they come to town only few days and now they dance here. One, her name is Sal, is the big one with straw hair and nice white skin. She my sweetheart one time at Agua Prieta. I take her, eh? Now what you think of the other—the little morena . . ."

He thumbed over his shoulder and winked at Barby who turned casually upon the same wearying scene that he had known for days and nights uncounted. Standing with one arm on the bar, glass in hand, Barby did not move an eyelid. Then suddenly the tightness of mind and body gave way. He could feel his whole being drawn out through his helpless eyes by the apparition he had seen or dreamed the night before.

The girl was sitting alone at her assigned work table on the edge of the dance floor. She was small and well formed, her skin a light iodine. Only her hair was that of the pure Indian. Even after a busy hour under the whirling fans its two black wings lay folded smoothly upon her head. Nor did she reflect either the bold truculence or inviting softness of all the other percentage girls whose tables and ready company awaited any man. So that lured by her neat and self-sufficient little figure, there were many who marked her for a new prize. Hearing the approaching steps of another taker, the girl lifted her childish head and turned her face.

Thus it happened that Barby, for the second time, felt the shock of her unsheathed gaze. For an instant only—and again! —the glance of her steady black eyes never wavered from his. It had the queer agelessness, the flinty reptilian inscrutability of an Indian down from the sierras. And yet her eyes, large and darkly luminous under their long lashes, seemed to remain open before him with the sensuous softness of a fresh opened flower. It was as if with the stuporous lifting of her lids she had thrown open a profound darkness from which glittered a light for him alone. A faint flush leapt to his stolid face. Nothing could have convinced him that the girl, in her glance, did not recognize and understand him just as completely.

It was a moment that never in his life was he able to recapture. And she, casually turning her head away, rose and gave herself into the arms of a cholo who happened to have in his boleros the price of a drink.

"Guadalupe. The one I tell you about," Young Fuera was murmuring beside him. "You like her for sweetheart, eh?"

His voice recalled Barby as though from a distant past. He drank up, surprised at the froth still on his beer.

"I don' know where Sal go," grumbled Young Fuera. "She most always here too. An' I don' know Guadalupe so well. But we go Saturday night damn sure!"

Leading Barby out to a small lonchería, he sat down for a plate of beans and meat with the satisfied air of a man who has done a good day's work. "What do you say, compadre?" he laughed. "I fix it for you to fight and make love. María! How does she look to you, eh?"

Barby walked home through the thickening dusk, still hearing dull, precautionary instructions regarding Kid Mike in a clinch and the way to take a slow cross, still seeing the light in a pair of somber black eyes.

3

Tai Ling, serenely squatting behind his counter, marked with inexpressive silence Barby's passage through the room. So quiet was the old man that his impassivity matched that of the figure on the shelf behind him. It was an effigy of his favorite Bodhisattva, seated in the Buddha-posture, on a lotus-throne enhaloed by a rainbow; at his feet a fish immersed like all sentient beings in a sea of illusion, and a human skull symbolizing renunciation of this world of ignorance.

Tai Ling himself had chosen the same yogic path of spiritual deliverance from worldly illusion. But fortunately his appearance was not so forbidding. It was simply that of a gentle old man clad in a black sateen coat and ragged trousers, whose full, smiling face peered over the horizon of his counter like a ripe yellow moon.

Yet there was something about The Lamp Awake, as there was about its yogi who had chosen thus to be a lamp unto himself, that seemed impregnable to inquisitive thought. Both seemed set in the most unlikely circumstances.

Sunk in mud or dust at the end of the Callejon de los Chinos, the shop faced the railroad tracks with a serene immobility of expression. But flanking it on side and rear lay the Plaza de las Cucarachas. A dim-lit maze of lewd patios and shrieking courtyards, Cockroach Court was aptly named for the prostitutes who filled its cribs—the inafortunadas, putas and parjaritas who here were known as cucarachas.

Tai Ling found nothing incongruous in pursuing his calling among them. Where else could he find so strorg an incentive as in the court's raging evil and rampant passion?

Inside, the musty little shop was cluttered. Barrels of fish brought up from the gulf; lengths of sugar cane stacked against the wall; dusty packages of tea and rolls of matting; prepared lily roots, lotus seeds, stem ginger, lychee nuts—all the strange delicacies which crammed the jars long forgotten in the window and on the shelves. Strips of meat dried in the sun to the color and consistency of foot leather. Garbanzas. Pinto beans. Bright butcher knives. Sticky, candied sweet potatoes and Mexican dulces. Rattan slippers, leather huaraches. Paper-backed novels printed in Spanish: El Tesoro del Maelstrom; La Esposa del Sol; Luna Benamor; Sombras de Aguilas. Two pairs of faded pink rayon panties. American blue denim overalls. . . .

Ostensibly all this was for sale. Actually little sold. Like Tai Ling they seemed permanent fixtures of the shop itself..

Twice a week he distributed a barrel of fresh fish. Occasionally someone stopped for a pinch of healing herbs. On rarer occasions a stranger peeked in at the shop's placid interior before retreating back up the alley. But Tai Ling did not stir for profit or flinch from poverty. Therefore for him neither existed. And so his Lamp neither flared nor died, but remained steadily awake thoughout the years.

Chewlee Singkee, a prosperous butcher and an old friend, once asked him why he did not read newspapers and show more interest in the world at large.

"Why should I?" queried the old man. "I need but look out my door. I see women prostituting their bodies, my friends sticking knives in each others' backs, Mexicans and Chinese quarreling among themselves and both with Americans. Of course there are wars between nations, crime waves, bread riots!"

But once Tai Ling did walk across the Line to an American movie. It left a great impression upon him. For years afterward he often referred to it. "These moving people of pictures mirror our civilization more truly than anything I know," he would say. "They are always in a hurry to get nowhere. But if they ever stopped to think, the machine would break down, the illusion be dispelled."

Thereafter he stayed in his shop. But while his neighbors forever sat reckoning profit and loss, Tai Ling sat meditating on mind and matter, the non-reality of birth and death, and the threefold illusion of past, present and future.

He had accepted an Ingersoll watch in trade. He sat with it on the counter, and picking out a designated minute on the dial, watched the hand creep toward it. "This minute does not exist; it is in the future," he observed. "But now it does not exist either, it is already being carried away into the past. . . . There, it is gone!" He shook his head. "Now what were my corresponding thoughts? Clearly they cannot be identified as being the present, for they are inseparable from both the future, whence they arose as the present, and the past, into which they vanished. Certainly then, past, present and future are one; it is we who divide them." So he dispensed with the watch, hanging it on a nail with a price tag affixed, and conducted his day by the tasks to be done.

His friends were horrified.

"What would you say, old friend, if during your crazy philosophizing you find out that Chino Juan has stolen all your business?"

Tai Ling grinned.

"In that American movie I saw a man more clearly than ever I saw Chino Juan. He was alone at night and counting his money. Oh, much money! It covered the whole table. It was close enough to touch. I could have reached out and filled my pockets. But I stopped to think. And I walked out. . . . That is what I would say, my good friends. Chino Juan would steal only an illusion. But I have walked out into reality."

He broke out into a chuckle and watched them shuffle away, shaking their heads. They did not come back. So much the better. He had more time for meditation.

4

To this shop and its yogi of Chinese Alley and Cockroach Court, Barby had wandered years ago. Tai Ling did not put him out. He did not bid him stay, even with the compulsion of kindness. And for the boy it remained simply what it had been—a cluttered old shop with an open door and a bed under the baking roof.

His contributions had been little and irregular. Early each

evening Tai Ling slipped around the boy's neck the leather strap of a wooden tray loaded with salted peanuts and cashews. "There are many dualities even in our coarse material existence, and there is a strange affinity between all of them," said Tai Ling with high humor. "Salt and beer are one. Keep to the bars, boy." So Barby, a ragged little chamaco with big eyes and bare feet, would trudge back and forth between the cabarets, cantinas and casinos, his trade keeping pace with their barkeeps' wet hands to the beer spouts.

When he lengthened out into a gangling youth with sharp black eyes and a pinched brown face, he substituted a white apron for his tray and was on call in the biggest cantina. By eight o'clock the place was full, and there was plenty to meet all feverish demands: Azteca and bock beer, American whiskies, tequila and cheap mezcal; women of every size and hue in the back courts; and every game of chance—panguingui and écarté, fan-tan, parchisi, blackjack, pocar garanona and pocar robado—stud and draw, chuck-a-luck and machines in every corner. And more and more often rose the cry, "Bar boy!"

Without looking up from his smooth hands, better kept than any woman's, a dealer sang out in a sonorous voice, "Bar-r-r-by!"

A barkeep relayed the call. "Bar-by!"—Barby!—Where in hell's that boy?"

And Barby would slip through the crowd to take and receive orders. Yet night after night he returned to Tai Ling and his shop; it was his only home. He had six months schooling in the parochial school, but assaulted the priest when caught stealing sacramental wine and never returned. A sturdy lad then, wide-shouldered, thick-necked, with round solid legs, he joined a group of laborers recruited to open up another desert tract for cotton. Like a bird leaving his nest, he merely grabbed up a blanket and waved ungratefully at Tai Ling as he went out.

A year later, in town for a spree, he found himself asprawl in the gutter with a cracked head, pockets empty, and the shrieks of four prostitutes laughing into his buzzing ears. Without volitition or conscious thought he rose and staggered down the street into The Lamp Awake. Tai Ling was at his counter. Without a flicker of his eyes, he watched the boy stumble past him and upstairs to bed.

Early that melon season Barby found his next work across the Border. The ranch overseer was an American named Massey. Within a month he took the boy from the canals and put him to work around the yard. He gave him a cheap straw sombrero, let him eat second helping at the mess table, and once slapped him on the back with a jovial, "Bueno! One damn fine worker!"

Barby amply repaid him with work that would have killed off a mule in the summer heat. He spoke only English, bought a striped silk shirt, and strutted insolently among his fellows on their way back across the Border each Saturday.

On one of these nights, when he was sitting on the edge of the walk just outside the glare of the Foreign Club, he looked up to see Massey and his woman coming out. She was dressed in white silk, every movement of her body visible beneath it, her hair gleaming amber in the light. Emboldened by enough tequila to assert his presence and grinning with frank approval, Barby got to his feet and lounged up to them.

The woman gave a tiny cry. Massey, with one look, thrust out a straight arm to the boy's chin and stuck out his foot. As Barby fell, neatly tripped, he heard the man's contemptuous laugh as he walked off with the woman.

"—just one of these cowardly, stinkin' drunk greasers! A

white man's got to teach them their place ever so often. He won't do anything!"

The words kept burning into his mind long after he had rolled to one side, and still asprawl, reached into his pocket for a cigarette. Sitting up, he smoked it through, rose slowly to his feet, and slouched off into the darkness. That night he bought a knife, long bladed and well hafted with bone, fitting snugly into hand and belt. He never went back to the ranch.

For a week he waited, lounging each night in the shadows beside the casino doorway. Then again on a late Saturday Massey strolled out of the door, alone. Dropping his cigarette and softly crushing out its glow as he stealthily drew himself erect, Barby replaced it with the knife.

It was not yet ten o'clock; and in the glare of light escaping from inside the casino, the man's body stood clearly revealed against the soft blackness of the desert night. The boy could see his wide muscular shoulders expanding his soft white shirt, the resolute profile under his soiled panama. Massey had been lucky at cards; a handful of silver pesos rattled in the pocket of his trousers as he approached across the wide portal. Still Barby waited in the shadows, casting quick apprehensive glances down and up the deserted street. Massey yawned, pushed back his hat on his head, and lit his pipe.

The boy gulped a deep breath, lifted his right hand to his belt. His fingers closed comfortingly about the heavy bone haft; his thumb at the back to drive it securely home; the long cool blade along his wrist, well hidden from any chance gleam of light. He felt clean and sharp with desire, keen for his purpose as his own knife.

Abruptly the man turned toward him. When so close that the boy could see the bulge of shirt pocket, the very button beside which he meant to strike, Massey turned his head. Involuntarily Barby flicked up his own glance to meet Massey's steady eyes. Despite himself he could not move. An unaccountable absence of desire, a sudden lack of will, seemed to paralyze his mind and limbs so that he could not even shrink away. Held helpless by the contemptuous sneer of the man before him, by the comprehending sharpness of the eyes that pierced and drained him until he felt hollow within, he stood rooted to the ground in an awkward posture of arrested flight.

Massey threw back his head and laughed. A coarse mirthless derision that struck the boy like a blow. Barby stumbled back against the wall. Never in all those days of waiting had he hated the man as at that moment. And yet, with a nauseous commotion in the pit of his stomach, in a helpless lassitude that drenched him in sweat, he could not make a move.

"Well I'll be God-damned!" Massey spit beside him. "You poor, spineless, brown-skinned bastard!"

Barby crouched staring into the darkness that soon swallowed even the sound of the man's departing steps.

It was this which finally drove him back to The Lamp Awake. He lay on the squeaky bed tortured with hate and cowardice that ate into him like an incurable disease. The dreary solitude of the room, broken only by the light intruding through the broken pane and the dull rumble of a passing freight, enclosed him like a shell. Not even Tai Ling came up the steps.

Never again did he cross the Border to the American side. Everything suggestive of that rich, superior and contemptuous world of the white curdled within him a violent denunciation. Yet brutal but without courage, lonely and impoverished, he craved what he denounced.

Little by little he ventured forth again. At first by night until he found the world uninformed of his secret thought. But always with a terrifying sense of his persistent isolation.

Occasionally he fought a three-round preliminary in the arena behind the Nuevo Mundo, for he was strong and brutal enough to exchange blows with unimpassioned oxlike stolidity. With the money it brought he got drunk and obtained a woman in any of the back courts. Without money he helped Tai Ling about the shop.

Thus his days, prowling the streets and disappearing at night down the Callejon de los Chinos. And forever around him a vast swarm of faces loomed indistinctly in the darkness and vanished again as he. Only one leapt forth from that timeless stream. A single face glimpsed for an instant through the window of a cabaret. Madre de Mío! What did it mean?

5

Downstairs on his stool behind the counter Tai Ling heard the boy cry out in sleep. What could be troubling him so? Compassion flooded his heart; he let it ebb. Instead he sought that complete quiescence of soul, that pure objectivity of mind, wherewith he might contemplate "The Ten Causes of Regret" free from vain emotion.

The prime of youth being the period of development of the body, speech and mind, it was indeed a cause of regret that Barby should waste it so.

Yet his own mind being of the nature of the uncreated, it would also be a cause of regret to let it be swallowed up likewise in the morass of the world's illusions.

The passions, the illusions of the flesh! Who can break their hold upon another and free him from his bondage? So Tai Ling struggled to free himself from helpless pity for the prisoner above him.

But that same night there came those who sought to bind him in his own bonds. He knew it the instant the three men slid quietly in the door. Discreetly Tai Ling turned down the lamp on his counter and led them to his own back room. He greeted each in turn.

Chugoku he knew: a scrawny fishmonger who sent him fish from a remote fishing village at the head of the Gulf. "I am always delighted to see an old business acquaintance," said Tai Ling courteously. "The fish you send are fresh and sound. They sell well; I regret I cannot use more. But I must thank you more for helping to indulge an old man's hobby. The last live perch you sent for my small collection was a most interesting specimen. Please continue to send me any strange varieties that come in. I shall try to pay you, not what they are worth to me, but what a poor shopkeeper can afford."

Chugoku grinned slyly, his begrimed face betraying a life that had been a ripe field for evil to harvest, and furtive eyes that were on the alert to escape any sight of human virtue.

Beside him sat a young, flashily dressed Mexican named Mendoza, a former pimp, whose chief business was known to be greasing the palms of Border authorities to expedite various shady ventures.

"Señor Mendoza, it has been some time since you honored me with a call," Tai Ling said gravely.

"It worked out O.K. too, didn't it?" replied Mendoza with a wink.

Tai Ling did not answer. He turned to his portly third visitor. The man was part white, part Chinese, perhaps only an Americanized Chinese of the third generation. Obviously he was from out of town. His clothes were inconspicuous and expensive, his manner urbane. About him Tai Ling sensed evil in all its most sophisticated disguises: power, wealth, influence, a business acumen he meant to avoid.

"I bid you a gracious welcome to my home," said Tai Ling softly. "May I have the honor of offering you tea?"

The man ignored both his idiom and his subtlety. "No thanks. It is too late and too conspicuous to send out for it. Besides, we have come only for a short business chat. . . . I hear you have a young man about." He peered out into the shop.

"He is not available for discussion," replied Tai Ling drily. "He has retired upstairs."

On soft voices the visitors crept to the point. This Border district was expanding rapidly. Vast tracts of desert were being reclaimed for the growth of cotton. For cheap labor the Mexican government had assented to the importation of Chinese workers. As a result this town, this quarter in particular, had built up into a sizable Chinese colony.

Tai Ling nodded. It was his own biography of the last twenty years. He remembered the filthy hold of the steamer into which he had been jammed with hundreds of his compatriots; the backbreaking labor of clearing illimitable expanses of cactus and mesquite in a new land; and subsequent years of penury no white man could endure and which no yellow one would desire to remember. But Tai Ling had won through them to a little adobe shop in the village which had sprung up on the Border as a shipping center.

This Gentleman—as Mendoza called him—continued. Chinese laborers were still coming in. Conditions were bad: vice, disease, poverty, racial prejudice, no work. As many of the great mercantile establishments were Chinese, financed by wealthy backers in Los Angeles and San Francisco, These Gentlemen were naturally interested in helping out their unfortunate immigrant compatriots. They could use them farther north; work, better conditions were available. But unfortunately the International Line interposed.

"They can't get passports," explained Mendoza tersely. "See?"

Tai Ling began to understand.

The matter was not too complicated, really. Chugoku's lonely shack at the edge of a remote fishing village would readily accommodate a few selected refugees at a time as they were taken off a boat. Mendoza's truck could easily bring them up from the gulf with barrels of fish, and transport them across the Line; his friendship with local rurales and Border officials would facilitate matters greatly. Thereafter This Gentleman would be wholly responsible for insuring them a proper and prosperous life.

It was all very simple. But for one thing. A place was needed here where they might be kept overnight, pending passage across the Line. Tai Ling's shop was suitable. It was at the quiet end of the alley; he himself was discreet; besides there was a small cellar underneath. Would he oblige?

Tai Ling answered softly but firmly. He felt unworthy of the responsibility of sharing in such a worthy enterprise. "My days of large profit are over. I am content with little, being but a poor shopkeeper treasuring only my fish and my peace."

Mendoza grinned. "Tell it to the tax collector and Chino Juan!"

Tai Ling sighed. The tax collector had come indeed just a week before and bullied him penniless. Moreover Chino Juan was ever pushing him closer to eventual ruin. It was his own fault; an evil cause that was due to bring its compensating effect.

For in those horrible, penurious days of his past, The Lamp Awake had gained discreet repute. In its cellar, buried alike from the scorching desert sun and the gaze of a chance rurale, his wretched companions could seek solace in a pipe of the inspissated juice of the poppy. Tai Ling, then, had been a purveyor of yenshee from cans of the excellent "Rooster and Elephant" brand.

The old man was not conscious of wrongdoing. It was that or starve. So he sat on the fulcrum of his conscience dispensing drug or kindness with equal equanimity; he gave away as much as he sold, thus balancing his illicit traffic with an unwarranted generosity.

Why not? Those who did not accept the transient illusion of heart's desire from his wrinkled hand for a few pesos were sure to have it forced upon them by Chino Juan for ten times more. And Chinese John had become a dangerous rival. His shop faced The Lamp Awake across the railroad tracks. Too, it was known that it was he who owned the Casino Chino, the low gambling rooms down the street. But worse! Rumor had it now that he contemplated still another establishment, a crib of forty girls.

Opium and marihuana, gambling, the carnal sale of girls! —Tai Ling shrank in horror. Straightway he gave up his own casual peddling, and depended utterly upon his shop for a simple livelihood.

Unfortunately no one believed it. Not Chino Juan who swore to run him out of business. Nor Tai Ling's own few friends, to whom it was unthinkable that he should turn tail to his dangerous rival. They all believed that behind his crazy philosophizing he hid a lucrative scheme of his own. Of course! Can a man live on a barrel or two of fish a week?

But all this was nebulous. Never did it congeal in actual facts or become audible in a single word. This was a quarter where a careless man was likely to be found on any night with a knife in his back.

Tai Ling was no coward. Confronted now with evil and conjecture, he relied upon truth to defeat them. "I have no quarrel with Chino Juan. Our interests do not coincide, but neither do our business ventures conflict. I would be friends with him as with every man."

Mendoza laughed. "What about Francisco Cheon's old place? I hear you've just got it."

He was surprisingly well informed, thought Tai Ling. "That is true," he assented. "Business of late has been very bad here at the end of this quiet lane. I thought another in a more auspicious location might help. It is an old place—a short bar with a table or two in back, no more. And Cheon is my friend."

Mendoza laughed again, this time a nasty chuckle. "I suppose you didn't know that you stole it from right under Chino Juan's nose—the very place he had his eye on for a crib!"

Tai Ling quietly opened his hands, palm up, on his threadbare knees. His three visitors watched him squirm a bit, then This Gentleman spoke.

He did not wish to become involved in local affairs or Tai Ling's personal business. But speaking as a disinterested observer, he saw that Tai Ling would do well to accept his proposition. First, the money would help him to open up his new place. Second, the new place would mask the financial returns he would receive for merely giving harbor to a few passing travelers. Third, Mendoza's influence would protect him from ófficial annoyance. And fourth, if it were true that Tai Ling were in danger of actual molestation from an embittered competitor, he might find it to advantage to be allied with influential and powerful friends.

He rose to his feet. Mendoza had little to add to his cold logic. Both he and Chugoku rose also.

Tai Ling did not budge from his seat or his principles. "Still I must refuse," he smiled. "You know, I hold to the belief that evolutionary progress proves that a leopard is constantly changing his spots. Mine also have changed."

This Gentleman frowned. "Would you like to prove that to the police?"

Tai Ling sighed as he rose. He felt caught in those circumstances of his own past which he knew yogically as his individual karma. How could he expiate it, with this annoying expediency of the moment which involved such material trivialities as his daily rice, the police or a possible knife-thrust in his ribs?

6

It was past midnight when Tai Ling let his three visitors out of the back door. For a long time he stood staring down the alley. The rain had stopped. The glow of cantina signs had faded. The night was sticky and starless.

Out of this viscous gloom darted two squeaks from a snake-belly fiddle. Again the two weird screeches repeated themselves at odd intervals. As he listened, memories of other songs fluttered to him like moths drawn from the darkness. Songs of the Pear Tree, the Budding of the Lotus, a Chant of Autumn, a Melancholy Emperor's Love—all so short, harsh and squeaky that the same few notes served to express them all. Yet like all familiar songs their different meanings awakened images in his heart. In the lonely fluted notes of the ti-tzu he heard the lapping music of the Whangpoo, smelled saffron and the far flood tide. The tinkle of a three-stringed san-hien echoed the sound of temple bells, reflected the pale sheen of water lilies in moonlight.

Courageously Tai Ling put it all from him for what it was—excessively romantic and unreal, a poetic illusion created by an old man's idle fancy. From across Cockroach Court, so far away that a mechanical piano could hardly carry, a woman's sudden scream rang out. Tai Ling bent his head half an inch but did not stir. He stood staring into the world he knew, knowing that it too was just as unreal and immaterial, created only in the mind of man.

From the railroad tracks to the deep arroyo of Rio Nuevo, from the Border gates to the blue picachos trembling in the desert haze, it was a world apart; a world a stranger has no eyes to see, no pulse to echo. And soon it too would vanish completely; no man would know that it ever existed.

To Tai Ling it was a vast grey brain: its cerebral halves divided by the arroyo; its lobes wrinkled by the convolutions of its winding streets and furtive alleys; clotted with sparse growths of tamarisk and chinaberry; and containing deep in its cerebrum, like a lateral ventricle, the central cavity of Cockroach Court which hid the pineal gland of his tiny shop. Festering in sun and heat and dust, this corrupt grey brain yet lived and pulsed and spumed forth its dreams of faces, its memories of faces, the fabulous and incredible visages of all the thoughts it had known and the sensations it had felt. . . .

There were the faces of all its wandering tribes, its vanished races and enduring breeds. The dark Aztec masks, hard and clean-cut as obsidian. The faces of the few remaining Cocopahs and Mojaves, decadent, pock-marked, eaten by disease and malnutrition; faces hopeless, resigned and yet retaining the unconscious dignity of racial death.

The faces of all the mixed-bloods: those of the mestizo yellow and cunning, with sly eyes and thin lips; those of the cholo broad cheeked and brutal, swinging forward with splendid animal strength and immeasurable vitality; those of the coyotes stained dark red beneath the brown; of the creoles and criollos, sharp featured with purplish lips.

The coarse peon faces swarming into the streets from squalid mud huts across the arroyo; earthy faces of men whose very lives were undeviating journeys from earthen womb to earthen grave.

Endlessly the yellow faces of China, suave and silent. The big nosed, arrogant faces of brawny, turbaned Hindu cotton pickers. Of giant laughing black children transplanted from the Congo to the Mississippi and drifting hence to this delta of the Colorado.

Streamed also the frank open faces of American Yanquis. The bluff red faces of ranchers. The pallid city faces of merchants, buyers, cotton and melon brokers. The tense pale faces lining the bars and gambling tables.

And all the perpetual animal-faces: of the bloodthirsty tiger man, the lustful swine man, the deceitful fox man, the thieving monkey man, the groveling worm man, the industrious ant man, the stupid and strong ox man.

And the vicious faces of all the petty criminals and poor unfortunates who filled this Border slum: the rateros, the pimps, the human cucarachas, the prostitutes, in their scuffed slippers and sweat-stained shifts, the beggars, the hop-heads and marihuana reefers, all the drunk and the dissolute, the perverted, damned and diseased. . . .

Faces, faces, a thousand faces seen a thousand times, they glided from the convolutions and cavities of this great grey brain like nebulous and disembodied visages of thought. To Tai Ling nothing in their shouts and gestures, nothing of the savage, violent and unfathomed energy of their figures came alive. Only the endless stream of their faces flowing past his door seemed touched by a monstrous enchantment.

Conceived in misery and evil, enslaved by greed and desire, they constantly perpetuated their own untruth, passing and repassing before him silently or with strident tongues to love, to hate, to folly and rapture, power and despair. And forever their efforts were rebuked by the unreality of their existence. In a monstrous enchantment they floated by without real meaning, the strange and fabulous nature of their origin their only truth.

Tai Ling stirred uneasily in the dark doorway. He had reached the core of his real problem. For just as his own past constituted what he called an individual character or karma, so did all these manifested thoughts swarming around him create a karma of locality. A complete objectivity alone would free him. Against this vast grey brain his own was pitted.

Tai Ling was too far down the path of liberation to underestimate his difficulties. It was a dangerous game, as martyrs of many faiths have testified. And he was humorous enough to recognize the paradox. For while most men endeavor to accomplish undetected a bit of evil in a world of good, here he was aspiring to do secret good in a world of evil. This was his only clue to the object of his existence.

The notes of the snake-belly fiddle had died away. The alley was deserted. The vast grey brain slept. There was nothing to remind him of its corrupt fantasies.

He went to his own room, and composing himself for sleep endeavored to remember "The Ten Things to Forget."

CHAPTER TWO

THAT SATURDAY evening near ten o'clock two girls remained standing on the corner outside the The Fifteen Letters cabaret, Las Quince Letras.

Inside, the cabaret was closing for the night. The great fans above the dance floor stopped churning the thick, still air. The brilliant lights hanging over the panguingui, poker and écarté tables were quenched, and men moved through the casino covering the green felt with protective canvas. Bartenders, dealers, entertainers and percentage girls joined the exodus back across the Line before the gates were shut.

The street lamp illumined the big-boned, straw-haired and coarse-featured figure of the larger girl waiting behind. With a grinning, expectant face she was jiggling about on restless heels and humming, "I wanta bee—in Tenna-see." The smaller leaned quietly against the dark wall.

"What's the matter, honey?" asked Sal, snapping her fingers under the other's nose. "Ain't you happy?"

"My feet are tired," answered Guadalupe. "It has been a busy night and I have danced all the time."

Sal laughed loudly. "You just got cold feet, that's all! They don't hurt. Watch me and you'll forget them tootsie-wootsies. I ain't had a night since the drought and I'm rarin' to go. Fuera's the boy who can show us a good time."

She squeezed Guadalupe's arm and began humming again, "Ta—ta-ta—da, te—de-de—dum," when through the darkness came the resonant thunder of a crowd in full cry. Sal stopped. "That scrappin' again behind the New World bar. A nigger and a white I suppose from all the noise. Well, it'd better be over. I told Fuera we wasn't goin' to stand here all night waitin' for him and that Barby. They'd better show up quick, eh honey?"

Together they stared down the street.

Already a trickle of people from the Nuevo Mundo was swelling the stream flowing north. Yet the open arena in back was still packed. All the bouts were over: a tame preliminary, a bloody three-round filler, and the main match between that beautiful big black boy, the Deuce of Spades, and the whiskered Border mauler, Bruiser Buck. But the evening's fighting seemed to have just begun. In the blood-smeared canvas ring the seconds of the principals were banging each other with their water buckets; the referee was threatening the time-keeper. All around them on the plank seats their supporters were shouting and stamping feet. A thrown beer bottle crashed against the enclosing wall of sheet iron. "Andale!—Andale!" shouted the few rurales trying to herd the crowd outside. Above all this din and clatter sounded the sudden raucous scream of a siren announcing five minutes to Border-closing time. It was the final winner. Swiftly, desperately, the place cleared. The trickle became a flood pouring down the street, swirling through the great wire gates.

In its ebb walked Young Fuera still grumbling at Barby. "What I tell you? Very fas' an' easy the first roun', to feel his wind. Trade the punch with him the second. Then you fight, everything you give. No? But what you do? Like you was asleep, more slow as an old woman. You do nothing like I say. Mother of God! I think Bud was go to have twins!"

Barby did not answer. The very thought of meeting face to face that dark oval ahead, of watching it emerge from the thousand faces of a thousand nights with all their mystery and yet with a meaning for him alone, filled him with consternation. And at the same time, and just as strongly, the desire raged within him.

This paradox of attraction and repulsion had persisted all week. Yet nothing could have driven him inside the cabaret. Each time that he passed Las Quince Letras he shuffled by with lowered head. Often he saw Sal; the streets were filled with such as she, older or less tawny-haired perhaps, but with the same coarse features and throaty laugh. But it was the face of the younger girl he could not escape. There was no need to see it; it was before him constantly. And now, step after step, he listened to his own heels carrying him closer to something he had no power nor will to avoid.

"That slow cross I say. You remember? No! You forget. Chihuahua! You take it in the face. A pasting. Yes!"

Barby cut loose a torrent of expletive. He had become suddenly wet and shaking with mortification at the thought of his cut eye and puffed left cheek.

Young Fuera stopped him with a kindly shake. "Forget. Forget, my frien'. I think you see your new sweetheart tonight and not Kid Mike. Don' I tell you you need a woman? But come, we make hurry. Now."

They swung round the corner; Young Fuera with a shout: "Cómo está, mi media naranja!"

Sal grinned. "Your little half-orange nothin'! Where do you get that sweetheart stuff so early in the evenin'? We only been waitin' an hour. I can see your friend ain't pressed for time."

"He come!" winked Young Fuera, as Barby lurched awkwardly into the group. "Don' mind his face; we bump into a wall hunting for you."

Sal snorted and turned to Guadalupe. "Come here honey and meet the boys. But say, don't your friend talk no English?"

"Yes," Barby answered sullenly.

"Well let's get off the se-habla stuff then. I ain't so hot on the Spic when I don't have to. Guadalupe, this here is your fella. Hope he ain't no worse than the one I got!" Sal laughed, squirming in the arm already around her waist.

Barby stood looking down at the ripe childish figure beside him. How small and vibrantly alive she was—his first impression of her nearness. He steeled himself for a glance at her face. It was as he remembered it, but even more beautiful and compelling than from a distance: this dark oval with its smooth wings of hair black as night itself, and its lips small, red and smiling as a serpent's. Now it was done! She had raised her face and he had looked into her eyes. They were wide, fully opened and darkly fathomless; they gave no sign that they remembered. Instantly he relaxed, feeling the tenseness dissolve within him.

"How are you?" he said abruptly and quietly under her straight open gaze.

"And you?" she answered simply.

He took her warm dry hand. Ahead of them Sal with Young Fuera was humming a happy way down the street. They followed.

The exodus across the Border was over. The gates had clanged shut. The lights of Las Quince Letras and all the great gaudy cabarets were out. But slowly in the flocculent desert night the dreary back streets were coming alive. By lamp and candlelight drab little loncherías offered tortillas, tacos, greasy plates of beans and meat. Somber mud-floored drinking dens began to fill. In the flicker of torches at the street turnings Chinese lottery vendors took up their stands. Dim-lit bars became noisy, and the cribs behind them.

2

"What the hell's wrong with this place?" shouted Sal.

They turned into the Xochimilco and sat down at a dusty table in the corner. Across the room a stout bar held up a row of cholos and Negro cotton pickers. In the opposite corner a rickety player-piano was banging out a piece of American jazz. To this a few random couples, cheek to cheek, scraped back and forth across the plank floor.

"What are we waitin' for!" Without waiting herself for an answer, Sal lunged toward the bar, followed by Young Fuera.

Barby rose to his feet. Without taking her glance from the dancers out on the floor, Guadalupe silently swung against him. The first pressure of her body against his shattered the spell of her face. He felt an overpowering sensuous softness, the flow of an intense and consuming vitality. But with it a mindless absorption in mere sensory motion that seemed unaware of his quicker breathing and the hungry touch of his hands. The warning of this contradiction he had no mind to perceive, though he knew that she was as unconscious of him as of herself. She danced lightly, without effort, her head resting against his muscular throat. And he, feeling the pressure of her firm little breast, the hand resting on his heaving shoulder, her strong supple back, was content to plod awkwardly across the planks in the paradise of her embrace. The music ended suddenly. Guadalupe opened her eyes and abruptly drew away from him.

"Let her alone, you. Her feet hurt. We been dancin' all day!"

Barby spun around. Sal was watching them with a truculent frown.

"No, Sal! I love to dance. Always!"

"Jesu! How she dance!" cried Young Fuera, with a patronizing jab at Barby's ribs. "But Barby here is too tired from Kid Mike." He slapped Sal's thigh again. "Come, we dance before you get jealous."

The boy watched them moving across the floor through the haze of smoke and lamplight. Halfway across, Sal broke free with a shrug and listlessly walked over to the bar. Barby slumped down at the table and stared at Guadalupe, idly watching a couple on the floor. As his glance played hurriedly over the swell of her small breast smoothly expanding its skin of cheap black silk, he knew her figure gave the lie to her childish face. Again he sensed his indefinable first warning. There was about her soft sensuousness a peculiar impersonality; something fragile and indestructable yet changeful as the wind. There was something in her he could never touch.

She looked up and smiled. "You don't wish me to dance with you?"

He considered it and her for some time. "You like to dance with everybody?"

Guadalupe laughed. "Of course I dance with anybody who will buy me a drink. But I drink red lemonade that only Joe knows is not wine. That is business. But I dance for myself, too. That is more. All the time I love it, both. It is still dancing."

Her face no longer held its quality of nebulous remoteness. It was so close he could see the red showing through the iodine of her cheeks, the tiny beads of sweat on her rounded forehead, the pinkness of her full lower lip where the crimson stain had rubbed away, a small mole below her left ear. A face like the surface of a moon seen often from afar, but now glimpsed for the first time as through a telescope.

"Lord! What a night!"

It was Sal returning from the bar with Young Fuera and another bottle. She slumped down in a chair and carelessly crossed her long voluptuous legs. Her garrulous voice had thickened perceptibly.

"Yep. Ory-eyed drunk ever night. We had to. Why? Well, I'm tellin' you: cause it ain't natural to sit at no window from Monday till Saturday lookin' down a street a block long and nobody on it. A dusty piece of road runnin' out to the jumpin'-off-place. Just them dry crazy-lookin' hills. The San Jose and the Mules. And the lonesome empty feelin' gettin' so thick you can't breathe. So what? You go to bed. And you get tired of sleepin' and get up. And there's them wrinkled old hills a-shinin' in moonlight same as in the sun. Pretty soon you can't sleep no more at all. You're just sittin' at the window watchin' them wrinkled up old hills shinin' away in moonlight and sunshine till you don't know which it is. Then it happened sure as shootin', sure as God made little green monkeys. Them hills would begin puffin' up like balloons till you thought they'd bust. Why, you could feel your head puffin' up till you had to hold it from explodin' too. Nuts we were. Goin' plumb nuts. And me that was in a good house once in Kansas City with pretty curtains on the window, yellow roses and all, and a streetcar clangin' by outside. The conductor always waved."

Sal took another deep swig. "Yes Siree. You had to be ory-eyed to stave off them dried up mountains till Saturday night. What then? Blessed little, I can tell you. There was only enough miners comin' in to stake you to tortillas and tequila for another week. And they didn't always pay up. The poor bastards! We used to have to get the stubborn ones in one at a time. You know, Luisa layin' stretched out on the bed while I stood behind the door with a pick handle wrapped up in a sheet. We'd blame it on the crazy Chink cook afterwards. They never did get wise. But it stopped 'em comin'. God Almighty! Saturday night. My first real nice one since I got away."

For a while longer they sat emptying the bottle. Sal drew out a vial of "Black Narcissus." Wetting her forefinger with this, she drew a perfumed line down the length of successive cigarettes and passed them around. Young Fuera had begun again to fondle her knee. Barby quietly reached an arm around Guadalupe's waist. She declined her head upon his shoulder and closed her eyes. The piano was still, its row of keys shining like discolored teeth in a derisive grin. The smoke thickened; the room stank of tequila, rotgut whiskey and spilled beer. Occasionally a woman ambled in from the back court, waiting for a stranded prospect.

Abruptly Sal reared up in her chair. "What the hell!" she demanded. "We been dancin' all day and drinkin' all night. I ain't goin' to do no more. I want to eat."

Young Fuera drew her down again. For a minute they whispered together, then Fuera spoke to Barby. The four rose from the table. Happy enough together and a little drunk, they quitted the Xochimilco and went out again into the heat and silence of the night.

3

They walked slowly in the middle of the road in order to keep Sal from traveling with one foot in the gutter and the other up on the patches of board walk. She had become play-ful again. From time to time she butted Young Fuera out of step with her hip.

The street was plunged in dark and silence, touched with the faint, indescribable odor of acrid dust and urine. Above the flat azoteas the stars had paled to the gritty grey of bottle glass. The underworld, moving slowly and cautiously like a snake, had begun to circulate. A crawling beggar, a prowling prostitute, the rateros, pimps, petty criminals—all shadows briefly outlined in the light of the Hong-Kong at the far cor-ner. Here Sal stopped, cocking her head toward the debilitated clatter of a mechanical piano.

"I wanta bee—in Tenna-see . . ." she began to shout.

"Shut up once, can't you!" growled Barby, conscious of his growing resentment toward her.

Sal turned around to give him an owlish stare, then broke into a shriek. "Shay some more! I wantcher talk like no man's talked like you to me before. A perfick gemmelman, s'wat ch'ar—you Goddam ignorant bum!"

Young Fuera jerked at her arm; together they moved on. The lights of the Hong-Kong lagged and fell behind. Others appeared beyond the turn, greasy blue windowpanes or dim yellow globes inscribed with chopsticks. Steadily now about them gathered the new smells and sounds of the quarter with its slight yellow men lounging in the doorways.

At the Nuevo Paris they turned into the Alley and went quietly up the cobbled, narrow lane. Barby stopped for a word with old Chan Foo squatting in one of the low doorways. Then down the steps they went to a small cafe ill-lit by a smoking lamp. Sal settled heavily in the nearest chair and be-gan to roll down her stockings over plump white knees. "Well Goddam it! We're here to eat," she muttered.

There were eggs, rice and pork, a second pot of tea. Long

after the others had finished, Sal continued to stuff. Young Fuera too ate ravenously but hurriedly, with only one thought in mind. Lest it be lost he ordered a bottle of rice brandy. Guadalupe still held Barby's fixed attention. He sat staring at her with rapt adoration. She ate sparingly, said little and looked at him seldom—completely at ease, and oblivious of the tense undercurrents around her.

The moment approached. Barby broke out into a sweat. Still he sat immobile between desire and fear, called by her soft sensuousness and stopped abruptly by her clear glances. Sal already had pushed back her dishes and slipped lower in her chair. Young Fuera could wait no longer.

"Call the old man over," he demanded forthrightly. "Let's see if he's got a room."

Barby began to tremble; he dared not face Guadalupe's eyes; he could not speak. No word was necessary. Old Chan Foo had appeared in the back doorway with an upraised finger.

They rose and followed him up a flight of squeaky steps. At the end of the dark hall he opened a door and set his candle on the floor. They followed him inside.

The room was bare save for two mattresses spread on the floor. Over the lower half of the single narrow window was hung a scrap of ragged quilt. A young boy came in with a wicker tray which Chan Foo took from his hands to place on the floor. For a moment there was low talk among the three men and the clink of money. Then silently the old man left, closing the door behind him.

When Barby turned around Sal was squatting before the wicker tray. It held a pot of tea, four cups and a bunch of hand-rolled marihuana cigarettes. Young Fuera dropped to his knees behind her, reached out both arms and drew her back against him.

Barby turned to Guadalupe. She stood quietly fingering a string of beads around her throat, the candlelight from the floor playing over her slim body and dark oval face. Their glances met and held unbroken. The boy's face was still expressionless of feature, but its wall of impassiveness had crumbled. The hidden glow behind his eyes shone forth, illumining their dark depths. The hunger was there, but something more. And in that moment, for perhaps the only time in her life, she saw him as he was.

He removed his hat and dropped it to the floor. Then gently he took her hand, and together they too sat down.

4

The room was quiet as a cell.

From the two couples on their respective mattresses came no sound or word. On the floor between them the candle stub was burning low. In its guttering light their humped, close bodies struck hierophantic attitudes on either wall.

Young Fuera still crouched beside Sal, his demanding hands moving slowly over her lush body. "No; don't rush me. Not till I get a kick out this first." She leaned forward and lit a cigarette. Again she stretched out, her head in his lap, the thin smoke spiraling upward from her lips.

The other couple did not move. Sunk in a posture of hebetude, legs crooked beneath him, Barby squatted with his arms round Guadalupe, staring at the candle. She raised on her elbow, coughing from the thick marihuana smoke. Barby watched her crawl to the window for a breath of air. Over her crouching body a ray from the moon hung as if pinned to the wall. From outside came the rumble of an empty freight moving to the packing sheds.

"This stuff's no good. Too much trouble for nothin',"

muttered Sal unsteadily across the room. A deep sigh was Young Fuera's answer. He tipped over the candle with his foot and snuffed it out on the bare floor.

Now silence and darkness held the room. Barby sat still and rigid, his senses preternaturally attuned to the sound of Guadalupe crawling slowly back from the window. He was not aware of a violent throbbing over his cut eye, that his battered left ribs pained him at every breath. He was resolved into nothing but a rigid organism that tightened with every faint sound beside him. He heard her cross the bare floor and sink down upon the foot of the mattress. He heard the soft impact of her hands upon the canvas, the rustle of her dress, the slight scrape of her shoetips. The sounds played upon his imagination. They clamored within him, beat wildly into his brain. Fresh perspiration broke out upon him. And still he could not turn around. He could not put out an arm.

Always there had hovered about him a veil of unreality, a strange sense of aloofness. Always its thin edge interposed at the moment of contact to shut off the deep flow of human communion. He had gutted himself with drink and women. But always still isolated in a growing aloneness, cut off somehow from the quick of communion. All were faces, unreal and without meaning. Then suddenly a single glance from a single face had torn the veil aside. In the profound mystery of one woman's eyes he had glimpsed, like a star, a meaning to his life.

She was there! she was real and touchable; and no power on earth could give him the strength to command her answer. And trembling in the sweaty darkness whose profound stillness intensified every faint scuff of her approaching slippers, all his senses cried out their one appeal. A single gesture that must come to him freely and unbidden.

He first felt her warm breath on the back of his neck;

she had knelt down at his shoulder. Then she slumped down beside him and laid a hand on his arm. His reaction at the light and meaningless touch was immediate and unexpected. He turned, flung both arms around her, and threw her roughly down across his lap. Not until she cried out softly as his teeth bruised her lips did he come to himself. But before he could release his arms, she relaxed and drew more closely to him.

For a moment he lay still, then leaned back against the wall, her head on his breast. Little by little now he saw her in the darkness with his finger tips. The firm little breasts that rose spasmodically to meet his touch; the velvet smoothness of her arms; all the slim, supple beauty of her waist and back. He caressed her cheeks and retraced the warm oval of her face. He ran his fingers over her smooth hair. Unbelievable mystery! She did not stir.

There was a rustle on the opposite mattress. Upthrust through the ray of moonlight over them a head reared erect. Over it Fuera slipped his shirt. "Chispas! I'm hot!" he muttered. "Gimme a drink," Sal whispered back. His fingers rattled the cups in the tray, seeking a sip of lukewarm tea. As he lay down the silence washed over him again.

Barby leaned down and whispered Guadalupe's name to see if she were still awake. For answer she turned easily in his arms and allowed herself to be enwrapped closer still. Yet for all the growing intimacy of his hands there was a restraint in their demand, faint and unfathomable, that long afterwards she was to remember with contempt.

For still he hesitated. Always that strange duality which impelled him forward, then jerked him back again. Even now, so close to her utter capitulation, he felt a dim presentiment of ultimate frustration. Thus they lay embraced upon the brink of that profound chasm wherein lay the last fusion and the last dissolution, the final rendezvous and battlefield of their separate selves.

Outside in the hall a door clicked open, giving forth the sound of slippered feet before it closed again. Barby dropped his hands, raised his head. Now in the dark hour before dawn the room was beginning to cool a bit. The ribbon of moonlight was gone. From the opposite mattress came the echo of their own quick breathing, though he could not see the figures. Barby rose to his knees to bend over Guadalupe, whispering.

Immediately she rose to her feet. At the door they turned from the couple lying locked in love on the floor. Then he closed it behind them and led Guadalupe down the dark hall.

Quietly they crept up the steps from the deserted cafe and into the alley. Save for a few pale ambiguous lights the lane was dark. Silence breathed with bated breath. The plaza was empty. Suddenly Guadalupe bit back a scream and shrank closer to Barby. He looked around.

An old woman was crouched on the lower step of a decrepit stairway, dimly outlined by a light on the landing above. For an hour she had waited here for the night to pass. Applying the flame to a cigarette butt, her cupped hands revealed themselves prehensile and bony as a hawk's. In the same flash her loose and evil face leapt out from a straggle of unkempt hair. Then again she relapsed into shadow and silence.

"Forget it; nothing!" whispered Barby as they walked past, putting his arm around the girl's waist. At the far end of the passage he stopped and swung open a rusty screen door. Together they stepped inside.

5

The day was auspicious. Tai Ling did not question why. He simply knew it to be so the instant he awakened and shuffled out to open his front door. The whole shop seemed permeated with a new, warm vitality. Quiescent in the early dawn, he settled on his stool for his hour of morning meditation on "The Ten Things Not to be Avoided."

As he meditated, the sun crept over the threshold, hesitated, strode boldly into the room. With swift fingers it touched up the walls from black and grey to brown and yellow. On the shelves it unwrapped a copper kettle, a brass lamp; polished a steel plow in the corner; shined the butcher knives in their dusty case. Then reaching the bird cages swung from the rafters, it set off the morning carnival of song.

With the first cadenza from his canaries Tai Ling returned from his meditations. He had just finished, "That which cometh of itself, being a divine gift, is not to be avoided." Another of the ten remained, "The thought of helping others, howsoever limited one's ability to help others may be, is not to be avoided." But the morning hour was over, and Tai Ling did not avoid its natural termination. He simply sat a few minutes longer contemplating the possible relationship of the happy texts to this auspicious day.

Then quietly he gave himself up to his fish. This was his single hour of daily pleasure, when the sunlight flowed like a stream down the dark aisle behind his counter. One after another the long row of bowls, jars and bottles on the back shelf were touched and enlivened with light. The water sparkled at every movement within, or lay in brilliant silent pools like tiny marine worlds lifted bodily from their watery universe. As he ambled up and down, pausing in front of a jar, lifting another to his counter to study the queer-shaped form within, the glass seemed nonexistent. He stood immersed in a shimmering water-world, at one with the single creature within.

A fish turned lazily on its side as if bathing in the sun;

another lay motionless on the bottom, only its rhythmical gills keeping time with life; the eels were curled in their slimy everlasting sleep. Their inactivity pleased Tai Ling. It was appropriate to the long evolutionary process through which they would be reborn out of water to air and earth, toward the only true and final activity. Too, he admitted to a mere sensuous delight in their colors. Form and color—this was what pleased him. And for their infinite variations he imported little domestic gold fish from across the Border as well as the huge specimens brought him in oil cans and barrels from the warm waters of the Gulf.

Red as the huachinago; green as the spotted rock bass, cabrilla; ferociously formed as the pez-gallo; marked peculiarly like the palometa with four dark lines across its back; odd as the bagre with mustaches long as those on any human lip; round, flat or with the swift, sinuous lines of the pez-sierra; gleaming in the sunlight blue, gold, pink and coral; how strange and wonderful they were, how like their human counterparts, illusionary all, dipped as they were from the ceaseless stream of life!

Tai Ling selected a huge can and lugged it toward the window. A new specimen had been sent him by truck last night from the Gulf. It was a large dorado, ripe gold in the water. As he watched it, the finch rolled slightly to one side. On its underside was a small spot that seemed faintly tarnished and lifeless in the sunlight. Tai Ling ignored the blemish, poured it into fresh water and added it to his shelf.

Now at last he began the day's work. For no apparent reason he moved a sack of pinto beans, dragged a stack of sugar cane into a new corner. He dusted packets of tea on his trousers, and from one rafter to another looped a string of drying chile peppers red and crinkly as a rope of coral.

Soon a boy from Chan Foo's came in with tea and breakfast. Morning was well on its way, Tai Ling observed, and Barby was not yet down. This was not unusual, but this was an auspicious day. After some hesitation, for he never went up there, Tai Ling ascended the stairs to the room aloft. Softly, slyly almost, he pushed the door open a crack and looked inside.

Barby was awake, with dungarees on, standing at the foot of the bed. The sun streamed through the window upon his broad muscular shoulders and bare brown chest. He was gripping the foot rail, leaning half forward in a posture of utter supplication. His lips, parted in a gentle smile, lent his face a strange power and grace that Tai Ling had never seen before. And his eyes, in that one instant before surprise veiled their blind adoration as he turned around, confirmed his unconscious posture.

On the bed, still sleeping, lay Guadalupe.

With one quick glance Tai Ling took in the situation. Observantly he noted the youthful fullness of the girl's body; the smooth round arm thrown across the dirty pillow to shut off the sunlight; the gentle profile like an amber cameo against the bed; the smooth black wings of hair.

As he looked he smiled. "Well. Well," he muttered, withdrawing from the door. In a moment he was back; on a chair he placed his breakfast tray. Without a word to Barby or a second look at their auspicious guest, he closed the door behind him as he left.

CHAPTER THREE

H E HAD taken her; she was his. The whole world changed overnight. Barby awoke to find it populated with people rather than with shades of people.

A fat old ship of a Señora calling to her children, "Mi buques, mi buques!—my little boats!" A blind beggar dozing against a wall. A naked little muchacho pensively urinating on the street corner. All these held a strange aliveness he had never noticed before; their faces took on an absorbing reality. And lying in bed, studying minutely the one pillowed on his arm, he saw mirrored all their beauty and sadness, their joy and cruelty. She was his! Through her he possessed the world.

Yes; his hour had struck. But it stopped each morning when they parted, and not until the night when she came again did it begin anew. Young Fuera had vanished, but Sal was always on hand to drink away his few pesos and take Guadalupe home with her. Yet again and again Guadalupe went with him to the privacy of his upstairs room in The Lamp Awake.

It soon occurred to him that he always waited for Las Quince Letras to close before going to meet her. He felt no jealousy in watching her in other arms. Dancing was her business; her percentage from their drinks was her only pay; and through the routine she moved impersonally, nodding and smiling without conscious thought.

Tonight would be different! He was going early and dance with her like any man. Late in the afternoon he left the steaming irrigation ditch that he was helping to clear out, then trudged swiftly home. He washed, ate supper on the counter with Tai Ling. Then he went upstairs to put on his striped shirt and a pair of clean boleros.

Dusk thickened. Already the shuffle of feet had begun outside, the tinkle of a vendor's bell and his wail of "Pa-LE-tas He-LA-das!" Barby flung himself on the bed. One of the girl's stockings lay draped over the rail. He drew it to him and began to smooth out its wrinkles while daydreaming of Guadalupe. It was habitually the easiest way to pass the time until she should be his again. His fingernail suddenly caught in the silk. By the light of a match he saw that the torn threads had unraveled up the stocking to the knee. Furtively he stuffed it behind a box in the corner where she would not find it, then quickly went downstairs.

Tai Ling looked up. "You're not going to Chino Juan's?" Despite the pleasant Spanish his voice held a curious warning.

"No. Las Quince Letras!" the boy answered boastfully, jingling the money in his pocket.

"Pues." The word expressed neither surprise, concurrence nor condemnation of the unusual extravagance. Ignorance pursuing illusion! Still, the girl was a cheerful little thing and he hoped for the best.

Barby hurried out. By the time he had crossed the tracks to emerge into the glare of the brilliantly lit casinos his boastful pride had vanished. Always this private world of wealth and power and rich gringos robbed him of self-possession. Politely he pushed into Las Quince Letras.

Guadalupe was dancing. He could see her as he wedged through the crowd and leaned as though exhausted against the bar. Strengthened by a tequila, he loosened the hat cord under his chin and removed his sombrero. The music stopped. Guadalupe was walking back to her tiny table on the edge of the dance floor. Sight of her somber brown face and black unsmiling eyes restored the power of his resolve.

She was seated, back toward him; now was the time before the chair across from her was filled. Yet every rich Yanqui, every sneering white rancher in the room, seemed waiting to laugh at his first step forward to claim her. "The lousy greaser!"—"The dirty Mex!" Helplessly glancing about the room, he noticed Sal staring directly at him. Her contemptuous grin whipped him forward.

He stumbled awkwardly through the crowd, his lips murmuring continuously, "Permisso—con permisso, Señor" as he bumped a snowy linen sleeve, joggled a panama or cigar. Hat humbly in hand, his uncombed black hair falling to his eyes, he slid under the ropes. Reaching Guadalupe's table, he sank down abjectly upon the empty chair.

The faint slap of his hat on the table roused her. "Pues— Barby!" Her greeting was warm enough, but neither her glance nor manner expressed surprise and welcome.

Pathetically eager to assert his proprietorship, Barby dragged out his fistfull of silver. He had hardly laid it on the table before the bar boy came up. His low toned jest to Guadalupe before he hurried off for their drinks roused Barby to helpless fury. He gritted his teeth till the muscles of his jaw stood out like ropes; an angry red flush seeped through his brown cheeks.

THE YOGI OF COCKROACH COURT

Guadalupe did not notice him. With inscrutable black eyes she was watching the dancing which had begun again. Barby half rose, but Guadalupe raised her hand. A huge pock-marked Mexican had ascended the balcony steps and was shouting through cupped hands. A sudden hush fell over the room.

It was time for the first floor show. Guadalupe rose instantly. "You are in time to see us dance, no?" Without another word she hurried away to join the other percentage girls straggling through a back door marked "Entrada Para Las Artistas."

Abandoned, Barby looked around. Men were deserting bar and gambling tables, surging forward against the ropes. "You there!" shouted the announcer. "Get off the floor!" Apologetically the boy backed into the crowd. The orchestra began to sputter and was soon together in a whine. And with the opening of the back door, Barby watched the Seven Sweet Seductive Señoritas begin their One-Two-Three—Kick! across the floor.

A redheaded girl in checkered bloomers, a scrawny youngster from Sonora in purple tights, Sal, Guadalupe, two faded blonds, and a big-breasted, broad-hipped Mexican woman: listlessly, hands on each others' hips, they went through their paces in the cloying heat. And slowly the musica para baile fled round the room, pursued by the girls a measure behind.

Every night the same inept steps and dreary tunes. A whining La Paloma; a clattering La Cucaracha; Horsey-Keep-Your-Tail-Up with an appropriate wiggle of seven posteriors; old ragtimes whose echoes had drifted down to the Border; and snatches of old folk songs that had blown up from Mexico:

"Guadalajara en un llano,
Mexico en una laguna;
Me he de comer esa tuna,
Aunque me espine la mano!"

Around them the crowd stood without change of face, though here and there an eye gleamed at a moving thigh. Nights on end they had watched Gonzalez' row of girls straggle out and as soon as possible straggle back—a dreary revue to hold them for yet another beer. With amused tolerance they read in the snarling painted grins a contemptuous indifference to their own unresponsive stares.

All but the little morena, the little dark one. Since she had come everything seemed fresh, alive. Simpática! And only a niña, too. Good for the little morena!

Himself held in the crowd, his hat clutched to his breast with both hands, Barby could see nothing but Guadalupe in her cheap silk dress and scuffed red slippers. What had happened? She was awake as he had never awakened her. She was the soft heavy earth waiting for the plow, and birds screeching over the corn milpas, and the tules bent backward by the wind along the washes. Blood rushed to his face, his palms grew wet. He imagined he smelled again the perfume about her, felt the warm lushness of her flesh.

Slowly he began to be aware of other feet around him scraping uneasily on the floor, of other heavy breathing. A man beside him gave a loud hiss of approval. "Chiche!" Then somebody threw in a coin. Another, then another, all flipping money to the little morena.

Barby could have howled his consternation. Fear and rage and envy swept through him. Yet he was held there, crushed and silent, until the song ended. Five of the Seven Sweet Seductive Señoritas stood scowling while Sal dived to the floor helping Guadalupe to collect her money. Then dabbing furtively at their melting faces, all stood in line for a last song.

"HIN-dus-tan . . . where I stopped to rest my tired CAR-a-van . . ."

With a kick and fingers blown from mouths, they turned and scampered from the room. Barby fled out into the street. He had left her on his pillow, all his. And now! The very moon leered down remote and untouchable as she. The way she had looked at him when he had come in; the way she danced and sang, removed from him wholly. Mother of God, what had happened?

He knew well enough. That public orgasm of dancing and singing. That silent tremendous approbation, a more powerful stimulus than the hushed adoration of a lover. Yes, by God, the money! The tinkle of coins on the floor kept ringing in his ears, shaming the few unspent pesos in his pocket. It was all like dust in the darkness, filling the sweaty hollows of his eyes, gritting in his teeth, intangible and impersonal. He rushed headlong through the dark, stopping only to gulp mezcal or green tequilo at any grimy bar.

For the first time the thought struck him that he might lose her. Impossible! He could not imagine such a thing. He would beat the desire out of her, lock her in his room.

Before he knew it he had turned and was running back toward town. He was frantic lest it be ten o'clock and Guadalupe had gone home with Sal. The fear, like the intolerable loneliness of night without her, pursued him over the bridge.

2

Miguel Gonzales, a potbellied picture of indolent watchfulness, also had observed Guadalupe's reception by his customers.

He sat at his battered old desk on the mezzanine of Las Quince Letras, drinking beer and peering down upon his cabaret through the paper flowers entwined about the railing. From this point of vantage his sly, quick eyes followed the hands of his dealers below him. He could watch the bar, oversee his percentage girls, and later observe the antics of his ever-changing chorus.

When it came to money Gonzales was close as a snake's belly to the ground. His bartenders would no more have given out a free drink than they would have slapped him on the back. And when accompanied by his bouncer, the Big Fella, he waddled down the steps with his little black pig eyes snapping, somebody went out the side door into the gutter. Still, to give him his devil's due, he did a good business because he gave everyone a run for his money.

Ay de mí! Gonzales settled back with another bottle and considered the question of this new percentage girl he had just drafted into his chorus—the little morena. . . . Beer with business! What could be better?

She couldn't dance or sing worth a damn. Green as grass. But she had something: rampant, shouting, youthful and unconscious sex! A regular little bitch in heat without knowing it. Look at all that money thrown to her by his customers! Caray! It had to be diverted into his own till. Gonzales put his fingers together. He was prepared to do the royal thing. Without hesitation, he rang for another beer and ordered Guadalupe sent up. . . .

It was after the nightly revue and close to quitting time when the Big Fella brought Gonzales' message to Guadalupe. Sal was sitting with her at the table.

"What's he want?" Sal asked him.

"The little morena, I said," he growled. "Not you. Are you deaf?"

The woman nodded contemptuously. "Don't you be afraid, honey," she said to Guadalupe. "You ain't done nothin'. I'll be waitin' right here till you come back down."

"And tell Barby to wait. He will come soon."

"Oh sure," said Sal; and after the girl had gone, "Hell, yes!"

Ten minutes later Barby burst through the bar door upon her, his frantic glance sweeping the darkening casino and empty dance floor. "Where's Guadalupe?"

"Oh. The grand cabayera again, eh?" Sal grinned insolently at his rumpled, striped shirt and clean boleros. "All dressed up fit to kill. You'll be washin' next."

The boy's face darkened. "Where is she? It's time to close. She—"

Sal got up and edged along the bar. "Plenty of time for a drink while we're waitin' hey?" No amount of quarreling prevented her from cadging a nightcap whether she went home alone or managed to take Guadalupe with her.

"No!" he shouted. "I want to know where she's gone. Something's happened. You're hiding it from me."

His frantic concern and stubborn refusal roused Sal. "Yeah! I thought you smelled like a brewery. You can't even wait to buy us a two-bit whiskey for rushin' to drink up your money yourself. You cheap skate!" She spat on the floor. "I never saw a greaser yet with any brains. It's gettin' so now you've got to be hangin' round her during workin' hours. Out on the floor to spend your dollar where everybody can see you. The great cabayera! What does she get out of that? A chip and another glass of pink sop. And you keepin' away all the good spenders that'd give us dough. . . . Christ! You think I'm goin' to tell you what she asked me to or where she went? Now? After waitin' here dry as a bone? Why—"

"Chinga tu madre!" He flung down some money on the bar. "Now tell me, you bitch!"

Sal downed her whiskey in one gulp, then threw back her head and laughed. An uproarious guffaw of derision. "A fool and a dog in heat! She's sick and went home early. Can't you get that in your thick skull? Oh you fool, fool, fool!"

Barby flung his drink full in her face, then turned and fled. Sal, still grinning, sopped whiskey and tears from her face. From her pocket she fished money for another drink. The bartender callously thumbed over his shoulder.

"It's all right," she breezily answered. "My little pal's upstairs with the boss. He wants me to wait."

She got her drink, lit a cigarette and continued waiting. In a half hour Guadalupe returned, her eyes shining, her whole face alight.

"Well, let's have it!" demanded Sal.

"But listen! I am to dance and sing all alone. Every night. They like me. Señor Gonzales tell me so!"

It was not her words but the look on her face that stopped Sal's sarcastic remark. Still under the trance of Gonzales' promise, the girl stared at her as if seeing nothing but a remote and resplendent vision. Sal took her by the arm; together they walked to their back-street hotel.

"Sal! But isn't it wonderful? Simpática, that is what it makes me feel. I love everybody and you most!"

The woman grunted. Climbing wearily upstairs she unlocked the door and lit a lamp. Guadalupe dropped upon the bed.

"I think tonight of when I was a child, of all the sad people who just sit. Good Mother!" She flung her arms above her head as if at the memory of a hopeless immobility whose bondage still oppressed her. "It was me too. I could do nothing. I was dead, dead, dead. Sometimes I saw the girls dancing in the cantina. Then everything in me was different. I was alive inside. And I knew someday it would be so always."

Quiet now she drew off a stocking. "Now it has come. I feel inside that it is good." Rising from the bed she draped the other stocking over the chair and slid her dress over her head. In one thin undergarment she stretched on her toes and came down smiling and relaxed.

"I am so happy because they like me tonight. So much money they threw on the floor to me I am ashamed. But if I am good I shall dance twice every night and not have to work on the floor all day. It is all because of you, amiga mia. Perhaps you too shall sing and dance with me and make much money. Don't you be happy too?"

"Yeah," said Sal, peeling off her own stockings. "I'm happy and my damn feet's just killin' me. Say, there's your money stacked on the dresser. Better count it and see how much you'd of missed by standin' around ogle-eyed instead of watchin' where they rolled like I did."

Guadalupe strode forward and with a sweep of her hand leveled the stack of coins upon the tabletop. Then she leaned over behind Sal's chair and wrapped her arms around the woman.

"They are yours. I don't know about money. You keep it, Sal."

"All right. Scrape it in the drawer then. We got rent to pay and eats to buy. Somethin' else you don't know much about."

Guadalupe laughed and kissed her on the back of the neck. She smoothed the sheet upon the hot mattress, and spread out inert. "But Barby!" she suddenly sat up to inquire anxiously. "I forgot. He did not come?"

"That ham? God Almighty no! Now that's somethin' else you better be learnin' about. These cheap tail-chasers who never do anything for you, and always hang around to scare off guys that might. Have a good time with 'em once or twice if it bites you, then forget 'em. Like I do with that Fuera. But this shiftless tomcat Barby! He's been hangin' around screamin' ever since. Lay off him, honey, or you'll be havin' somethin' more than singin' and dancin' to worry about."

Guadalupe's face straightened. She could do and think of but one thing at a time. Still she said petulantly, "But I like him. And you make me sad and not happy when you say such things."

"It's your own funeral," said Sal. She was still slumped down on the chair, legs crossed. She had on a pink silk chemise beginning to show its wear, and chin in hand was staring out the window. "Damn, it's hot," she said after a time. "This old hotel's like an oven. I'm slimy already." She ran a wet hand up her bare legs and wiped it on the worn chemise.

Suddenly she spun around. "You ignorant little brat! You heard what that Goddam speckle-faced bouncer said to me and how he's been bellyachin' at me all the time. Just like he acted to Ina before he kicked her out one night for no reason at all. I ain't no fool; I got a hunch who's goin' to be next."

Guadalupe, her face half-hidden from the light, lay fingering the beads around her throat. Worry and hurry she could never understand. Things happened when they were ready.

"Oh, don' mind," she answered listlessly.

The tone of her inner unconcern roused Sal. She uncrossed her legs and rose slowly. "Who in the hell says I mind? Or anybody else? I'm takin' what's comin' same as I always done. Hell won't be no hotter'n this, though; I'll tell you that!"

3

Taking her time she washed at the stand in the corner, splashing her arms and legs from a tin bowl uncomfortably hot to her hands. Without wiping she stood before the lamp and stared at her reflection in the glass of the mirror. Even as she stood there, the hot dry air of the room evaporated the water on her skin. As her face dried, devoid now of powder and paint, the wrinkles crawled into place. With the fingers of both hands she drew her cheeks tight but the instant they were removed her face sagged. Sal gripped the edges of the dresser and bent closer. Unafraid, she saw herself clearly: the big bold face clammy white in the dusty glass; the too generous, large mouth; bitter smoke-blue eyes like glass marbles staring from nests of crow's-feet; the taffy-colored hair that once had been a glossy yellow. For a fleeting moment a wistful, almost childish look of pain transformed her face until she seemed transiently young again. Then it was gone and something of a sneer crawled into its place. Her cheeks appeared to lengthen and hollows deepened between their fleshy skeins. With a quick careless gesture she stuck a cigarette between her bloodless lips and lit it from the lamp. For a long time she stood looking down at Guadalupe sprawled out upon the bed in sleep—at her firm pointed breasts, the creamy thighs, close-knit knees and rounded arms, the delicate oval face.

"Jesus! So much and don't know what to do with it!" she muttered to herself. And then again, "You lucky ignorant little brat!"

She blew out the lamp and found the chair in the dark. Here she sat smoking and looking out the open window. Across the wide flat blackness of the railroad tracks a row of

lights still burned in the wooden shacks. Behind them rose
the square flat tops of brick and adobe barely outlined against
the night's horizon. Soon two laborers emerged from the little
bar on the corner below her; she could hear their voices
amiably quarreling down the street.

It wasn't like you could call at them here, or maybe they'd
stop of their own accord for a bit of joshin' like at that little
house in Yuma. Only four girls, but she had been a fool to leave.
Never could get that good house in Kansas City out of her
mind. Pretty yellow roses on the curtains, the little bell that
rang when somebody asked for you especial, and the streetcar
clangin' by outside. The Owl. The conductor always waved
from the back platform when you blinked your lights. A
Swedish boy. He took his cap off once and you could see his
curly hair more yellow than yours. But he never came in.
Bashful or broke. You just kept waitin', callin' yourself a
damn fool. A Swedish boy streetcar conductor on the Owl,
K.C., Mo., U.S.A. But you had a hunch if he ever came to
the third house from the corner and asked for the girl on
the second story, in the room with the curtains of yellow roses,
somethin' was bound to happen.

An engine puffed heavily by with a string of cars for the
night's switching. Their thunder shook the room. Within her
the clamor of their passing remained long after they were lost
in the shadows of the packing sheds. The injustice, the bitterness of living, shook her big frame.

Damn the Big Fella and his lousy hide! She had a hunch
what was coming. Ina, Lulu, Maria, Sonora Sue—each of them
symbols of a dozen others, they flashed from her mind where
happily forgotten they had lain so long. Sure, she knew what
was coming to her as to them, if not now then a month, a
year later. First gin and beer took your ginger, then sun and
dust your looks. And men took everything else. What more

did you have then, Sal wondered, besides a cigarette cough, a nasty hoarse voice, and a body like a sack? Staring into the darkness she was unable to find an answer.

After a time she rose and stood looking down at Guadalupe on the bed. Only for an instant a jealous thought flashed before her and was gone. Guadalupe had something and meant to keep it; damn everything else. You didn't know just what, but you could feel it. The girl was on her way up, and she was on her way down.

"You damned lucky little stiff!"

That's all she could say; her greeting and farewell as they passed. Slowly Sal passed a tired hand across her face and wiped the sweat on her thigh. Then she too flopped down on the bed.

4

Yet week by week she went to him more often. Neither Sal nor Barby could understand why. Gonzales had kept his promise. No longer did he chain her by necessity to a table for eight hours a day as a percentage girl. He kept her for his evening crowd. Her two brief appearances on the heels of the revue kept swelling it ever bigger. Las Quince Letras began to boast of its featured entertainer. Guadalupe became a name. She danced and sang, awkward but compelling, with an unpredictable repertoire of constantly changing moods.

Barby had not gone back into the cantina. He was biding his time, content to lie waiting for her in The Lamp Awake. But sometimes, a lonely silent figure with a cigarette drooping from his lips, he stood at the window where he had first seen her. She was there again, glance to glance, and singing a song —La Calle 12—as if to him alone:

"Que bello será
Dáme un beso y no me mires asi;
Toma otra y guarda todas para mi,
Que tus besos me estremecen de pasion
Y a ti solo me entreque."

The boy stood unresponsive. How it lied, and she! But there was something within her which could not lie. It gave him an assuaging sense of possessiveness. He slouched away into the darkness toward Tai Ling's, knowing that she would come to him again.

Sal was completely mystified by these repeated nocturnal peregrinations of a girl whose very character seemed to refute and abhor them by day. Every morning in their hotel room Guadalupe awoke instantly and fully alive. The first ray of the sun through the grimy curtains seemed to touch off her vitality like a match. Sal, worn to a frazzle by the night before, could only lie abed grumbling her protests at another day. Her earliest mutter never caught Guadalupe in bed. Invariably she was up sunning herself, naked and stretching on her toes, with the shades pulled back; or else kneeling before the open window and staring quietly over the azoteas while the sun warmed her scalp.

"Get up! Hurry, Sal. I am so hungry!"

Sal managed to get up and rinse out her mouth from the water bucket in the corner. After a cigarette which she smoked lying flat on her back while Guadalupe slid on her stockings, she felt better. "Why so damned early?" she kept muttering. "When you get as old as I am and lose some of that ginger you'll appreciate a cat nap in the mornin'." That she never failed to get up, for all her grumbling, was a measure of her attachment to the girl. Guadalupe had been coming home so seldom lately it behooved her to exchange an hour's sleep for their only private companionship.

What a child of the sun the girl was! Like a lizard, she could not move until the light had penetrated every fiber of her being. And then how suddenly and intensely alive she became and remained throughout the day. It was as though through every pore she absorbed an energy that impelled her every act. Curiously enough it carried her through the evening as if the casino's bright lights and music were a prolongation of her mood. Sunlight! It was her life as she was its symbol.

Night blotted her out instantly. With the abrupt change from light to dark, and with the last flicker of the casino, she became a different person. As abruptly different as night and day. Her life, her intense vitality, seemed to clot in her veins. She became stagnant.

Always it had been like that; as if night evoked a subtle metamorphosis within her. But Guadalupe—she knew the terrible nullity, the hopeless inutility of not-being. And she lay in a very Indian stupor, drawn in tight within herself against the oppressive dark. It had no voice, no comfort, no disturbing dreams—no reality; it was simply an utter negation from which she shrank with an overwhelming fear.

This passive acquiescence to that brought out in her at night, Barby supposed to be an eager response to his own demands. Nor did Guadalupe act otherwise. She was simply compliant.

As her evening in the cabaret drew to a close, she could feel it coming. Sal still had another hour to work. Gonzales had forbidden Guadalupe to wait for her in the cabaret; she was an artista now. The hotel room was dark and empty; she already had loafed all afternoon there. So she stood singing softly, cringing from the approaching claws of night. Suddenly her voice rose and broke into the loud vacilada of the peon, that taunting cry which expresses more than anything else the complete acceptance of his fate. With a flurry of skirts she collapsed upon the floor. The spotlight upon her went out.

It was her last song. She was through for the night, and the hopeless inutility washed over her in a dark wave. A few moments later she slipped out of the side door and fled to Tai Ling's upstairs room. Barby was always waiting. Wrapped in his arms she still felt the dark obliteration of night, but the nullity of not-being seemed less acute. To be wanted, to be loved! That was all she felt.

Gradually then she came to him more and more often. Half her clothes were strewn throughout the room in The Lamp Awake. That she left early each morning, hurriedly and completely, made little difference. With the night, like a thing passive, suddenly gone dead, she came again.

5

Tai Ling, watching her come and go, understood well these two poles of her being.

Like day and night, sun and moon, male and female, the wisdoms and the passions, they reflected that ultimate duality of the mundane consciousness, the phenomenal Sangsara and the noumenal Nirvana, which in reality were inseparably related and must at last be recognized as an indivisible unity.

The results of such a dualistic view Tai Ling observed all around him. In the room above him he heard it as the cause of antagonism between sexes. On the street outside he saw it causing racial hatreds and cracked heads. Persisted in as it was, it divided even the individual. Intuition strove with rationalization, flesh with spirit. Perverted, it roused its male and female principles to battle for command of the personal self.

Objectively, then, he suspected Guadalupe of being a battleground on which the dual poles of her nature fought for dominance. Constantly the pendulum swung back and forth. Where it would rest he did not know. He viewed both equally, admitting the sangsaric or earthly existence of each as an illusion, and denying them separately as apart from their real nirvanic or heavenly unity.

Such were Tai Ling's objective conclusions about Guadalupe. Personally he had taken a great fancy to her. Poor little songbird! Fluttering her wings against the ignorance that held her prisoner. But help her he could not. She simply had come like Barby, a welcome guest, and could draw no more from him than the capacity of her nature allowed.

Objectively, personally—these Tai Ling realized suddenly were themselves dual reflections of his own base nature. He settled down to reconcile them. Perhaps, weak as he was, she had something to give him.

He did not have long to wait before it was apparent. Late that night he was aroused by a discreet knock at the back door. A loaded truck stood in the alley. Mendoza had accompanied it.

"Five barrels of fish? In the middle of the week?" asked Tai Ling. "Chugoku knows better. I cannot handle them with my modest business."

Mendoza grinned slyly. "Yes you can, old boy. We'll just unload them quietly, and unpack them down in your cellar. You won't have too many fish to get rid of."

For a long time they looked steadily at each other.

"I told you and your friend, as you will remember, that I could not accept your offer," said Tai Ling firmly. "It is against my principles. I desire only to carry on my poor business without indulging in your venture. You will have to go elsewhere."

"No we won't. Look outside." Mendoza thumbed over his shoulder. Tai Ling saw standing at the end of the alley the figure of an armed rurale. "Drive us away and he will fire two shots in the air. That will bring out all the Border police-men from the garrison. You will be arrested for harboring and trying to transport illegally five aliens. I will be a witness, and testify to your previous sales of contraband drugs. If you don't belive me, try it!"

Tai Ling was caught. Even so, he gathered courage to sacrifice himself to those principles of right-doing in which he so devoutly believed. Meanwhile his mind frantically weighed as foolish pride the empty sacrifice of his mere personal self against the practical harm it might do his two innocent guests to deprive them thus of a home and endanger their immedi-ate future.

As he hesitated, Mendoza grabbed his arm. "You old fool! Don't be crazy. The Gentleman gave the order, not me. I only paid off the rurale to protect you. Nobody's going to know. They're only going to be here till tomorrow night."

"I will not be a party to such an illicit affair."

"I'll tell him so. This is an emergency. Quick, it'll soon be daylight!" Mendoza turned and ordered in the five barrels.

Wearily Tai Ling watched them being carried down into his cellar. When the truck had departed he went to his own back room. He could not sleep. Over and over he probed the "Eight Worldly Ambitions," dualistically expressed, for clues to his own weakness.

No, he had no worldly craving for Profit, and Avoidance of Loss; Fame, and Avoidance of Defamation; Praise, and Avoidance of Disparagement; Pleasure, and Avoidance of Pain. He was simply caught, like any fish, in the web of karmic illusion.

Tai Ling could not deny its existence, nor could he admit its ultimate reality. They were dual halves of something neither evil nor good. It was up to him to make the best of it. Like Guadalupe, he too must admit of two poles of being which must eventually coincide.

The thought swung him back to her sleeping upstairs. He listened intently. There was no sound. His poor little songbird! But with her boxed upstairs no one would suspect what went on in his cellar. And for this unconscious protection he would repay her in kind.

CHAPTER FOUR

SUMMER STRUCK. Town, sand hills and the chaparral-studded mountains beyond quivered in the shimmering heat waves as if afloat upon an invisible but restless sea. Over all hung the lilac desert haze.

From sunup till dusk men hid under the wide portales or slipped from shadow to shadow as if afraid of being seen. Only at dark they ventured forth, haunting the streets for a bit of breeze. Beset by swarms of crickets and cucarachas, scratching at heat rash and wiping off sweat, all seemed afflicted with a nervous ague.

By midnight it was little better. Barby and Guadalupe lay exhausted on the bed, reduced at last to physical apathy. It was as though the condensed heat of the upstairs room had drawn out the consuming fire in the boy.

For the first time they talked. Yet gradually their talk developed into an insidious persecution of the girl beside him. There was nothing about her that Barby did not want to know. Night after night he ruthlessly kept dragging from her those inconsequential facts of her simple life that had led her to Las Quince Letras, to Sal and him.

Guadalupe at first was not aware of how persistently he sought to draw her out. Nearly stupefied by the malignant torpor, she even welcomed his prodding voice.

"Go on! You can tell me, can't you? What the hell!"

His dark eyes, metallic in the moonlight, never left her face. She could not pause for long until his low insistent voice compelled her to go on. With the touch of his hand on her knee, she answered to his intimate questioning as though the dark called forth her thoughts. And as she heard the faint wash of drunken song, the debilitated clatter of a far piano, there returned to her with misgivings that persistent, forewarning sense of imprisonment which never left her free.

2

There had been nothing in her childhood on the Reservation suggestive of imprisonment. Lazy and sweet, the days were all alike. Morning Mass. Simple lessons in the Mission School. The Indians straggling down hill to hoe their scrubby fields, then plodding back.

The sense of constriction she often felt came from something within her that beat its wings seeking escape. Out into the courtyard it drove her in a whirlwind of arms and legs, pelting the stolid other children with long bean pods of mesquite. Then suddenly seeing the worried gaze of Sister Teresa, she spun into the nun's arms. Something appeased for the moment. Something inside her that would try again to escape.

What did Sister Teresa think of her then?

Sister Teresa. . . .

Guadalupe could hardly recall the tall, stiff pillar hung

with black or the white marble face mounted on it under the starched band of its cowl. That long, lean face, ascetic and impersonal, cold white as that of a corpse! She could only remember Sister Teresa's hands. Long and blue-veined, they seemed to hold all the life and repressed desires denied the nun's face and body. Constantly fingering the beads about her throat or clasping each other in prayer, they were never still. They seemed always to be searching, demanding, imploring— even that night when Guadalupe was ill and Sister Teresa slept with her.

How tender they were, caressing the girl's body as they wiped off the perspiration; so protective as they clasped her closer and closer in the darkness. Suddenly the girl awoke from a fitful doze with a scream of terror. The nun's body held her prisoner. Her bloodless lips were covering her with kisses. Her hands . . . Guadalupe's cry aroused the whole ward. Lights flashed on. An attendant came running. Instantly the nightmare was dispelled. Sister Teresa herself said so.

"A bad, bad dream! All gone, my child. See, here is your Sister Teresa beside you."

Indeed she was. Her cowl was straight again on her cropped head. Her bluish lips were smiling with solicitude. Her hands—those horrible, nervous, outlaw hands—were gently smoothing bed and pillow.

"Now Sister Teresa will ask Our Father to protect us against evil, temptation and bad dreams. Then she will put out the lights and sit here on a chair beside you. Yes, my child. A dream, nothing but a dream. All gone."

It was all a dream, of a woman with a dying urge for living ceaselessly praying to the image of a limp dead Man on a cross. Guadalupe fed instead from a stronger god—the dark Madonna of the blue robe, the Virgin of Guadalupe, the old goddess of Indian Mexico canonized by the Church.

The story never grew old: how as a child, wrapped in a black rebozo with an old carven image, she had been found under a mesquite and brought up here under the Virgin's own name. Time and again she listened to descriptions of that dreary Sonoran mesa, the broken wagon, and the nearby bodies of a group of Mexican peons who had tried to flee from the revolution. To these she added little from the haze of her own childish memory; slowly the outline of her plundered village in the sierras faded. But the vitality of her patron saint persisted, and her own ecstatic adoration which she soon learned to keep hidden.

"Our Lady, Guadalupe the Virgin . . ." she recited glibly aloud.

But silently and secretly from the cavern of her mindless memory welled a truer invocation:

"O Dark Madonna of the Tepeyac, clad in your blue mantle dotted with stars like toasted grains of maize, do not forget us, our Guadalupana! Poor, dark and humble like ourselves, O Guadalupe, leave us your image on your fine ayate. We are the feather, the flower, the drum and mirror of the old gods. So lend us your breath, O Tonantzin, Ancient Mother of the Gods, with your new name, that we may remember you also. Dark goddess, ancient mother, come to us in your mantle of sweeping rain! Let the tall drum *huelhueltl*, the flat drum *teponaztle*, be beat again! O Dark Madonna, we wait longingly till you come again."

She, the child, had forgotten the chant, but the dark madonna made her blood remember. And she remained a stubborn little pagan. Whereas the decadent Cocopahs, Mojaves and Yumas about her were slow and apathetic, Guadalupe was vigorous and alive. She was explosive, with a mood for every moment. But she had a sullen, black negation too.

She puzzled the authorities, wrecked routine with a laugh,

and burned holes in all their blanket attempts at submission with her furious little rages. She simply couldn't be good when virtue demanded stupidity. So that Father Ignatius, with repetitive solemnity, periodically recommended her removal at the earliest opportunity. Only in Sister Teresa she had a friend.

Another horrible night came. This time Sister Teresa lay in bed surrounded by candles, and it was Guadalupe who was allowed to kneel and say a prayer. The dream ended.

The girl rose and walked outside. The calm of night still lurked among the pepper trees. Only the twitter of birds in the palms made music in the air. Slowly the sun rose, touching the adobe walls of the church and the mission school. At the edge of the hill Guadalupe stopped and sat down.

How strangely unfamiliar now it all appeared. The unkempt corn and cotton patches on one side, and the bleak dun sand stretching away beyond to the wrinkled desert mountains on the horizon. On the crest of the opposite hill the crumbling old fort prison with its latticed iron doors hanging rusty and broken on their hinges; the dusty road creeping toward town. And just below, the great slow curve of the river crawling like a brown wet serpent between the sandy bluffs. The "River of Good Guidance," named nearly four hundred years ago.

Quietly Guadalupe sat there, arrested for one fleeting moment of reflection between the desert of the past and that river which was like her to flow forever onward without return. Then the thin voice of a bell rose into the morning. Another joined with a brazen cry. The bells of Santo Tomás calling her to a last early morning mass.

The girl walked quietly back.

Father Ignatius had been both exceedingly busy and kind. There in his study, his bald head round as the globe of the world on its squeaky standard, he told her what plans he had made.

"A very good place, my girl, and an excellent opportunity. A quiet, homelike atmosphere you will find in it, I'm sure. The duties will be very light: a few beds in the morning, a hand with the dishes. Very fortunate you are; due entirely to the interest we have taken in you, my dear. We felt we must assure ourselves of your new home.

"Just a few words of caution though." His pudgy fingers sent the world spinning on its axis. "You are growing, you know. Quite time for you to take your place in the world. It wants dignified young women. I know you'll be all those things which we recommended so highly to Mrs. Lascelles. Won't you, my child?"

Paternally he reached out a hand to pat her own before she withdrew it to her lap. "Even the fall of a sparrow the Lord sees. Remember His eyes will always be upon you. Shall we not offer up a prayer for the protection of one of His lambs before she leaves the fold?" Thereafter came crisp words of instruction, definite things to be done in the way of her few clothes.

A solemn Requiem Mass was said for Sister Teresa. The great doors of the church swung open. Slowly the throng marched in: the priests and nuns, the older women in their cotton blankets and the men with their hair plastered down with water, then the children; Guadalupe, with the girls, stiff in starchy Sunday gingham. At the worn threshold the sign of the cross was made. Thence the figures dispersed throughout the high, vaulted room and were lost in rows of seats. Dark blurs in a musty sepulchral gloom lit only by clumps of flickering candles. None individual. All supine, restrained, anonymous as Sister Teresa lying in her box up front.

Guadalupe was suddenly aware of her hungry belly, the small tips of her breasts chafed by starchy gingham, the buzzing in her head. A tear fell on her hand. She brushed it away angrily. She meant to keep alive. But obediently enough she slumped forward on her knees with the others.

Far up ahead, against an ornate altar, a white robed figure began to mumble. The girl was not aware of the voice changing from Latin to Spanish and thence to English. She knelt or sat there inflexible as an arrow in the bow, her dark face raised, her dry black eyes piercing the gloom before her.

The droning voice ceased. The white robed figure turned and began the movements of an incomprehensible pantomine. Guadalupe as always watched him curiously. He had none of the rapt absorption of the Indians before him. His steps were quick and jerky. He shook a little water sprinkler with pompous impatience. His hands were brittle; they clapped together across his breast, broke, and joined again as he knelt with a back stiff as a pine tree.

At last it was finished. Once again each face and figure was human and individual as they passed out into the bright sunlight.

The two trucks were filled. Behind them in marching order were drawn up the other Sisters, the attendants and children of the school. The cavalcade wound out of the courtyard toward the cemetery.

It was early spring. The desert was lit by a transient loveliness. The long whiplash ocotillos were tipped with crimson. On the hillside stood pale Candles of Our Lord, the yucca, La Vela del Nuestro Señor. Yellow cactus flowers bloomed in barren sandy washes; matted purple verbena; the wild shy poppies called Las Dormideras, the Drowsy Ones.

All so sweet and still, waiting for Sister Teresa.

At the Campo de Santo the procession stopped. The trucks in the center; encircled by the nuns, the tired and dusty children; and they in turn enclosed by a thick fence of barbed wire, a protection from nocturnal coyotes. There it was, saw

Guadalupe, like a dark deep wound in the flesh-colored sand. Beside it she watched the box being lowered from one of the trucks. Nothing could quite convince her of its contents.

For Guadalupe the nun would always be back there, a cold white face mounted on its tall stiff pillar. Then unaccountably she thought of those long, blue-veined hands still clawing inside the box, still searching in death as in life. A sudden tremor shook her body as if they passed over her again.

A tall nun shook her arm. "Sing, child, sing! Can you not remember your own Sister Teresa?"

Guadalupe moved her lips but the words made so sound. The hymn drifted away over the vast dry plain as the coffin was lowered. She opened her eyes to the mountains on the horizon, looming up with outflung arms on the edge of another world. They were covered with a dark blue mantle and dotted with specks of light, like toasted maize grains, by the bright morning sun. She was free.

3

Lascelles' Boardinghouse, located on the Arizona side of the Line, was a stubborn survivor of feudal Border days. Its massive adobe walls were pitted with bullet wounds. The cobbled courtyard that once rang with the boasts of caballero and vacquero was now overgrown with weeds. The great vigas beaming the rooms had turned, like smoke-cured hams, to a rich dark brown.

Built too soundly for decay, the old ranch house had later been used as a gambling resort. The dining room where Guadalupe served Ma Lascelles' hungry boarders had been the roulette room. Flanking the door through which she slid with her tray still stood a section of the bar effective as a large buffet. The other half served for a hotel desk in the front hall.

The present guests for the most part were dealers, bartenders and percentage girls who worked at night across the Border. Seated together for the evening meal they presented to Guadalupe an incongruous picture of domesticity. Moving down and back the long table, her black eyes wide to every detail, she had a chance to observe them closely.

On one side were the girls, like a row of painted dolls. Catita, almost black and smaller than herself. Adelaide, fat and sloppy, almost asleep on one elbow and still stuffing green olives into her cheeks. Taffy-haired Grace, easily the beauty of the table with a glow just beginning to lose its forced flare. Demure Emily, the cash girl. Sorena, tall and slim as the cigarette in her bony fingers. And on Ma Lascelles' right, a contemptuous girl in red silk who made Guadalupe's mornings miserable by calling continually for lukewarm tea—Benita, Ma's pet by reason of her double pay.

Across from them sat the men, most of them dealers, who dispatched their food with the same rapidity and silence with which they dealt poker, blackjack and écarté. They might have been a convention of undertakers in white shirts and black bow ties.

On their right sat a big sandy-haired man named Toberman. He always finished first and excused himself with a "Good luck for the evening, friends!" that would have sounded ridiculous were his eyes not so bleak and blue. Guadalupe could sense the others' relief at his departure for the gold table at the largest casino. Once he had left, Jose and Luis, two young fellows in one of the cabaret orchestras, began joking with the girls. The fun lasted for perhaps a half hour. Across the hotel desk George and the little cash girl played checkers till time to go to work. Then by two and three they drifted out and across the Line.

There remained only the Lascelles. Until long after

Guadalupe had cleared the table Ma Lascelles remained at its head. Small and lumpy, her brown greasy face seemed to ooze nicotine as she sat smoking innumerable cigarettes. She had a decided preference for brown-paper Mexican cigarros which Benita brought her from over the border. Gradually their smoked stubs mounted in the thick saucer at her hand. Occasionally, as she lifted a stubby hand to push back her thin hair, the ashes caught in her hair or dropped upon her face without notice. Save for a sharp command in Spanish to Guadalupe clearing the table, she seemed lost in a reverie of blue smoke. It was the only time Guadalupe ever saw her relax.

But it was Jim Lascelles at the foot of the table whom Guadalupe watched most carefully. Each time she entered the room she suffered an instinctive revulsion at sight of his red meaty neck and close cropped hair growing grey above his small ears. His own glance seemed to strip her like a sweaty hand. As she leaned across him to clear the table, he slyly reached down under the tablecloth and pinched her leg. Guadalupe jumped; two glasses shattered on the floor.

"Niña! Los vasos! Please be more careful," came the woman's quick reproof. Her sharp eyes fastened themselves upon her husband for an instant before their stare became blank again. Then Guadalupe began upon the dishes in the kitchen; the woman joined her; and Lascelles strolled out into the night.

Ma Lascelles was an exacting taskmaster. A woman who had known work all her life, she expected as much from all except her husband who dozed all day behind the bar-desk in the front hallway. Guadalupe spent the mornings cooking bacon and warming coffee for the boarders who straggled down at all hours. She was continually trotting upstairs with lukewarm tea for the cranky pet, Benita. At noon she and Ma Lascelles made the beds together, swept the house. After a late lunch her siesta hour in the weed-grown garden under the pepper tree was made miserable with sheets to be mended and buttons to be sewed on. By then it was time to start dinner.

The short interlude until sleep was her only leisure. This too she spent alone. Something about Ma Lascelles' busy body and vacuous stare forebade intimacy. Nor had she any friends among the boarders. They had no chance to detain for talk the dark young girl flitting busily among them like a shadow; and she had no time. In the solitude of her attic room she lay thinking of Father Ignatius' sly smile, of Sister Teresa's hands, of Lascelles' small ears.

The old sense of imprisonment returned. There persisted something within her she could not control. Once the freshness of her new home wore off, it kept tantalizing her with an intolerable ache. Terribly she wanted something, but what it was she did not know. All the world outside was just as far away.

For an hour she fretted. Another moment and she sat upright, listening to Ma Lascelles preparing for bed in the room below. It was early, scarce ten o'clock, and all in the inn was quiet.

A little later she slipped quietly out and across the Line. Sight and sound of the turbulent evening life became a drug to her starved senses which continually called for more. But afraid of being seen by any of the boarders, she could not satisfy the longing that drove her night after night down the dark streets. Only for a few minutes she dared to loiter in the shadows of the gay cabarets and casinos. Then still unsatisfied she returned to the old inn.

One night Ma Lascelles opened the door upon her as she crept upstairs.

"Niña! Qué hace? What are you doing?"

The girl's face went suddenly hard as stone.

"If you wish a drink take a glass with you when you go upstairs. I do not wish you to go downstairs so late."

"Sí, Señora. I go quickly." Sullenly she slouched upstairs.

Both of them knew the lie; both thought of Lascelles. For a week the girl did not leave her room. Then again she resumed her nightly peregrinations. The aching hunger to fill that empty void of self! It would not let her rest.

The night came, slowly drawing down from the hills. Outside the window a stray dog howled answer to the faint yap of a coyote. Almost immediately the sound was muffled in the black velvet night. All again was quiet. It was nearly midnight.

Guadalupe slid out of bed and dressed quietly in the dark. She could visualize her destination clearly as on the morning she had first seen the old dry well across town. An old wishing shrine, its waist-high walls still stood in the middle of the road. There were many in town who still believed in its powers, when properly invoked with a secret midnight candle and a shy whispered prayer to the Virgin; and each morning their burned candles added to the innumerable stubs stuck in every crevice of the rocks and on the tallow smeared top.

Dressed, Guadalupe felt her way to the big comoda. Opening a drawer she felt for her small heap of silver dollars. These she knotted in the foot of a stocking and thrust into her dress. Now, shoes in hand, she slid out into the hall.

At the head of the stairs she paused, and crept softly down. Away from the hotel she knelt to put on her shoes. With the sharp click of her hard heels echoing the beating of her heart, she walked swiftly down the street. It was later than she thought; a slow influx from across the Border was beginning to swell the street. At the last of the open shops she turned in quickly. "La vela! Yes. The big candle there on the shelf!" Without quibbling she paid the price and hurried out.

She had just turned the corner when she heard steps behind her. Even as she turned with a presentiment of detection, the man spoke.

"Well! What's the hurry, kiddo?"

As she flung about, the long candle held behind her, Lascelles caught her arm.

"Sure enough! Thought I saw you slippin' around the corner. Now tell me you're just out on a pasearse to take the evenin' air! Go on! I knew you wasn't so quiet and tame as you looked." He chuckled deep in his sunburned throat. "Bet the old woman don't know you're out. You sly little devil! Got a novio down here somewheres, eh? Let's see what else you're takin' him."

Guadalupe shook under the grip of his hand, then held out the candle.

"No, Señor. I do not understand. I go to burn a candle to the Virgin."

Lascelles reared back to laugh. Then seeing the cold black stare of the girl's eyes, he nodded sagely. "Oh-ho. On the outs with the boy, eh? And this is to get him back. Sure, I savvy."

The girl did not flinch from his stale breath. "What do you do, Señor?" she asked in a quiet, hard voice.

"Do?" he chuckled absentmindedly. "Why, we're goin' on down to the well to light that candle—unless you want me to take you home to the old woman."

Guadalupe turned stiffly, and with his arm through hers, crossed the street. She was forced to hurry to keep up with his swift lumbering body. Beside his long strides her little slippers beat a quick tattoo in the dust. Lascelles seemed engrossed in deep, pleasant thought. At the well he stopped and removed his arm.

"Well, we're here kiddo," he said with a slight tremor in his thick voice.

The old well was yet unlighted for the night. The road was dark; there was no moon. The few lights of town seemed far away as stars. Nor could she hear a car or hoofbeat.

"Señor, give me a match. I have forgotten a light for the Virgin's candle."

Lascelles dug into his pocket. As he extended the match his hand reached for hers. Guadalupe retreated around the well. "It is a big candle, Señor. I think it will stick in these rocks better." She thrust it deeper into the inside wall, then rasped the match across a stone. In the flicker of the light she could see the man's face resting on his hairy arms: the broad nose, his dark stubble of beard and hungry eyes. He was silent and breathing heavily, and had forgotten his jocular mood of the moment before.

She bent her head, watching him between her fingers. Then remembering her prayer, she closed her eyes. In that instant, quicker than she could raise her head, Lascelles was behind her. One arm went round her waist. With the other hand a wedge under her chin, he kissed her long and greedily on the mouth.

His tension broken for an instant, he raised his head and laughed. "Burnin' a candle for love, eh? And ain't I glad it's a big one! Didn't take long to bring you luck did it?" He bent down to her again, very confident.

The girl's arm had been released. Now, too swift to be ducked, it flashed up and then down, her fingers raking marks across his cheek.

"You little cat!" he growled. "Claw my eyes out, would you. . . ."

Immediately she was pinioned to the wall. Slowly he forced her back, his broad chest crushing her breasts, his beard already brushing her face. She was suddenly conscious of a searing flame; her arm, flung backward down into the well, had moved into the flame of the candle wedged between the stones. Swiftly, with a "Sweet Mother!" and a quick hand, she jerked it free and drove the burning end into his face.

A minute later she was crouching in the darkness at the corner. Lascelles, half-blinded and burned by the hot tallow, was still cursing at the well. Quickly she made up her mind, and slipped out into the open road that led from town. Only once she looked back, and it was with the disturbing sensation of the man's kiss still running through her.

4

All this and more Barby drew from her as night after night they lay together in the sweaty blackness of Tai Ling's upstairs room.

"And then what?" he would ask, rising on one elbow to stare into the dark eyes that remained open and fixed upon the memories recalled at his bidding. He was insatiable. There seemed nothing, however trivial, that he did not want to know about her. Her throat dry from talking she would lie silent in the lethargic darkness. Barby would get up and bring her back a drink from the water jar in the corner. For minutes he would sit on the edge of the bed smoking. Then lying down beside her once more he would demand again, "And then what? How did you happen to come here?"

There was something in his insistent tone she could not refuse. And remembering the night she had fled from Lascelles, the old stage and those within it, Guadalupe talked on.

She had been sitting beside the road to rest her aching feet when the stage swept past. Then, five lengths ahead, it

screamed to a sudden stop. The driver leaned out and called.
"Come on! I ain't got all night!"

Wearily she climbed in; with a clatter of gears the car
rumbled on. It was an old auto-stage fit only for the rough
travel of desert roads. In the middle of the roof was a small
yellow light. It showed an old woman, three Mexican laborers
bumping sleepily from side to side, and in the back seat a girl
curled up under an old coat.

"Hi kid!" the latter called, rousing. "How's walkin'? Put
a leg over and have a smoke."

Before she could answer, the old woman moved beside
her. There was a rotten decay about her which made her seem
older than she was. Several of her teeth were missing; she kept
thrusting a pink tongue in the vacancy. Her watery grey eyes
watched the girl's every move.

The driver turned sidewise, and stuck out a hand. "Two
bucks, girlie. Or do you want to go on through?"

Guadalupe got out her knotted stocking. Where the stage
was going or where she wanted to go she did not know. The
darkness kept rushing past.

"Aw c'mon," came the voice from the back seat again.
"Can't you see the kid's flat? Turn around and forget it. Nobody ain't seein' you give a lift."

"You dry up, Sal!" the driver yelled back, changing gears.
"And keep your nose out. If I made as many pickups as you'd
like, I'd be payin' to ride myself. Now come on, girlie. Two
bucks or off you go. I done you a favor already by stoppin' out
here at night against the rules."

The old woman had watched the stocking being untied.
"Here, dearie. Pay the man your fare. Let me help yeh." Her
prehensile fingers poked stealthily in the little pile of silver
dollars which Guadalupe emptied into her lap, and selected

two which she passed to the driver. Then watching the girl wrap up the others again, she edged closer.

The girl called Sal yelled out once more. "Kid, you better keep away from them claws or that old bitch will get more outa you than that dinero. You come on back here in good company."

The old woman's thin lips drew back; she turned around and began to swear. Sal propped up on one arm and lit a cigarette. "Oh pipe down, Oakie. I know what you're after. And girlie, get me straight: you stick to Sister if them big eyes of yours ain't blind."

By the time Guadalupe had turned around, Sal was covered up again; she could see nothing but a mop of taffy hair. Old Oakie had put her arm around the girl and was patting her clumsily.

"Go to hell, then, both of you!" Sal cried, flipping her cigarette stub at the old woman.

Guadalupe remained silent, watching the blackness rush by the window. In the fuliginous hour preceding dawn the stage stopped at a grimy garage. The three Mexican laborers got out and crossed a little plaza toward the railroad depot. On the other side of the plaza a few pale lights gleamed sleepily: an all-night lunch counter, a pool hall, a two-story frame building. When she got out she saw that Sal had left the stage without another word and was vanishing up the street. Deadened by the spell of night, as always, Guadalupe had ignored the girl's hearty warning. Now suddenly a queer foreboding leapt out at her; Sal had turned the corner.

The old woman was plucking at her sleeve and pointing to the ramshackle building. Above its doorway, lighted by one small and unshaded electric globe, appeared the words, "Cuartos de Renta—Baños."

Guadalupe hesitated. Chortling to herself, the old woman led her forward.

"What then?" asked Barby after waiting for her to continue.

Guadalupe did not answer. She lay beside him, one arm flung across her eyes as if to shut out a memory too painfully vivid for words.

"Come on now. It's not late." He drew her arm from her face, sunk a kiss in its crook, and held it across his breast so that she could not turn away. "Then we go to sleep, eh?"

When she still did not answer, he reached down stealthily and gripped her just above the knee. The sudden painful clutch freed her from the spell of an experience she could not put into words. With a jerk she tore herself from him and jumped out of bed. Lighting the lamp on the cómoda she stood looking upon his sprawled figure and touseled head resting upon the bed railing.

For the first time she sensed the way he loved her, the passionate voracity with which he tried to consume her wholly. It was as if he were forcing from her, little by little, every phase of her life until he had drained her of that one clot in her consciousness which would enslave her to him completely.

"Questions! Questions! Questions! Mother of God!" she yelled. "All the time you ask me questions. What does it matter what I do so long ago? Why don't you leave me alone?"

Barby flung out an arm that just failed to touch her as she stepped back. In his eyes a slumbering intensity warned her of ever betraying that which must remain hers alone. "Give me a cigarette," he demanded, out of humor.

She put it in his hand, watched him light it and lie back down.

"What's wrong with you tonight?" he asked petulantly.

"How can I understand your coming here with Sal when you just said she left you? How did you get rid of old Oakie?"

"It is nothing! Nothing I say! Everything you want to know. Every little thing I cannot remember. The old woman is evil. Sal took me from her. Then we lived together and came here where we went to work in Las Quince Letras. Pues! There is no more."

Guadalupe laughed. It had a metallic, mirthless sound. She was suddenly again a woman—less human but more coquettish.

"Maria! How is it you think only of asking me so many questions of those things so long ago when I am here now? You forget how you miss me when I do not come."

Barby leaned out from the bed, put both arms around her, and pulled her down beside him.

And yet an hour later when he had fallen asleep Guadalupe lay staring into the dark. Oblivious of his rhythmical hot breath on her shoulder, the sweaty arm flung across her thigh as if to hold her even in sleep, she fought to extinguish the vision that burned before her. Oppressed by the darkness she felt herself as horrified, as powerless in its bondage as then.

"Sweet Mother!" she prayed to herself. "Will the darkness never end?"

5

Downstairs, as upstairs, the merciless questioning went on. The yogi of Cockroach Court was also reviewing his past life.

In imaginary retrospect he saw himself being born countless millions of years ago when the planetesimal earth itself was cooling from a molten mass. A living organism created by the agency action of the sun's ultraviolet rays on water which was charged with mineral salts and carbonic acid. A spark of life in the immeasurable illusion of space and time—no more than that. From this unicellular protoplasm he watched himself evolve into the plant kingdom, and thence into the animal world of form. Slowly he kept on evolving. Through triassic theriodent reptile, bird, quadruped, simian, anthropoid ape. To man ape, primitive man, modern man.

Like Guadalupe's, his had been a long journey to Cockroach Court. It too had held many nights when he had experienced the nullity of not-being; when his life had retreated from wakeful aliveness into the obliteration of darkness.

The yogi recognized these long periods of discarnate existence as death. And he knew they were not interruptions in his development. Between day and night there was for Guadalupe a break in the continuity of her consciousness, but not in her subconsciousness. Similarly for the yogi death was a mere break in the continuity of his mundane consciousness, but not in the supramundane consciousness that was his real self. Reborn again, he resumed his evolutionary journey.

No; there was no real difference between the girl reviewing her life in fitful murmurs upstairs, and the yogi reviewing in reflective meditation his own life below. For just as each of her experiences had contributed to the summation of her worldly personality and character, so each of his incarnate existences had helped to form his individual karma or cosmic character.

The only difference between them lay in their viewpoints. Guadalupe identified herself with each of her environmental experiences. The yogi bent his efforts toward disassociating himself.

He observed the shopkeeper, Tai Ling, set down in the midst of the yowling confusion of Cockroach Court. It was a strange place, but no stranger than those many places in which he had been incarnated before, in other worldly forms. Like them, it now clutched at Tai Ling with circumstance and desire to imprison him in its illusionary world. But Tai Ling had a master; that consciousness of self which would not be bound, which would free him to continue his evolutionary journey toward the ultimate realization of his oneness with the divine consciousness imbuing all matter.

So the yogi was merciless with Tai Ling. Every worldly thought and fleshly desire he called forth, like moths, to the destructive light of self-realization. Not to bind to him the transient identity of a fleshly mortal. But to sever himself completely, the immortal consciousness of his only real self, from the impermanent, often ludicrous, old shopkeeper of Cockroach Court.

Guadalupe also had a master. "Goddamnit! Go on, can't you! What you stoppin' for?" In the hot stillness of the night Barby's persistent demand echoed faintly in the darkness. Every detail of her life, every thought and desire, he wanted to probe toward the end that he might bind her to him wholly.

He did not realize what he was doing. For just as the reflective meditation of the yogi frees the higher self from the tyranny of its mundane consciousness, so on a lower plane does the questioning psychological method, which he unwittingly enforced, release the conscious self from the bondage of its dark unconscious.

"What are you?"

"What am I?"

In the ghostly dark stillness of the night, upstairs and downstairs, the merciless questioning went on.

CHAPTER FIVE

M EANWHILE TAI LING nursed into bloom the flower of his hope.

Somehow, from somewhere, cash had been forthcoming. With it work had gone on for weeks upon the abandoned little side-street cantina that had been Francisco Cheon's place. Windows were scrubbed. Strips of paper were pasted over the cracks in the bar mirror. Bare hand-soaped tables cluttered the scrubbed plank floor.

Still more cash appeared, and Tai Ling went on with his plans. He leased a slot machine and installed a game of chuck-a-luck. He stocked the bar with all that Cheon knew how to mix and ladle. He even acquired a piano almost complete of keys, and demanded a raised platform for it in the corner.

At last one late afternoon it was almost done. With annoying exactitude Tai Ling directed the placing of the sign above the door, painted with brave black letters and a great yellow sun. Cheon hoisted the frame; Barby hammered it into place.

Tai Ling stepped back and surveyed their work proudly. It was not just another dreary adobe cantina. It was a song of his making, an epic of persistent frugality of which he was proud author. Into it, as into a pattern, he had woven many threads unraveled from a fantastic snarl as he sat behind his counter. With it he would insure Barby's future, repay Guadalupe's auspicious stay, confound his enemies and face the growing prestige of Chinese John. With it he bought his freedom from the material world.

In every way it was to be a worthy sequel to The Lamp Awake. He had named it El Sol de Mayo—The Sun of May.

Sweating copiously, Barby descended the ladder and walked home with Tai Ling. "Well, she's all set for Saturday night! That barrel of free beer ought to bring a crowd. Now all you need is some entertaining."

A delicate smile flitted across the old man's face like a breath of wind over a placid pool, disturbing gently his many wrinkles.

"You better give me some money for them handbills. I'll scatter them," added Barby.

Tai Ling ambled across the room and returned with a stack of silver. "Plenty mully," he joked in the foolish idiom he always employed when touchy subjects were discussed. "Llou pay lil' girl come, eh?" Then casually he added, "Thlink llou buy something llou too."

Barby seized the silver and went upstairs to count it. The old man had not been too generous; he had probably spent all he owned. But it was enough—just the excuse he had been waiting for. From its hiding place the boy drew out a bill Mendoza had given him. A lucky friendship over a glass of beer! And with a smart, well-dressed fellow like Mendoza! Strangely, they had taken to each other right off. Mendoza, confidentially, had heard Tai Ling was going to open up a new place; he was glad Barby would be around to look after the old man's interests. There was talk, you know. . . . Yes, Barby remembered hazily a bit somewhere he had heard sometime, himself. They walked over to the place. Barby showed him around; the storeroom where the bar liquor was to be locked interested Mendoza especially.

"I think you and I are going to be good friends," Mendoza said casually, shaking hands as they parted. "But don't mention it to Tai Ling, that fine old patrón of yours. I don't want to cause him any worry, you know. Or do you."

In his hand had been this bill. Now with it and Tai Ling's silver, Barby hurried across the Line to a general store on the American side. There he bought a pink silk shirt, a Stetson with a high round crown he did not indent, a leather wristband, and then by way of novelty a snakeskin cord to go round his new hat. This done he busied himself with purchases for Guadalupe. There was money left to pay for the handbills.

By the time he had distributed these and wolfed some meat and beans at a lonchería, he was ready to meet Guadalupe. Waiting for her at the dark side-door entrance, he adjusted the new Stetson to his liking and tied a fancy knot in the snakeskin cord. He felt like a new man. Wait till she saw what was in these packages for her!

When she came out he called thickly, "Mijita!", and grabbed her by the arm. Guadalupe let herself be led to the Xochimilco for a drink. He was in a high humor, excited about the new cantina's opening.

"Pues! But certainly, Barby, Saturday night, as quickly as I finish at Las Quince Letras. Most gladly will I sing and dance. . . . But now. I ask you two times what these packages are you push in my lap! You buy them for me?"

He ignored her incredulous amazement. "Me and Tai

Ling," he boasted. "So you'll help entertain at the opening. We got a keg of beer to give away. It'll be a big send-off."

The girl's eyes glittered like black glass buttons as she opened the big package and drew out a dress. It was screaming yellow, full and flounced with ruffles. In the smaller box was a pair of high heeled pink slippers. Guadalupe let out a squeal of delight, then leaned back to stare at an entrancing vision of herself in new fluffy yellow under the spotlight of Las Quince Letras.

"They will yell and clap louder than ever!" she murmured. "Won't Señor Gonzales be surprised? It will make him want to buy me many more to dance in, no?"

It had been several days since Barby had seen her. Now he wanted her as a dog a bone—alone, wholly, and with a hunger that forbade interruption. He suggested that they go to The Lamp Awake to try on the dress.

But no. She wanted to be alone with it, to admire its color and texture, to posture in it before the mirror and see herself as others saw her. "It must be a surprise. No-one must see Guadalupe in her new dress before Saturday night. Oh, how they will love me! The little morena will be a lady. . . . How much did it cost, very much, no?"

"You and your Goddamned entertaining!" he answered thickly, halfway down the bottle. "You can't think of nothing else. . . . I said let's go home. What we waiting for?"

In the midst of this argument, just as the whistles were blowing for the Border gates to close, Sal drifted into the cantina. "My eye!" she snorted, slouching up to the table. "What's all this getup? You must be goin' to a Fireman's Ball."

"See, it is what Barby bought me for the opening of Tai Ling's new cantina."

Sal shrugged and dropped into a seat opposite them, her back to the door. After calling loudly for another glass, she calmly poured herself a drink. The. in answer to Barby's scowl she tossed off another.

"What do you do with it all," he growled, "pour it in your pockets?"

"Sure. Wets my pants just to hear you crab about it." Contemptuously she flipped her cigarette stub past his head so close it almost singed his ear.

It was all the boy could stand. He half rose, raised his hand, then sullenly settled back. Sal's fingers had closed around the neck of the bottle; she was still staring at him with a nasty smile.

"Stop it!" cried Guadalupe. "All the time you fight! I don't like you both."

Sal yawned and rose. "Pretty tired tonight. Let's you and me go hit the hay, honey."

"No! You're coming with me. I been waitin' too long. I . . ." Barby lunged forward, shoving away Sal, and trying to grab Guadalupe.

The girl dropped to her knees and twisted from him like a cat. At that moment something happened behind boy and woman which only Guadalupe saw. An old woman appeared in the doorway, smiled and beckoned to her with a skinny forefinger.

When Barby straightened up it was to see Sal staring at Guadalupe with a look of amazed unbelief. He spun around. The girl was standing there as if frozen into stone. Her face had set; her eyes were clouded; she had gone suddenly and completely dead.

"Why, kiddo! Christ, honey!" Sal ejaculated, grabbing up the bottle. "Don't be scared of *him*. Hell, he's just a drunk bastard. You know I've just been waitin' for a chance to bust him one!"

Guadalupe came bac. to life as swiftly as if some switch inside her had been snapped off and on again.

"No! Don't fight with Barby. I love him too. . . . But Sal, I go home with you."

"Hell yes. We're on our way!" Without more ado Sal grabbed the girl by the arm and hustled her outside.

Old Oakie, like an apparition flushed out of the street's darkness, had disappeared. Gradually Guadalupe came to herself. Throughout the day she forgot it completely. But at night she knew it was still alive. A prowling monster of secret desire and nameless fear that Barby was forever trying to call forth. How could she forget? When in the darkness inside her it lay hidden, when in the darkness outside it waited to spring forth again!

The presence of Sal reassured her. There was something about the woman's blunt and gruff manner that bound them close together despite the girl's growing intimacy with Barby. Guadalupe had only to catch sight of their old hotel to experience a new sense of security.

There was a sudden shout. Barby, gathering up the new dress and shoes in their boxes, and draining what was left of the spilled bottle, had finally caught up with them. They quarreled all the way across the railroad tracks: Barby drunkenly trying to pry apart the linked arms of the two women, Sal cursing, and Guadalupe protesting to both.

At the stairway entrance to the hotel, Sal stopped and flung off Guadalupe's arm. "Oh hell with you! You don't want him and then you do. Like any Goddamned woman. Make up your own mind. I'm goin' on in. You can come or not!" She went on in.

"I come, Sal!" the girl cried. But first she caught Barby by the arms. "I go now, Barby, like I say. But we come Saturday night sure. Do not forget."

Barby watched her retreat slowly up the stairs. He straightened unsteadily, pushed his new Stetson to the back of his head, and spat after her. Stumbling forward he clumsily hurled the dress box inside the doorway. Then regaining his balance, he made off across the tracks.

2

That Saturday night El Sol de Mayo opened its doors. Lamps and lanterns shattered the dark. Colored placards written with cryptic signs smiled welcome in the windows. Streamers of twisted paper gesticulated from the doorway. And to every street and corner the word passed that in Tai Ling's new back-street cantina were to be had free beer and cheer.

Tai Ling sat in the back room, a genial host to his old friends from the Alley. They sat quietly smoking and sipping tea. He had saved for this moment an important announcement. All listened carefully.

El Sol de Mayo, Tai Ling said quietly, was being given over tonight, on its auspicious opening, to another. He had no son, no business associate, being fatherless and an old man having no material ambitions beyond the modest income from his small shop. Nevertheless he owed some mark of gratitude to that young man who, since childhood, had loyally lightened his days with work and companionship.

Gravely Tai Ling poured more tea and continued. Now this young man had crossed the threshold of manhood; he needed the responsibility of a legitimate enterprise of his own. There was another inducement. It was well known that his protegee was discreetly intimate with an irreproachable, talented and charming young entertainer. What was more natural than that? Tai Ling approved of it completely. He hoped that the affair would soon come to its expected consummation, and that the couple would continue to make his poor home theirs. To hasten that end he believed the gift of this modest cantina would give the boy an assured income wherewith to match that of his talented mistress. Hence it was not being withheld as a wedding gift. He had spoken plainly, not to embarrass either, but to fully enlighten these, his trusted friends and honored guests, with the full truth of his motives and actions.

He hoped, therefore, that they would hereafter regard this cantina as wholly Barby's and give him their esteemed patronage and friendship as they had himself.

These fustian phrases finished, Tai Ling called abruptly for Barby. "This is your cantina. I have just informed our neighbors," he said quietly in excellent Spanish to the boy standing beside him. "See, here is the deed in your name. It will be in my box."

The boy's eyes widened with initial incomprehension, then he grinned foolishly. There came a sudden crash of a beer pitcher from the front room, a loud shout. "Go tend to your guests," said Tai Ling. With a gentle smile and an eloquent gesture he passed around the salted cashews.

Barby, his head in a whirl, rushed out front. The room was packed; the thick air was hideous with noise. Cheon at the bar was busy drawing beer for a crowd of Mexican, Chinese and Hindu laborers. Somebody was banging the piano; a phonograph screeched from a tabletop. To this two Negro cotton pickers were trying to shuffle on the plank floor. Watching them sat three old Señoras, like the three wise monkeys, swathed to the eyes in dark blue rebozos. And peering in the door, as if afraid to enter, was the usual ragged Cocopah Indian.

It was to this enlivened setting that Guadalupe now brought Sal and a group of percentage girls from Las Quince

Letras. She had on the yellow dress and pink slippers; and as if they had never quarreled, she warmly greeted Barby.

"Listen!" he muttered swiftly. "I'm a rich man! Tai Ling . . ."

"I want to see Tai Ling!" She brushed by him to the back room. Tai Ling received her warmly, poured tea and passed the ginger and pistachios. Then he introduced her to each of his callers, taking care that they understood she had brought the noisy group of girls expressly to divert his guests.

Indeed, the girls were doing their damndest: dancing, drinking and warbling, "I wanta bee—in Tenne-see." Gradually as the kegs ran dry, the blare developed a fuzzy-tongued sound of sentimentality.

The little morena was here. Give the little morena a chance. Hadn't they all stood in that big barn of a casino, giving good money after bad to that cabrón of a Gonzales, just to see her? Now she was here, right here, where the beer was free. So shut up, you he-goat! The little dark one is going to sing. Quiet, fool!

In the corner drowsed a guitar player; from a tattered shirt sleeve his hand kept reaching out to catch the instrument before it slid from his lap. Now mournfully and as though still asleep, with all the cloying harmony of his race, he began to pluck at the strings. Instantly the place toned down. Guadalupe, one hand resting on his shoulder, began to sing. The little niña, herself, in her yellow dress.

Barby's own eyes never left her face. As usual it had assumed an impassive, trancelike placidity. He knew it reflected her mind, preoccupied with the physical effort but thinking of nothing at all. She had moved back into another world to which he did not have the key.

All evening he had carried about him a new, secret and bloated sense of proprietorship and self-importance. Tai Ling had given him this cantina. He would be rich and powerful. He would take Guadalupe out of Las Quince Letras, install her here to sing and dance. His cantina would be known along the whole Border. And she would not only love him but respect him as her patrón.

But Guadalupe had shattered this grandiloquent dream the moment she started to sing; with the mere look on her face she proved its lie. Why, by God, he hadn't had a chance yet to tell her who was boss of the place—as if she would give a damn when she heard. All this singing and dancing! No! He meant to have her alone, the only thing he had ever loved and owned. Nothing could take her away.

There was every reason for his jealous anger. Though neither of them knew it, Guadalupe also was reaching another turning of her road.

She had just finished singing. As she bowed, flipping up her dress, one of her lavender silk garters—a present from Sal—was revealed. A man beside her reached out and jerked the band down her leg. With a tolerant laugh Guadalupe lifted her foot and sent the gaudy silk spinning into the crowd.

Barby lunged forth to catch it, then brought up with a jerk. A man, half-hidden by an enormous woman sitting beside him, was staring fixedly at Guadalupe. He was middle-aged, swarthy, with spotches of grey hair in his long sideburns. Even as the boy noticed that both of his legs had been cut off at the knees, the man brought one of the stumps down with an angry thump on the edge of his stool.

"Here! A zapateado, girl!"

Guadalupe turned around with surprise.

The man grabbed the guitar from its sleepy owner. Waving his hand toward her, he growled, "All that fol-de-rol on your legs. Andale! Let's see if you know how to use them."

Guadalupe smiled, tossed her other garter to the crowd.

Rolling down her stockings, she stood poised before the man. The fellow lifted his hand, swept it lightly across the strings, and began to play. Barby watched Guadalupe dance down the length of the bar and back. Finished, she stopped in front of the cripple and awaited his approbation.

He looked her up and down. His long thin face was divided into thirds by two dark horizontal lines; one formed by his black eyebrows, and the other by his thin compressed lips. Each appeared locked at the ends by a maze of tiny vertical wrinkles. Those at the corners of his eyes suggested a strong concentrative will; those at his mouth the power to enforce it. His sarcastic voice confirmed both.

"A zapateado, girl! I ask you for a single zapateado, and you fling yourself up and down the whole floor." He turned to the big woman beside him. "Peña, did you not hear my simple request?"

"Shh, Trinidad. What do you always expect? The child did very well. I like her. Come here!" she called to Guadalupe, and put a big arm around the girl.

For awhile they talked in voices too low for Barby to distinguish while the crowd resumed its fun. Then Trinidad raised his voice. "Now. You say you understand. We will see!" Again he struck a chord.

Guadalupe pulled up her skirt, dug hard with the ball of her right foot. As one stump of the cripple came down on the stool, she dropped her right heel to the floor making two swift clicks. Trindad's other stump came down. She struck the heel of her left foot, then stamped the whole foot flat.

The cripple's voice broke out as she repeated the turn. Then bringing down both legs with an exasperated thump, he burst into a short laugh.

Guadalupe stood as if undecided whether to break out in tears or throw her slipper in his face.

"Here child! Let me show you."

The woman Peña rose, big enough to make two of Guadalupe. But incredibly light and decisive, her heels beat on the floor. Her body, save for a slight turn, never moved. "It is so simple. I keep time for you now." From her great bosom she brought out a pair of castanets and adjusted them to her thumbs.

A rapid roll of four clicks with one hand, followed by a single golpe with her left; their crisp staccato shattered Trinidad's sarcastic grin. He leaned back and took up his guitar.

"You go easy," she warned him.

With the clear, dry snap of the castanets punctuating each measure of music, things went better for Guadalupe. In the clear space between the piano and the end of the bar she repeated over and over the steps Peña showed her, while Trinidad lay back playing. None in the room paid them any attention. Even Barby lounged away disgusted. The click of the castanets followed him across the room. He looked back. The big woman was showing the girl how to move her arms. In the dim, smoky light she looked like a child playing with a puppet.

3

Tai Ling was tired and bored. Almost never did he go out. Tonight had been a special occasion, a momentous event. But in his one short speech he had done it justice. Never again would he have to spend such an evening at the cost of a quiet meditation alone before the effigy of his rainbow-enhaloed Bodhisattva. Nevertheless he suffered this last one more and more acutely.

One by one his own guests had departed, leaving him seated alone in the back room. The tea was cold; besides, he had had his four small cups. The air was foul with cigarette smoke, alcohol fumes and perspiration. The noise was deafening—drunken laughter, curses, the scratch of dancing feet; and he knew that the gelatinous gloom of even the street outside quivered to the bang of the piano and a chorus of hysterical shrieks.

All this, he reflected calmly enough, was the worldly pleasure called fun by the curious materialistic age into which he had been placed for a brief sojourn. Of just what did it consist?

He observed the Mexican and Chinese laborers, the Hindu and Negro cotton pickers, staggering up to the bar for still more drinks; the Cocopah Indian still stuffing all the remains of the rice cakes, tostados and salted nuts he could find. He observed the percentage girls screaming delightedly, with mock rage, as their partners' fingers pinched them on their behinds or fumbled at their breasts. There was Guadalupe, obsessed with a new variation of physical motion. It was being taught her, appropriately enough, by a cripple; his sensuality of kind, deprived of legs for expression, perversely seeking yet another pair. Tai Ling caught a glimpse of the woman Peña's eyes as her hand slyly caressed the girl's hip. Lastly there was Barby himself—inflamed with drink as usual despite his new responsibility, seething with jealously, sulking with rage.

To what end was all this directed? He saw Sal. She sat slumped against the wall, hair disheveled, staring disconsolately out the door with eyes like cooling coals.

Lust, Ill Will and Stupidity, the Three Fires of Desire; by these all their lives were lighted. None of them was free.

Compassionately Tai Ling called the ragged Cocopah to him and gave him what was left of the delicacies on the table. How could he impute blame to his fellows for obeying the carnal appetites of the flesh, the passions of the senses? Not until the Three Fires of Desire had been cooled and transmuted into Purity, Good Will and Wisdom, would there dawn in them the Perfect Knowledge. Tai Ling, under the self-impelled necessity of making his own lamp to shine, could no longer sit and watch these rampant unrealities manifesting themselves before him. He rose stiffly to his feet.

The room had suddenly quieted; the keg had run dry; everyone began to leave. Trinidad, a little drunk, laid aside the guitar. Peña lifted him down and together they walked out the door. Guadalupe ran after them to give the woman a last hug. "I come, Peña! Sure!" The girl's face as she turned back seemed lit with new life by their promise to teach her more new steps.

"My God! Ain't you through yet? Let's go," grumbled Sal.

Barby, still sulking, turned back to help Cheon tidy up and close. They had just rolled the empty keg to the floor when Cheon happened to glance out the window. His eyes snapped with sudden fear. He ducked; it was too late to warn Tai Ling. The old man already had reached the doorway.

Chinese John stood on the threshold, looking in. Tai Ling stepped calmly back, letting his hand fall in a gracious gesture of invitation. His enemy did not accept it. The light from inside reflected the ironic smile on his thin lips. "This is the young man's new cantina?" The straight stare of his black eyes refuted his words. Tai Ling looked at him impassively; then without speaking, he walked past him and went slowly home to The Lamp Awake.

4

From its first night El Sol de Mayo prospered. Tai Ling ascribed this to the rousing opening made possible by Guadalupe and her girls. Gratefully he presented her a secondhand phonograph and several double-faced records: *A Hunt in the Black Forest, A Good Woman's Blues, Over the Waves,* and the *Beautiful Blue Danube.* Thereafter the shop was seldom without the noise of one being ground out by a dull needle.

Hardly did he finish his early morning meditation before there sounded above him the patter of bare feet, a gritty scratching, then the blare of Guadalupe's small phonograph. Aroused by the music every canary in the place burst into frenzied song. Tai Ling beamed. And to Johann Strauss' waltz and the chirping accompaniment began the first movement of another symphonic day.

By eight o'clock Tai Ling was done with his day's pleasure. He closed his eyes to his fish, his ears to his canaries. His frugal breakfast was brought in. But now *A Good Woman's Blues* began to yowl disconsolately in a deep rich voice:

"If a thing ain't right, you bet it mus' be wrong;
An' so, fo' evah good woman, I'se singin' dis song . . ."

To this accompaniment Tai Ling reviewed the details which reflected El Sol de Mayo's surprising success—questioning Cheon, now the barkeep, about its clientele and supplies; examining the bills for a cracked window, a broken beer spout. It was not his business, of course. He assured Barby that when the boy came down. He merely wanted to see the boy off to a good start, then he would wash his hands entirely.

Yes, the new cantina was making money. Barby was there all day, making the most of his opportunity. By noon only two things were left to trouble him: what Barby did with the profits, and the crass misinterpretation by his enemies that the cantina only masked his secret schemes.

In the afternoon after Sal had gone to work and while

Barby was away, Guadalupe brought down the phonograph
and set it on the counter. When *Over the Waves* began she
stepped out upon the empty floor. She had removed her stockings. With her dress pinned up to her hips, her slim bare legs
pantomimed an ecstasy of motion before him. He could see
the tiny scars on her shins, the drops of sweat gathering on her
forehead.

When the record ran out she demanded impudently,
"Turn it over and give it a wind," and went on dancing,
blank-eyed, as if he were not there.

Tai Ling meekly bent over and did as he was told. No one
came in. The room was still save for the spasmodic running
of the records and the click of her heels on the floor. It kept
up for an hour or more as with arms and legs, head and eyes,
she directed a forceful campaign of line and curve against
his impassive stare. Tai Ling watched her with amused tolerance.

In a sweat she stopped and leaned against the counter.
"Pues. Don't I get better?"

The old man sank limply to the floor, cross-legged. Bending forward, he touched his forehead to the planks. Then
straightening up, he stuck out his left leg and rose on his right
toes. It was quickly and gracefully done with a sinous ease
Guadalupe was unable to match. She drew back gasping.

Tai Ling grinned. "So you master the body to become a
servant of the dance, hey?"

"Yes! Just like Trinidad tell me!"

Tai Ling chuckled. "Then the dance vanishes and you
are the servant of an illusion, the slave of your body. . . .
Hoh!"

"But the art of Spain won't vanish. It's immortal. Trinidad says so!"

"Not only the art but the civilization which created it will disappear. So will all this." Tai Ling waved his hand toward the open doorway. "The day will come when you will not believe it existed. Here!"

He reached to a shelf behind him and offered her a piece of ginger. "Now while you wash and dress I shall have some tea and cakes sent in. No?"

Quiet in the late afternoon they sat talking.

"What do you keep so limber for?" Guadalupe asked impudently.

"For an old man?" Tai Ling added. And then with a twinkle in his eyes, "It seems that you master your body so as to think about it all the time, while I master my body that I may forget it entirely. . . . But you are not eating your cakes."

"Too fattening. Bad for the wind."

Tai Ling laughed delightedly.

"Now I must go," the girl announced without moving.

"What's the matter?" Tai Ling observed gravely, opening the cash drawer. "Doesn't Barby give you money?"

Guadalupe grinned assent. "Yes, but I need some castanets." She snapped her fingers to show him what she meant.

"How many dollars?" he asked warily.

"Oh, good ones cost five dollars."

"Heh!" He gave her three.

The girl was delighted and scampered out.

Till ten o'clock, when Barby and Guadalupe returned, the shop was quiet. Tai Ling, settling down to his evening medi-tation, then heard the phonograph begin again upstairs. While it ground out faintly its *Hunt in the Black Forest,* he searched diligently in his own blacker woods for the "Twelve Indispensable Things."

Among these, as he recalled, an art of living which would enable one to utilize each activity of body, speech and mind as an aid on the Path was indispensable.

The noise upstairs washed down reassuringly. That small battered phonograph was itself serving him indispensably. Heard in the street outside, it lent the shop a disarming air to passers-by. With it playing, he was freed from worry to pursue uninterrupted his meditations.

Morning, afternoon and night, then, the phonograph clamored raucously. Its same worn-out tunes were heard by Barby too. But, as if polyphonic, it spoke to him with a separate meaning. It was also prophetic.

5

The first scratch of its needle every morning rasped across his nerve ends. An instant later the sudden music blasted him awake. He rolled over in bed. Already Guadalupe was up and standing at the window. The sun, striking through her thin cotton shift, revealed the rise and fall of her small breast as she hummed *The Beautiful Blue Danube* being ground out by the phonograph beside her.

"Turn off that damn thing! Every morning you've got to wake me up at sunrise. I'm goin' to throw it out the window if you don't let me sleep."

Guadalupe glanced casually over her shoulder at him without answering. Dropping to her knees, she leaned against the sill to be completely immersed in the showering gold. The phonograph kept on playing. In the bright becalmed morning the waltz reiterated with melodic clarity a freshness and limpid cheerfulness which the boy on the bed seemed powerless to combat. Ever afterward a bright early morning or the chance strains of a Strauss waltz evoked the other in his mind. Already they seemed inseparable. He lay silent, watching the girl kneading the sunlight into her hair with indolent fingers.

He loved her so! The sight of her oval face, half turned

toward him in the sunlight, struck him as it always did with its tragic freshness enhanced by the early morning. He had not seen her since night—so long an absence even in restless sleep. Always she awakened before him fresh and eager for the day, as if the first touch of sun kindled a flame within her. Watching the flow of color to her sepia cheeks, the glint in her black eyes, he could see it eating away all the residue of night. Each morning the resurrection took place before his eyes, and with it he felt an agonizing perception of her unquenchable vitality.

He himself knew only an incessant misery that never entirely left him. Thoughts, suspicions and fears kept heaping their burdens upon him. His very body ached. And the phonograph mocked his misery. It was a symbol of that inconquerable vitality of the girl herself, and upon it he vented an unceasing acerbity.

"Cut it out!" he yelled again. "You been playin' that music box a half hour now. Ain't you got enough?"

Guadalupe rose deliberately, stretching on her toes. Without giving him a look she tossed a pack of cigarettes on the bed and put on a new record. She began to dress slowly behind him, stopping frequently to listen to the words:

". . . so listen, Daddy, if you don' like my way of livin',
Take up yo' trunks and move!
There ain't goin' to be no fussin',
You better kiss you ma good-by.
That ain't no lie; I mean you gonna die,
You gonna die!"

Barby whirled around in bed. "You like that too, huh?"

Still the girl did not look up. Lifting one foot to the cómoda she drew a stocking up her leg rolled it down at the knee, and gave it a careful twist.

"What did you say?" he yelled again into the silence.

"That you like the music? It ain't the words? They don't say nothin' you're afraid to say? No?"

Guadalupe rose quietly and smoothed down her skirt. Taking a box of matches from off the chest of drawers she handed it to him and raised her eyes to his. "Yes," she said simply. "I like it very much. Don' you?"

Barby rasped a match across the bed railing and lit his cigarette. He could not tell by her voice whether she was taunting him, but he could not bear to meet her eyes. Their darkness would be unfathomable as stagnant water. Or over them would quiver the papery fine-veined lids. Her whole face mirrored an expression of profound placidity which he had found he could not disturb. He had come to fear it more than her occasional outbursts. Rising to his knees, both hands gripping the footrail of the bed, cigarette in mouth, he watched her wind a light blue rebozo about her shoulders. She walked past him without speaking. It was like her to stand waiting at the window, back toward him, until the record ran out. Quietly she turned off the switch. He was suddenly contrite. The moment of parting, like the moment they met again, held for him a peculiar fascination.

"Adios," she called, brushing by the bed. She always greeted him with the same word.

He flung out an arm, caught her around the waist, and bent his head to her breast. Looking over his head with an expressionless face, she stood in his embrace as long as he cared to hold her. Then flipping the end of the scarf over her shoulder she moved away.

"Wait!" he called. "Where are you goin'?"

The girl flung around at the door. "Where I go? Why I go? All the time questions! Can I never move without you know? I go where I go every day. Where else you think?"

Turning, she pattered down the steps and the boy could hear her cheerful greeting to Tai Ling.

He leapt out of bed to the window. Standing behind the grimy curtains he watched her across the sunlit road, walk down the railroad tracks, and turn off in the direction of Sal's hotel. She did not glance back. The instant she had vanished from sight the tenseness went from him like life run out of a clock. Wearily he flung himself on the bed again where he lay, unable to sleep, until time to begin work.

He was beginning to lose his first feeling of importance at being the owner of a cantina. For one thing, there was so much work to do—cleaning up last night's mess, mopping floor and tables, and puzzling over his simple accounts. The janitor work, suggested Tai Ling, should be done by Cheon. But no. Barby preferred to drag out of bed in the morning and open up himself. It gave him an excuse to leave Cheon to close at night, so he could meet Guadalupe the instant she was through at Las Quince Letras; he dared not trust her to wait for him. Still, there was the money in the cashbox he locked away daily.

Before counting it, he subtracted a bit to buy Guadalupe a present. Saturday, a twenty-dollar Mexican fire opal. Today, a fifty-cent plaster-of-Paris model of an American soap advertisement. Whatever caught his eye; money was inconsequential; he had only to mark down in his book for the day's take an amount minus the sum.

Guadalupe cared little for the presents. What pleased her was the novelty of getting them. He fancied that her curiosity helped bring her home. Tonight, as every night, her first words to him as she entered the room were, "Well, and what you bring me today?"

He thumbed at the box on the cómoda, watched her tear it open and bring out the cheap plaster miniature of a dancing fairy. A smile of delight lighted her face. "I like it! Oh yes! Much better than this old ring—it's so smoky in the daytime." She took off the opal and chucked it in a dresser drawer. Everything else suffered the same fate. They pleased her only for the moment; like him, she gave no thought to their intrinsic worth.

Yet day by day he loved her more. He lived only from her "Adios" at morning until her "Adios" again that night. Yet something within him revolted increasingly at his bondage. Between these extremes he seemed continually tortured. Even in their closest embrace he was conscious of a pain that would soon break out afresh. And day by day he hated more that part of her which would not be his.

Now as they lay together in darkness and he reached an arm around her, Guadalupe's laugh rang out suddenly.

"What's that for?" he demanded sullenly.

Like a child she pointed to the little plaster cast faintly distinguishable in the moonlight. She had been imagining how it would feel to dance off one cloud to another like that fairy poised on its labeled soapbox. A foolish thing like that! It showed him what a flimsy hold he had upon her. As if he held her captive in his hands and the instant he closed upon her she was gone.

It only made him hold her closer. And this roused in her an antagonistic repudiation of his will. But less and less often they quarreled openly. She had found other ways of isolating herself from him completely. A straight impersonal look in the eyes as he bent to kiss her stopped him more effectually than an outthrust arm. She could stiffen in his arms and his passion was instantly dissipated. A casual remark about her dancing, interposed during his continual questioning, would check him like a gag. A look, a gesture, a word—they were a woman's blows under which he suffered the ignominy of defeat daily.

But try as he might, he could not find what kept her from him. He railed at her singing and dancing. He hated Sal. The phonograph became a cause for new bickering. And still he continued his efforts to drag from her every remembered incident in her life.

"Mother of God!" she cried out, leaping from the bed to stand fearfully looking down upon him. "What is it you want? What of me is not yours already that you must have?"

The clarity of her blunt question terrified the boy. He could think of nothing that could be put in words. Instead he began a long tirade to cover up his fears.

She shut him off by turning on the phonograph. It was her surest defense.

CHAPTER SIX

FTER A TIME he began to spy upon her movements throughout the day. These efforts aroused in him a feverish anxiety lest he discovered something to confirm his suspicions. Profoundly relieved that he did not, he turned contritely back to her each night. And again the next day he redoubled his efforts.

The moment she vanished in the morning he would jerk back from the upstairs window where he had been watching. Grabbing his hat, he clattered down the stairs and out the back door. He ran up the alley emerging at the Nuevo Paris, and slouched inconspicuously across the corner to the maze of railroad tracks. Crossing the upper end of the yards he halted opposite Chewlee Singkee's carnicería, strolled past the loading platform of a cotton gin, and sank down in the shadow of a car along the siding.

He was not too soon. She swung into sight less than a hundred yards below him. He could see the slight yet jaunty meneo of her hips, the precise balance of her head, the graceful lift of a hand to adjust her rebozo. Each was a movement with which he was long familiar, as he was familiar with every variation of the same movement. They were unconscious gestures of moods which he had learned to read like the changing expressions on her face.

Lighting a cigarette he watched her cross the tracks and enter the saurian throat of a hotel which jutted out on a narrow reef between the maze of tracks and a dusty side street. The sun was climbing. The lines of steel glittered brightly; one by one the windows of the hotel blazed forth.

Barby knew which one to watch: the dark one on the top floor. Its shade was always down until Guadalupe arrived. For a moment he waited. Then like a wink the shade shot up. He saw a figure he knew to be Guadalupe's tugging at the window, watched her as long as she stood breathing the morning air. Then he rose and slouched back to El Sol de Mayo.

He came to know at what hour during midmorning she went across the street with Sal for the woman's first pitcher of beer. Leaving the cantina on any excuse, he learned where she ate at noon, at what time she walked with Sal to Las Quince Letras. He knew to what shop across the Line she went for an hour while a smirking pock-marked clerk played for her new phonograph records. He traced the invariable route she followed home, stopping on the bridge across the arroyo to watch the cabaret lights go on—her favorite leisurely walk before work.

What he thought to discover by his espionage Barby never knew. But so well he came to know her habits, the inconsequential happenings in her daily life, that her talk at night sounded like a meaningless repetition of something he had heard already and knew as well as she.

Then one morning the discovery came. Without realizing

it, he had become suspicious of the long morning hours which she shared with Sal.

He began at first to loiter at the hotel, ready to flee at the sound of her steps. Then growing more resolute he went inside. The proprietors, a family of Chinese always economical of space, had appropriated most of the lobby for their own living quarters. The office was a mere dark cubbyhole underneath the stairway. Here one rang a bell, scrawled a name in a tattered journal, and received a key.

In this dusty gloom Barby quietly climbed the stairs. On the top landing he would stand staring down the long hall at the row of doors. No one came out. No one went in. In the pallid morning light diffused through the dusty skylight overhead, the corridor lay before him like a swath cut through silence. Hurriedly he would walk past Sal's door as if she and Guadalupe heard and knew his steps. After a time he became bolder. He sauntered down the hall, listening intently as he passed the room. At the far end he would flash a look backward as he stepped out upon the fire escape. He had heard nothing. He never heard anything!

But this morning just as he reached the head of the stairs Sal came out. Barby slunk back against the wall as she brushed by him in the darkness and clattered down the steps for cigarettes. He walked quickly down the hall. She had left the door ajar; and turning his head as he slouched past, the boy saw the room was empty.

Empty! The fact reached inside his head and scooped out the comforting illusion of days. He had imagined Guadalupe spent all morning with Sal. She was always in a hurry to leave him. For what? The question rattled in his empty head derisively. The memory of her jaunty air grew unbearable.

At the end of the hall he stopped to look back, wondering

if he could have been mistaken. But no. The small empty room could not have lied. She was gone.

He was about to retrace his steps when from behind the door at his side her voice rang out clearly in the silent hall.

"Oh but you will! You will take me with you. Yes? Yes! I mus' go!"

The sound of her voice, the peculiar timber to which she pitched her most exhorbitant demands when well pleased, struck him like a blow. He whirled half around as if expecting to see her standing behind him. Surprise and anger chased through his veins like liquid fire, suddenly turning into ice-water. Still the meaning of her words had not fully penetrated his mind. He stood cringing outside the door like a man awaiting the second lash of a whip from which he could not flee.

It came. A man's voice answered hers with a mocking reply that did not disguise his unspoken assent. It was enough! The boy fled outside to crouch on the fire escape. For minutes he waited there staring back at the dark hall. Slowly the words burnt into his mind and stood there flaming until he could see nothing else. He felt compelled to go back, to confirm the incomprehensible fact which his mind refused to admit. The man's voice held him still. It had sounded vaguely familiar; there was no denying its mocking yet gentle tone. The distant sound of steps ascending the stairs, and the slam of Sal's door finally released him. He fled down the steps.

That night he was quiet. He did not reply to Guadalupe's cheerful "Adios" when she came in. There was no present for her. She flashed him a queer look and turned on the phonograph. Barby, smoking on the bed, turned his face away. He could not meet her eyes.

Only when she had undressed and lain down beside him in the darkness did he feel at ease. She talked little and he seemed not to hear. In a few moments she was asleep. He

rose on one eblow, looked down at her face illumined by a
shard of moonlight. It was almost childishly vacant of expression. With lips barely closed she seemed not to breathe.
She slept like a flower gone dead for the night. It gave him
a peculiar feeling of mastery to see her so inert. For the first
time he felt time and decision at his own finger tips. He
brushed back from her eye a black feather of hair to its smooth
wing with a steady hand. And smiling derisively in the darkness he lay down carefully again beside her.

2

It was not quite seven o'clock when Guadalupe left the
shop. The morning was cold, clear and dry; and in the brittle
desert air the sierras stood out fawn-pink and close as a stone's
throw. These the girl arrogantly surveyed as if about to lift
them from the plain and carry off in her shawl. Then with a
jaunty swing to her hips she walked swiftly across the tracks
and entered Sal's hotel.

The woman, aroused by her knock, loosed the catch on
the door and jumped back in bed. Guadalupe strode to the
window, raised both curtain and sash, and stood immersed in
the sunlight.

"Sal! Get up! I am late today."

"Late, my eye! You're gettin' earlier ever' mornin'," mumbled the woman again wrapped in blankets, knees up and chin
down. "God, it's a cold one!"

The girl laughed. "Cold? Never! The sun is warm like
yellow wine. See—even the dog below tries to bite it in his
mouth."

"Wine hell!" the woman muttered, then stretching out an
arm, "Hand me that bottle on the dresser."

Guadalupe tilted the pint against the light. "Is there left no more than this? And you buy it last night?"

The woman took it from her without answering. Taking the last two fingers in one gulp, she slid the empty flask under the bed and ducked back under the covers.

As the whiskey gradually worked down inside her she relaxed, stretched out her legs. For minutes she lay staring at the girl. Then with a curse she flung back the covers and began to crawl hastily into her clothes. The effort was greater than the resolve. Half-dressed, she slumped back down on the bed. Elbows on knees, both hands clasping her bent head, she sat damning another day through the snarl of taffy hair hanging over her eyes.

Guadalupe stooped down to push back the woman's hair, and gave her a cigarette. "Don' feel bad, sweet'art. Soon we have breakfast. Then you be all right."

Leaning forward to reach for a match on the dresser, the woman suddenly stopped before the mirror. "Jesus, what a face! Ever' day it's worse." She grabbed up a small tin of rouge and haphazardly smeared a splotch of color over the clammy whiteness of her cheeks. The brilliant smears only accentuated her cold blue lips.

Guadalupe lit the woman's cigarette and watched her inhale deeply.

"God damn his lousy hide!" burst out the woman in a hoarse vehement voice as if the thought, frozen all night, had suddenly thawed and spouted out. "I seen him talkin' to Gonzales about me again yesterday. He's after me. I know it."

"No Sal. Don' mind the Big Fella. It is Gonzales who is the big boss. He know you are my friend."

"Well that don't help me none. It's plenty tough now. No pay and dance chips gettin' scarcer ever day with all this cold weather. Besides he's always raggin' at me. He don't ever let up."

"Don' worry I say. Soon spring will come with lots of business again. Now the dance chips you get buy your dinner every day. Don' you have this room too, only a dollar a day?"

"No! Who the hell has been payin' for it the last three weeks even though she don't stay in it?"

"Not me!" Guadalupe answered cheerfully. "Look! I have brought you two dollars again today."

"What'd you tell him it was for this time—castanets, dancin' shoes, God knows what! Chink or no Chink he'll be gettin' on to this business of tradin' back phonograph records instead of buyin' new ones."

Guadalupe laughed. "But Tai Ling like me very much! He don' come upstairs, and besides I have many records. Now hurry! I am so hungry and there is so much work before I go away. Oh but I am happy!"

Listlessly the woman dressed and followed the girl downstairs. In an hour they were back. With breakfast and a beer inside her, Sal went in her room to lounge in bed until time for work. Guadalupe walked on down to the end of the hall.

She never had to knock on the door but once for Peña to let her in. Trinidad was always waiting. There was hardly time for her to return the woman's "Buenos dias!" and close embrace before the cripple was urging her to change into an old shirt and a pair of dungarees cut off above the knees. He sat in the dark corner, impatiently thumping a guitar. The light streaming through the one small window beside him made a glare almost impossible for the girl to face. And it almost hid him, with his deformity, from her sight. He had become to her no more than a voice. It was the only tool with which he whipped, clubbed and cajoled, frightened and flattered her into submission.

The moment she rose from fastening her shoes he called out, "Listo!" impatiently drawing his fingers across the strings of the guitar.

Immediately the girl struck her pose, left arm up and curved, right arm hanging at her side. At the first beat she began a single zapateado. Before the four heel clicks had beat on the bare floor she stopped, confused by sudden silence. Again she tried the step, faltered, and stood staring into the dusky corner where Trinidad sat silent, both hands resting on his guitar.

"Dull, dull," he announced caustically. "You think you learn how to dance by dreaming what a fine girl you are?"

The girl had learned not to take the bait. There was no arguing with a voice which struck out at her like a snake from its hole.

"What is the matter! Are you in Las Quince Letras that you listen for applause before you have even danced?" He leaned forward into the light, head turned, listening. "But me—I hear nothing. Peña, do my ears fail me?"

"I have practiced! All afternoon after I leave here yesterday until I am so tired, Trinidad . . ."

The man silenced her with the single gesture of a hand. "Till you are tired? Oh too much, too much! When there are so many people to clap for a pretty face you practice steps for one old man until you feel tired! Madre! The great dancer she get tired!"

"Let the child alone till she warms up," broke out Peña.

Trinidad sighed deeply, "Sí, sí. It makes Peña's big heart bleed too."

The girl's face hardened.

"Come, come. A slow waltz perhaps now you have rested. Lazy long steps, verdad?" Instead he broke out into a lively

paso doble that lashed the girl into a frenzy of motion on the
bare floor.

The instant she finished Guadalupe flung around toward
him. "Trinidad! I cannot!" she begged. "Not till you tell me
if I can go. All day, all night, I think of what you say. That
perhaps I can go with you. Perhaps! It drive me crazy. I hear
no music, nothing but 'perhaps,' 'perhaps' in my ears. Tell me
if I go with you or no. Favór!"

The man's voice suddenly changed tone. "I promised nothing," he said kindly. "I say only that if you dance well perhaps
I take you with me. But how can I tell if you dance well or
poorly when you stand and do nothing?"

"Of course you will go with us, child," soothed the big
woman leaning against the wall. "Don't be nervous. Trinidad
has promised you. Show him how well you know all the
steps."

"Don' stand so!" the man's voice bit at her again. "How
many times I tell you to stand evenly on both feet? Look now!
You stand on one leg. The other it hangs like a cow's tail. And
the hip—Madre Mio! Does your novio hang his hat upon it
that you stand with it stuck out so? Come to me!"

Obediently the girl approached him.

"Once again I tell you," he began petulantly. "Every momentito you must think how you stand, how you walk, how
you sit. The body it must be taught all over how to move.
The legs, the arms, the head: you must fasten them together
so that not one moves unless it is balanced by the others. The
stiff wrist, the clumsy fingers, even they spoil the step. You
must forget the empty motion the people clap at if you dance
for Trinidad. In the foolish ruffle of skirts he sees the clumsy
whirl. From him you cannot hide the crooked hands in the
mad waving of arms. And the pirouette! Santíssima!—I tell
you there is no pirouette! There are one thousand poses like

the faces of a jewel which the body must form before it can be flashed before the eye. Remember this: you must dance as if God might strike you dead at any moment and turn you into stone. In that one posture, for every man to see forever, would you be judged for the dancer you are. When thus the body has learned to have grace and dignity in every movement, you must train the mind to think of the dance as the artist thinks of the picture he will paint. And then, child— then, if you have the heart, you may begin to learn to speak that language which only the eye knows and the heart understands."

For a moment he was silent. Then in a voice which seemed to bring him back to the girl standing before him, he said abruptly, "You see now what it is to dance for Trinidad? The dance is everything. But Trinidad knows. He will take you only because you have worked hard and will work harder."

The girl leaned forward, began to smile. "I go then? I go sure!"

Trinidad grunted. "A bull must smell the blood. No more. But understand: you are nothing. Nothing but a dull child who has been dreaming much. To Trinidad a body that is tired already—look at the knees trembling! You must make it one of steel like that of Toledo which can be bent only because it cannot be broken. Me—I have the mind! I think and your body it must act! And the heart only God knows if such a foolish child has the heart to dance. But for a little while yet because it pleases me I shall teach you more."

3

This was the cripple whom Guadalupe had met at the opening of El Sol de Mayo. Twice a year perhaps he crawled back and forth along the Border, picking up a girl here, a likely couple there, to present at any of the big cabarets. At most they never exceeded five, and he was lucky to keep one at the miserable pay be gave them. Usually they were young Mexican girls whom he advertised as Spanish—girls of whom Peña approved on personal grounds as he did professionally. And invariably they left as soon as they learned a few simple turns, or ran into Peña's disapproval.

It did not matter. He stoutly maintained his dramatic pose as a master of the dance exiled from Spain and reduced to teaching miserable girls to wring a smile from a back-street bar. He—Trinidad!—who had swayed thousands with his poetry of movement upon a Madrid stage.

In this he was a complete hoax. Actually he had been only a young apprenticed dancer in Spain when he was run over by a street car during a political riot. All his speeches were almost exact duplicates of those made by his old master over thirty years ago. Remembering them, his eyes grew misty with the fanciful past.

"In the soil of Spain," he would say then, "there, niña, grows the dance. Seek south of Madrid where the caliphs ruled. Do not unsaddle until falls that day's shadow upon the ruins of a Moorish castle. You will know then that you have come to a land of grapes and fighting bulls, of destitution and wit, guitar and song. Dismount there, child, and take root. On that soil blooms the dance!"

Yes, the dance, he would continue. "Not the indolent waltz, the stiff minuet, the vulgarity of the gypsy. These lack dignity and are thus without beauty. But that of Andalusia. Sweet Mother! It feeds the soul with its majesty of posture, its strong and simple lines, its speed and grace."

Trinidad then, thwarted and warped and crippled, believed only in Spain and the Jota of Aragon. And to its world of motion he just as devoutly believed he held the key, like castanets, "in the hollow of the hand." Even these were important. He advised minding their pitch and whims. On cold days to carry them next to the skin. To mate them carefully. The larger one, the deep-voiced male, in the left hand; with the smaller, the female, to answer in the right.

These flights of metaphorical fancies no one understood—neither his simple, peasant protogees nor his impatient Border audiences. All knew him for a crank. And because of his infernal persistence in pronunciation, always using the Spanish "th" sound for the Mexican "c," he was commonly called "Señor Thinco Thentavos de Athucar"—Mr. Five-Cents'-Worth-of-Sugar.

But his resplendent talk and simple teaching opened a world to Guadalupe she had never dreamed existed. He did know the rudiments of the dance. Each took on for her an engrossing character: bolero, jota, and fandango; the panaderos requiring a flexible waist and back; the garrotin in which the hands invited or repelled; even the tango danced as a solo by man or woman—as a woman supple and relaxed; as a man, rigid and intense. Marvelous those hours in an empty room down the hall from Sal! She went to them as instinctively as a moth to the flame.

Now, ready to drop from fatigue after her morning's work, Guadalupe stood wiping the sweat from her face. Peña, as if hearing something in the hall, turned her head toward the door. Then again she faced Trinidad and Guadalupe. "Muy bien, niña," she said, winking.

"Not badly," echoed Trinidad. "Perhaps one dance I let you do. These Americans are so busy and eat so much they see nothing. If we are busy only—"

"Oh but you will!" Guadalupe begged. "You will take me with you! Yes! I mus' go . . ."

Trinidad's face did not change. But his glance swept past and fastened on the door behind her.

Guadalupe whirled around to see the door close—slowly and quietly as it had opened—behind a figure standing motionless inside the room.

It was Barby. The odd stiff-backed crouch with one knee flexed inside his loose and baggy trousers, right hand resting limply on his belt buckle, the straight black hair protruding from under his Stetson—these details of his figure the girl's eyes caught in a flash. His face was unrecognizable. Unwashed and haggard, his lips drawn back to show ever so slightly a thin white line of teeth, his black eyes repelling the strong light of the opposite window, it was a face with more power, pride and madness than she had ever suspected in the whole man. She stood staring at him too paralyzed to scream.

"Pues; the jealous sweetheart comes to avenge his love!" came the deep sarcastic voice of Trinidad.

The boy whirled a glance around the room like a lasso. Then suddenly, without a word, he flung about and was gone. Peña jumped to the slammed door and flung it open to let out Trinidad's loud and scornful laugh.

4

With that derisive laughter pursuing him down the back steps, Barby fled out of the hotel and into the streets.

He had been so sure, had closed his heart like a man at last! Even in that instant when he knelt outside in the hall, his hand tightening on the doorknob, he had heard within him the first whisper of freedom. Free from the bondage of a face, of a woman who had never been really his! He had opened the door stealthily, knife ready, his eyes sure of the spectacle of his betrayal within—had opened the door upon the confounding and innocent sight of Mr. Five-Cents'-Worth-of-Sugar and his fat wife!

He lowered his head and began to run down the street like a madman. Still that derisive laugh pursued him. Again he had been made a fool. . . .

The quarrel began that night in the street when Guadalupe left Las Quince Letras. At midnight she managed to elude him and spend the night with Sal. But the next morning when she came out Barby was waiting.

"You lie, lie, lie! All the time you lie!" he stormed at her.

Guadalupe shrugged.

"You never tell me nothing! Even your silence lies!"

"I lie when I talk. I lie when I say nothing. What will you have me do, then?"

"Chispas! Don't you know the truth from one day to another?"

All afternoon in the upstairs room of the shop they bickered back and forth. Barby lay on the bed worn out from a sleepless night. Rising from her chair at the window to flare forth, the girl would sink down again. Strangely enough, she dared not play the phonograph. His face yesterday morning and the knife in his belt had frightened her a little. There might be something still hidden in him which she hesitated to bring out. And yet . . .

"Holy Mother! Don' I tell you I go but for two weeks? Trinidad he go to the big, wonderful place where all the rich Americans go. They pay him to bring some entertainers and a man to play the gourds. Perhaps I do but one dance. He take me just to learn. Two weeks."

"Why go if that's all? Don't you do your own dancin here? Don't they yell and throw you money? Stay here with me!"

It was his one appeal. He was sick of her dancing, sick

of the music ground out night and day by the phonograph
beside her, sick of her. And yet he was deathly afraid lest she
be removed from him wholly. Two weeks, a week—when
even a night without her seemed unbearable. He rose to his
knees and hands on the bed. His voice rose with him.

"The goddam cripple, and you too! All this jumpin' and
smirkin' around. Who cares?"

Wearily she shrugged her shoulders and turned to stare
out of the window at the cold twilight seeping down from
the hills. Her silence was more effective than any answer. It
marked the end of every quarrel. When the glaze outside
deepened from the color of a jacaranda bloom to the blue-
black darkness of early night, Guadalupe abruptly left for
work. He cursed her down the stairs, ran to the window and
shouted through the cracked pane as she emerged into the
street. She did not look up.

That night, though he waited with the lamp lit in the
window, she did not return. The next day Barby was more
contrite. He whined, pleaded, dragged what was left of his
pride at her heels. "Don't go. You stay here with me.
Don't go."

It was a monotonous refrain which soon lost its real meaning to them both. Guadalupe ignored it. She was only glad he
kept on crying; he was dangerous only when silent. And early
the next morning, as planned, she left town with Trinidad
and Peña.

Barby had half expected such a trick, unable to learn
when she expected to leave. He reached the portal of the Gambrinus Club just in time to see her stage pull out across the
Line. He returned to his room and flung himself on the bed.
Worked up to an emotional frenzy, the boy had scarcely eaten
or slept for three days. Utterly exhausted, he slept for twelve
hours without moving.

The mystery of sleep, that strange alchemy of subtle change! For now, upon awakening, he felt a different man. The phonograph for once was still. He was utterly alone. Yet he felt strangely alive, his soul at peace. No longer did his hands twitch, his whole body quiver in anticipation of a face, a voice, a step, a hand on his arm. She was gone, and he was again alive and whole. It was as if he had somehow miraculously re-entered a body that felt good to be his again.

He lay and enjoyed a cigarette. Then getting up, he stumbled upon one of Guadalupe's slippers in the middle of the floor. Elated at the discovery that it roused no feeling within him, he kicked it under the bed and went downstairs. Tai Ling gave him a long shrewd look, also a steamy bowl of pork and greens. With this inside him, fortifying still more the independence that so wonderfully had descended upon him, he went out upon the street.

To men he had not noticed for months he now spoke familiarly and effusively. Weather and beer, the new blackboard built in the Owl for the duration of the horse-racing meeting at Tijuana, and Young Fuera's last fight at Juarez, all seemed to have taken on an extraordinary interest. He worked, ate, slept and lounged through the streets with a wholehearted abandon not felt in years. Never had he felt so free. It was incomprehensible to him how one face could have chained him so abjectly to a woman's heels. He seemed to have been delivered from a bondage whose exactitude he had never known till now. And he gave himself all credit for his deliverance. How well he had got rid of her! The only thing that stung him with irritating repetition was that he had waited so long.

Gradually as his flush of freedom ebbed, he began to inflict himself with memories of the many ignominies Guadalupe had heaped upon him. If he had only peeked in the door

before entering—the damned cripple! What if he'd put her
out not days but weeks ago! Or given her the beating she de-
served without waiting. Incidents, words, a look, a shrug—
they all flew back to sting him again and again. And always
his warped pride suffered from the unforgivable; not the act,
but that others had seen it. The memory of himself cringed
before the memory of Trinidad and Peña, Sal, and Tai Ling.
Like him, they remembered his degradation.

Little by little then he began to envision the many re-
vengements he would have upon her. Daily his retaliative
mood expanded. He fed on fancies that were replaced by
others more absurd. Like jostling her in the street without a
glance, or dancing with a percentage girl in the casino as
though she were not there. He would wait until she reached
the door on the day of her return, then throw out her clothes
into the street and stand imperturbably watching her gather
them up, begging to return. Often he envisioned her, arms
around his neck as she clung to him breathing love. How still
he would stand, cigarette in mouth, until she dropped weeping
at his feet. Long gaudy curses took shape in his mind for the
time when they might decorate her in front of Sal. In the
middle of a cold night he would drive her from bed to Trinidad's room to dance. One by one in rancorous detail he went
over those imagined incidents by which he meant to shame
her, to break her pride, and bring her to his feet. Yet always,
though he gave this little thought, they all came to the same
end: his magnanimous forgiveness when he had degraded her
utterly. It was a picture he saw without perceiving what it
meant.

There came the day when he suddenly realized to what
focus rushed his vindictive aspirations. It came upon him unaware, as if he had trod upon an electric cable. It jerked him

erect and flung him forward with pounding heart though he had not missed a stride.

He was waiting for her to return, when all this time he had thought himself completely freed; but only, he convinced himself quickly, that he might wreak upon her his utmost will. The thought restored his composure, gave him confidence to look forward with some equanimity to the time of her return.

The days dragged by, the two weeks ended, and Guadalupe did not return. Daily he grew more nervous and apprehensive. He could not still the turmoil beginning to stir within him. Her increasing absence began to resolve itself into a prolonged torture which he could neither end nor alleviate. It was as though she read his thoughts and maliciously kept away. This allied itself in his mind with her stubborn silence, her careless shrug, and recalled these with a vivid freshness that made him sweat at night.

Still she did not return! Every day he hid himself behind the Gambrinus to watch the stage pull in without her. Unable heretofore to stand the sight of Sal, he now began to trail her back and forth from the cabaret to her hotel. He spied upon the floor of the cabaret, kept vigil upon the dark windows of Trinidad's room at night. And still for all his efforts, Guadalupe kept away.

The taste of his freedom went sour. Again his nerves seemed to screw themselves up into a knot. He forgot his intricate schemes for revenge, and began to be deathly afraid lest some day he come upon her unaware. Dreading the possibility of meeting her on the street with Sal, of seeing her in the cabaret, he ventured out warily. A sudden step behind him on the street, a voice in his ear, and he whirled around as if suddenly detected in a shameful act. Not to be seen by her first! It grew to be his one concern. Convincing himself that she was planning to circumvent him by the last monstrous ignominy of casually coming upon him, he grew to look for her with a consuming fear of detection.

And still she did not return.

He dropped off to sleep each night with the lamp glowing in the window lest the darkness hide her approach.

CHAPTER SEVEN

ONE BY one the yogi of Cockroach Court went over "The Ten Things Wherein One Doeth Good to Oneself."

He had done good to himself, negatively speaking, by abandoning worldly conventions; departing from home and kindred; relinquishing worldly activities; giving up social intercourse; and renouncing desire for luxury and ease.

Positively speaking, he had done good to himself by dwelling alone in solitude as much as was possible for him; enduring hardship; adhering to the resolution not to take advantage of others; disciplining the three doors to knowledge, the body, the speech, the mind; and devoting himself increasingly to the three religious activities—reflecting, analyzing his reflections, meditating.

Still Tai Ling was not pleased with the tenth. He could reflect and analyze his reflections with perfect composure. But for all his frugal diet and long hours alone in his shop, he could not meditate abstractedly with the utter tranquillity and complete objectiveness it required. He caught himself listening for Guadalupe's phonograph upstairs, and being interrupted by faint sounds in the cellar.

Reflecting on the former, Tai Ling could reject consideration of everything upstairs. The boy and the girl were each divided psychically; their separate selves fought constantly. Until they could integrate themselves, how could they attain peace with each other?

But he could not reject consideration of the sounds below. They created in his own mind a worldly image of evil. This was an illusion. To dispel it he sought its dual counterpart, its aspect of good. He no longer kept aloof upstairs as if they did not exist, but went downstairs to administer to his frightened, wretched compatriots as helplessly caught as he. He spoke simple words of kindliness, chafed their cramped and knotted limbs, salved torn patches of skin, gave them hot tea— all to the end that they and he might derive from their common brotherhood a minimum of good out of the evil enclosing them.

It was no use. Tai Ling still saw in their presence an image of evil-doing in which he was an unwilling participant.

Hence when Mendoza casually sauntered in The Lamp, Tai Ling's heart was resolute. He surveyed his visitor calmly— his expensive clothes, a new diamond ring on his middle finger, his air of smug satisfaction. Why is it, he wondered, that the poor in heart increasingly boast of the riches on their backs?

Mendoza flinched from the old man's appraising stare, then announced curtly, "Well, expect us again Friday night."

Tai Ling did not bat an eyelash. "Bring your rurale for me, the soldiers too. I will accommodate you no longer."

Mendoza pleaded.

"No," went on Tai Ling, "I have notified you before that

such a business is not to my liking. I desire neither fine clothes
for my person nor the acclaim of others. I am an old man with
nothing but this humble shop. I want the peace I find in it
alone. This you cannot understand."

Mendoza stormed.

"No," continued Tai Ling imperturbably as before.
"When the little girl was upstairs playing the phonograph I
assented to your compulsion. Her presence and the noise
masked your comings and goings. Now she is gone; Barby is
attending to his own business. I am alone and will have no
more of your charges. This you can understand. It is not my
excuse, but you can use it as yours."

"You damned old fool! We'll see!"

"I have paid my debts," answered Tai Ling. "To you, to
my friends and enemies. To everyone but myself. We shall
see indeed of what that consists. Circumstance will teach us."

He watched Mendoza fling around in a nasty mood and
saunter up the street, then settled back on his stool. Whatever
happened, he had done good to himself by removing the last
worldly obstacle to his complete devotion to spiritual activities.
Perhaps now, unworthy as he was, he could make more ad-
vancement along that Noble Eight-Fold Path which all sentient beings, even Mendoza, must eventually climb.

2

The third week had passed and most of the fourth; still
Guadalupe had not returned. But late that afternoon Barby
happened upon Young Fuera holding forth in a bar.

He was the same Young Fuera and yet a new one too:
in pleated trousers, a bright blue coat narrow waisted and
heavily padded in the shoulders, pointed patent leather slippers with pearl buttons, and a cream colored slouch hat. In

appearance, speech and manner, he gave out a cocksure independence that brought the girls in from the back courtyard and held the men about him. Young Fuera, the flashy new Mexican welter, was back home from his last campaign and telling what had happened.

"Por Dios! A straight right, his very best. I put down my arms and laugh it is so weak. I wave to him to come in and fight. And he!—he cover up, run around the ring, hang to me in every clinch. For three roun's the crowd laugh and yell. Then I get tired waiting for the great Martinez. It is the fifth roun', in his own corner, I catch him. One-two to the middle, very fas'. Then I bring up my right from the knee when he is bent over. Pues, amigos: his nose root up the groun' at my very feet!"

Grandiloquently he paid up for another beer and turned to the crowd. "The first one. Yes. It was nothing. But the last one in Juarez—a truly great fight. Only the next champion could win!" As a murmur of approbation ran along the bar, he put down his glass, squared off into his stance, and illustrated. "But you read in the papers, verdad? Mira!" He took out a sheaf of newspaper clippings to wave in their faces. " 'YOUNG FUERA, HOT TAMALE CHAMPION, WINS AGAIN!'—'YOUNG FUERA, THE MEXICAN VOLCANO, A REAL COMER!' Look! My picture every one. What do I tell you, eh?"

Belligerently staring into the admiring faces before him, he stopped short at sight of Barby. He shoved through the crowd, punched the boy lightly in the ribs and ducked back, hands high, grinning.

"How you like to take the next champion, eh? Or do you take some tacos first? Chispas, but I am hungry!"

Leading Barby to a small lonchería astride the gutter, he sat down on an empty box. In the glow of a charcoal brazier his clean brown face flushed with pleasure at the sizzle of fat. He leaned over the counter to slap a pair of buttocks wide as his own shoulders. "Madre Mio, more onions—la sauza, Madre!" Ravenous, vociferous and affectionate, he sat on his box in the gutter like a king returned from victory after months of rigorous abstemiousness.

"The devil take you, my frien'! Why you so sick and sad?" he ejaculated, suddenly noticing Barby's listless homage. "I tell you what you need is a woman. And for me it has been months since I have done nothing but fight, fight, fight. These two girls I know now—we go make love tonight and feel better. Pretty, with blue eyes, both of them. Santíssima! They will light the fire in your belly and make your heart warm. No?"

Sight of Barby answered him. The boy's brown face had turned yellow. His lips trembled, and the slight click of his teeth as he closed his jaws confirmed the fear that leaped from his eyes. Fuera bent over, shook him by the shoulder.

"Thought you meant Sal and . . ." Barby stuttered. "I remember the last time, we . . ."

"Sal?—Sal!—Oh sí. Sorda hija de tal! Now I remember that old fat chippy, a poor piece if I ever had one." And then with sudden comprehension, "The little one—what do you call her?—that little morena. You—well I'll be Goddamned!"

He had no need to finish, glimpsing the unassuageable misery in the boy's black eyes. No! No man could be so foolish for long. It was but a sickness, temporary as all ills. "Mother of God, compadre, what you think a woman is? The bright lights, the music, the money—that is where they go like moths every one, today, tomorrow, always!"

No; he could not comprehend it. Nor flushed with success, full of food, could he restrain that healthy animal vitality which oozed from every pore. He threw centavos to three chamacos in the street and rewarded the winner with a black cigar; shouted over his shoulder at passers-by; winked at every girl who slipped past. At last he let out his belt, lit a cigarette, and turned about on his box to see, leaning against a telephone pole, a man who had been watching them with an ironic smile on his thin lips.

The man dropped his cigarette, crushing it out with a toe of his expensive Oxfords. He brushed an imaginary speck off his suit with a hand whose diamond ring glittered brightly. Then he sauntered over.

"And who is your noisy friend, Barby? A noted politician beloved by all these people he benefits? Or a large cotton grower? Perhaps he owns a race horse which has just won the Coffroth Handicap at Agua Caliente?"

Barby recognized the ironic smooth voice before he whirled around. "Mendoza! Señor Mendoza! I—this is Young Fuera, the fighter, you—"

"A boxer? Oh yes. I seem to have heard the name somewhere." He smiled disdainfully.

Young Fuera flushed, clinched his hands. Mendoza's tailored clothes cheapened his own gaudy ones; Mendoza's oily voice in excellent Spanish shamed his own vulgar, loud idiom; indeed the whole man shrank at once his own success and put him in his place. But Fuera held his anger; obviously Mendoza was somebody; perhaps even a future backer.

"Well, I'm glad to meet you, Fuera," Mendoza smiled more openly. "I recall now that it was you who defeated Martinez in Juarez. An excellent match, I hear. Have a cigarette."

Young Fuera warmed; the case was of shiny silver.

"It's always good when two friends encounter success in their separate careers, no? I suppose Barby has been telling you what a businessman he has become? The owner of a new cantina. Making more money than any place of its size in the district."

"No! What the hell?" said Young Fuera.

"Oh, it isn't so much!" protested Barby, suddenly warmed by Mendoza's open approbation. "Just a small place. No entertaining. I—"

"Entirely too modest he is, Fuera. Why, to look at him you'd think he was a poor, shirtless labrador. Such clothes! Utter disregard for appearances!" Mendoza swept over Barby a swift, discerning glance, then turned to Young Fuera. "One thing I must say for a boxer that I can't say for a businessman, speaking personally of course. A coming champion doesn't neglect appearances, does he, Fuera? But then we've been around a bit more, eh? Barby has been tending too strictly to business perhaps."

"That's right. You got to have a front. Yes sir! Why all us sportin' people know you can't look cheap."

"It's not that he doesn't have the money," went on Mendoza, edging up to Barby. "My guess is that he's got something else on his mind. A little tiff with that sweetheart of his! Pues, what is that!" He winked at Fuera; suddenly plunged his hand into Barby's pocket. When it came out it held some crumpled bills.

"Fuera, you and I are going to take this friend of ours across the Line this instant and spend his money for him! A whole new outfit! I myself will select his ties. I depend on you, as his other friend, to add a silk shirt or two. What do you say, Fuera? New clothes will make him feel like a different man when he sees that sweetheart of his again—and it will be good for his business. . . . We won't take no for an answer. Come along now!"

Young Fuera, thus appealed to as the sporting gentleman he was, beamed at Mendoza. Once in the shop he bought both shirts and ties with extravagant generosity while Mendoza calmly helped select a suit.

Barby's mind still whirled at Mendoza's sudden appearance, more friendly than before; his championing of the cantina; and more than all else his keen, sympathetic and yet jovial allusion to his trouble with Guadalupe. It seemed to lift a vast weight off his mind, to shrink his worry into nothing. Finally fitted in his new clothes, he strutted before the mirror. Wait till Guadalupe came back! It was no longer a doubt but a certainty.

The three men strolled back to El Sol de Mayo for a drink at Barby's invitation. They had several. For the first time the boy felt the glow of proprietorship. Mendoza was no less hospitable.

"Drop in—anytime," he urged Young Fuera as the boxer got up to leave. "Bring your friends. El Sol de Mayo is always open for you fellows to talk about your fights."

When he had gone Mendoza settled back in his chair and lit a cigar. "That's the way to draw a crowd, Barby. A good front. A sociable welcome. You have to spend money to make money. . . . In no time you'll be rolling in it." His voice had grown harder, sharper. His eyes narrowed.

Barby stirred uncomfortably in his new clothes. Now that Young Fuera had gone, he felt the necessity of admitting that the money which had bought them was not his but Mendoza's. Why, he didn't know. "These clothes—I . . ." and curiously abashed, "maybe some day I can do something for you, Señor Mendoza."

Mendoza relaxed. "Por nada, por nada." Then abruptly, "Come to think of it, there's a real favor you could do me. . . . Yes, perhaps you're just the man!"

He leaned forward confidentially. On Friday night he

wanted to store a half dozen barrels in a safe place for a couple of days.

But no! It wasn't quite as simple as the boy imagined. They could be kept in the back storeroom all right, but it had to be kept locked. In fact, it would be best if Cheon did not know they were there. . . . No. That would be asking too much. They should forget the whole thing.

"Why, Señor Mendoza!" Barby was indignant.

Mendoza hitched his chair closer. He wanted to be truthful. There was a certain faction on both sides of the Line engaged in stirring up trouble. It made things difficult for him as an export agent of an important business house. Strict confidence prevented him from saying more. But if Barby did insist on trusting his discretion, he, Mendoza, would be grateful as a friend and, moreover, see to it that his Company was also duly appreciative. There was no reason why Barby should not gradually work into something good if shipments continued.

Good!

They agreed on minor details. Cheon could be given a couple of nights off for a change, and open up Monday morning. Then only Barby would be there when the shipment was brought in. Enough supplies could be moved temporarily into the back room; the storeroom would not have to be entered.

Suddenly Mendoza whacked Barby on the back. "Better yet, compadre! Drive down to the gulf with me to pick up my shipment. Give you a chance to learn how to take my place if I'm delayed or need help. You're looking seedy. Too much work, too much worry about that absent sweetheart of yours. An outing will do you good. What do you say?"

3

On Thursday morning they rumbled off: Mendoza, Barby and a young Mexican-Chinese named Tony Wong who drove the old, deep-bottomed truck.

Wong handled the car with ease, his eyes fixed on the rutted dirt road that crept across the arroyo and led steadily southward through the empty desert. He was respectful, discreet, and answered only when addressed.

"You can depend on Tony," boasted Mendoza. "He knows the ropes, and better yet, how to keep his mouth shut." He was in high humor, kept up a bright chatter of all the places he had been, the sights he had seen. "Does you good to travel, eh Barby? How do you like getting out for a little cross-country run? Maybe Tony will teach you how to drive someday. What do you say, Tony? We're all going to get along fine, I can see that."

But a little later his voice turned sharp. "Only one thing, compadre. I'm stopping Chugoku from sending Tai Ling any more fish. I don't want you telling him you've been down here either. Don't ask me why. Let him stick to his business and you stick to yours. Understand?"

Barby shrugged. The old man would get along all right; he always did. He was more engrossed in the immeasurable landscape about him, the exhilarating sense of rushing through it. He had never felt so free.

The monotone of the long desert miles was broken when the truck reached the top of the sierras. Below him, for the first time since childhood, he saw the sea spread out like a vast blue blanket with the reticulated white surf turned down like lace upon the shore. For an instant it hung there fresh and vivid, like a picture in his memory, then the bumpy road dipped steeply down to the half-moon bay.

There was the fishing village again; and at its far end, like a clump of debris washed up on the smooth white beach, Chugoku's shack. Barby first discerned a net hung out to dry, then long ropes and leaves of seaweed hanging from the roof. A scrawny long-legged stork was drawn on the door, and on the single window were lettered a few thin and wavering ideographs. Behind it was a shelf of odds and ends. A half decomposed star fish, a pipe whose bowl was traced in ivory, pieces of pink jade, abalone shells, dried herbs, a rusty compass, a stack of shark's fins. Above all, in the window and inside the shack, fish: fresh fish, dried fish, fish raw, cooked, salted and pickled.

"You know Barby don't you, Chugoku?" said Mendoza. "Stays with Tai Ling. But now he's got a cantina of his own and is going to help us out. But we'll talk about that later."

Chugoku grinned; a miserable, sly wretch, he looked as scrawny as his ill-drawn stork and smelled as badly as his fish.

"Want to stretch your legs a bit while I talk business?" asked Mendoza. "Why don't you see if you can buy a case or two of Carta Blanca beer cheaper than in town?"

Dismissed, Barby walked back to the little fishing village. The melancholy cluster of huts, the smell of brine, the sound of the surf—all these brought back to the edge of his memory his first childish days with the Romeros. But there they stayed. Most of the palms had been destroyed by later storms. The village had grown and changed. A new pier had been built. There was no-one he remembered. An influx of Chinese had given the old Mexican village a new temper and rhythm. No; even the effortless peace and timeless calm in which he remembered being immersed as if in a vacuum was rent by thoughts of Guadalupe, of new pain over her absence, new fears that she would never return.

Disgruntled and disillusioned, he turned back. As Tai Ling would have said, it was a world that no longer existed as he remembered it; an illusion in his own mind.

That evening the old steamer Mendoza was expecting rounded the corner of the cliffs and crossed the half-moon bay. With all the villagers the four men waited for her at the pier. The boat was a wormy, waterlogged tub of perhaps sixty tons stinking with fish, fruit and the peon families bedded on her deck.

"Cargo, Captain! Did you bring any beer?"—"Tony, help Chugoku hustle off that fish!" Mendoza shouted officiously in the crowd. Then he took Barby aboard to wait while he talked to the slovenly unshaven skipper about his shipment in the hold.

"There's nothing to it," he confided to Barby that night. "Just be sure to get the barrels or boxes off and taken to Chugoku's. He's out in the back room now seeing nothing's been damaged. We don't have to bother."

Late next morning the truck was loaded: Mendoza's few big barrels, a few cases of Carta Blanca beer for El Sol de Mayo, and a box or two of merchandise Tony Wong was hauling to the stores in town. Chugoku fastened a tarpaulin over them. Tony filled the water bag. Then the three men drove off.

The truck stopped for inspection twice. Each time Mendoza merely leaned out of the cab, shouted effusively and familiarly at the officer, and was waved away.

"Good sports!" boasted Mendoza. "Just keep on the good side of them. Saves time."

Barby did not answer. He sat, knees up, staring blankly out upon the slow rushing miles. For just as their departure from town had lifted the misery burdening him, their arrival back lowered it again upon him. Mother of God! Where had Guadalupe gone, that week after week she stayed away? If indeed she ever intended to come back. The suspicion almost made him howl aloud with new anguish.

"Slow up, Tony! What the hell! I told you there's no need to get in before dark," shouted Mendoza angrily.

Obediently the truck slowed down, began a leisurely climb up the sierras. Then the wide dark plain, faintly lit by the brightening cluster of cantinas, began drawing Barby back into a vortex of searing recollections. The signs growing intelligible in darkness, the bridge across the arroyo, the buildings, the streets, the alleys—they all leapt at him anew with their associative memories of Guadalupe. Nothing had changed. Nothing!

"Well, here we are!" announced Mendoza. "Nine o'clock and nobody around. Barby, go in and tell Cheon he can go now. You can lock up. We'll wait out here in the alley before unloading."

The boy was too tired to care. Everything in his mind was out of focus except the old feeling of desolation and aloneness. Wearily he helped Tong Wong unload, and gave the storeroom key to Mendoza. When they drove off, he flopped down on the bar stool and poured himself a drink.

An hour later he was still sitting there, oppressed by an overpowering hopelessness; not a customer had come in. He locked up and stumbled home.

So stupefied was he by this cloying futility that Barby did not notice the dim glow of a light in his upstairs room at The Lamp Awake. He went in quietly lest he disturb Tai Ling in the back room, wiped off his face in cold water, and climbed the stairs.

Even then he had no presentiment as he turned the door

knob. A trickle of light ran out of the opening door. He raised his head. The lamp on the cómoda against the far wall was turned low but burning. In its light a figure in bed rose on one arm and turned her face toward him. He could not see her eyes, shadowed as they were by the wing of black hair spread fanwise upon her bare shoulder. Guadalupe, for her part, regarded him as silently. Then chilled by the cold from the cracked window she lay down again without a word, her face pressed into the pillow.

4

It was his greatest triumph—that she had come back to him at last. And yet it was on this first dawn of her return when he awakened to find her head once more on the pillow beside his, that he first knew he had really lost her.

He rose on one arm and bent down over her. The sun was not yet up, and in the room's splotchy darkness her black hair was still a part of night. Only the outline of her face with its stub nose and resolute chin coincided with its image in his mind. He could see her bare smooth shoulder curving out from the covers, the swell of her small firm breast below. She shivered slightly, still asleep.

Guadalupe was home and his again! It brought the blood rushing from his heart. He sank down carefully and lay holding her hand as a priest at prayer his crucifix.

The room gradually lightened. Gently he rose with mute adoration to look down upon her face again—that dark sweet oval he had not seen for weeks. It was like a child's, smiling in sleep. But there was something about that smile which froze his running blood. It betrayed, but did not reveal, some pleasant reflection of the past recalled in sleep. And deep inside him that secret voice which had told him she would not return now whispered with equal authority that she had been drawn from him forever.

Never! No voice, no-one, nothing could deny him! And as he had then ignored that small voice of his deepest self by brooding over her absence, so now he stilled it by closing his eyes to that mocking smile. He lay back down and fell asleep. . . .

Yes, everything at first seemed as before, even better. But gradually he perceived a change in the girl. The extreme placidity of her countenance became its disturbing symbol. Not a flicker of interest passed over it as he strutted his astounding new haberdashery before her, bragging of a secret business partner he had acquired. Nor did it light up with ecstasy or cloud over with resentment when he tried to make love to her. At best she was merely passive. Still she had come back, kept coming to him nearly every night. Why: habit, loneliness, company, money? The perpetual mystery of a woman's heart!

Often as he lay waiting for her light step, Barby felt those eager words which might tell her the agony of those empty weeks without her, the gladness, glory and tempestuous rush of life that now filled him at her return. They rose out of him unbidden and unbearable, trembled on his tongue. And the moment she came in the door, placid, unmoved and with only a curt "Adios" before turning on the phonograph, all these words and phrases, these spendthrift thoughts and emotions so fluid and fragrant, seemed suddenly dammed within him. The merest words of welcome grew stale and shriveled on his tongue. He could only lie back down again, sterile of expression at sight of her steady eyes and placid face.

But slowly it began to light up at something else.

5

"Oh, but it was so lovely! Never do I see such things before!"

For days it was all she talked about. That far, famous resort with its creamy walls and red tile roofs gleaming against the green hills, its towers hung with bells, the ballroom and the gaming room, the patio and its gurgling fountain, the race track and its crowded grandstand: all this magnificence and beauty still hung before her as if painted on a thin silk curtain through which she now saw but dimly the unimpressive surroundings and inconsequential actions of those about her.

Barby let her talk on.

"Magnífico! Exquísita!" She hardly dared define it with her most expressive words. And the people! Above all, la gente de razon! They had filled the gardens, thronged about the gold table under a chandelier jeweled and glittering with a thousand prisms like a royal crown suspended overhead. They flanked the long mahogany bar which softly gleamed with brass and nickel, langorously lifting tall slim glasses filled with drinks pink as jacaranda blossoms, honey-colored, or green as garden grass under the shaded lamps. In the patio they grouped thickly about the tables; rose and moved with a happy hum of voices upon the dance floor. An endless parade of wonderfully endowed creatures in a world so sublimely beautiful that it was just adequate for their needs.

Guadalupe could never imagine them in surroundings less than these. The women tall and slimly voluptuous as if they had been poured into their sheaths of silk and satin, their white arms and pale immobile faces coolly resisting the flaming colors. And the men, all in black and white, masters of

this world which spun endlessly as a machine which they kept
going with casual contributions from pockets that never
seemed empty of silver and rolls of bills. They were all perfect
and hence incomparable to any others. she had known. La
gente de razon! Guadalupe was but deeply grateful and happy
that she had been allowed among them.

For an hour in the tawdry upstairs room of The Lamp
Awake she would thus prattle till Barby would interrupt sav-
agely, "Turistas! Rich American Yanquis!" as though the
epithet were sharp enough to rend forever that curtain of unreality which hung before her eyes.

"But no! They love me!" Guadalupe would flash back,
her voice ringing with the passionate conviction of a childish
faith. "Barby! They love me too!" This was the phrase by
which she answered every doubt.

Trinidad, true to his promise, had let her dance. Besides
herself and Peña, his featured entertainers were a couple
picked up in Agua Prieta. The man—a boy not quite twenty-
four with a cavernous face and long curved sideburns—was
one of those long, angling, tubercular-looking oddities which
haunt like ghosts every cabaret along the Mexican Border. His
partner was a chunky Mexican girl who knew how to use her
hips, a sombrero, and a Chinese shawl. That she was his wife
was evident to Trinidad from his malicious pleasure in mis-
handling her on the floor; an attitude not concealed by his
toothy, mirthless grin, which turned into a penitent smirk the
moment he was off the floor. They were both gaily costumed
—charro and chinapoblano—and went through a series of foot
stamping and arm waving, the Chinese shawl flapping until
the figured roses almost flew off, which ended with the sombrero being thrown on the floor and being danced around, not
too closely lest one of its tiny bells be crushed. They were im-
mensely popular and repeated the last dance every night.

Trinidad sat watching them without change of expression. They were dependable, his bread and butter, and he never objected when the same foot stampings and arm wavings were successively announced as a bolero, a fandango and a jarabe.

Only when Peña came out with her castanets did he seem to come half-alive. He sat up on the dais, eyes half closed, his deformity hidden from the crowd below, and played his guitar. Peña's castanets did all the rest. They buzzed, purred, droned sleepily as bees in the summer sun; then they seemed to whirl aloft, becoming the whir of a bird on wing; again they were angry and ominous as the rattle of a snake; or divided their tone, the male loud and demanding and being answered softly by the female. Then they drew together, carrying along the rhythm of Trinidad's guitar. Guadalupe, amazed, sat looking out from the curtain behind Trinidad, aware of Peña's few graceful steps underneath her long black silk skirts. The turn drew enough applause to warrant the few minutes each night, and Trinidad at the last stroke put down his guitar as if it were too hot to hold.

Then one night soon after their arrival he raised his hand: a single gesture to the announcer out in front. The man got up, called out the girl's name through his trumpet, and turned to wait for her. For an instant Guadalupe sat as if petrified. No one, not even Peña, had told her she was to dance that night. Before she knew it, she was walking down the steps to the dance floor. Trinidad lazily raised his guitar. There was but one look from his eyes as she began to dance; and that look, casual but commanding, erased her nervousness completely.

"So I dance, Barby!" Every step and turn, every gesture of her hands, each posture completed as if for Trinidad alone. And he, immutable as a judge, gave her no sign or look of approbation or disfavor.

"But they love me! Yes! Just like in Las Quince Letras!"

All those people, bored and full of food or drink, that weary horde of resort guests which nothing could awake from a permanent lethargy, had looked out from their tables upon another cantina entertainer and had given her the same polite attention and casual applause that they would have accorded the antics of a trained dog or a juggling clown. She was to them no more than a dish of olives listed on the menu—something to be taken for granted and deserving no thought at all.

But to Guadalupe their applause seemed a tremendous welcome to that resplendent world which held her so entranced. The silly vapid smiles of the women turned on mechically as electric light switches the moment she had finished seemed lit by the radiance of her own childish gratitude. And the men, stolid and stuffed, and taking up their cigars and drinks again, seemed to have passed upon her the taciturn approval of lords who have no need for words. The hum of voices began again. To Guadalupe it was all about herself. She waved her arms to them, blew them a kiss, and went back behind the curtain. They loved her! La gente de razon!

Over and over it was the thing she talked about to Barby. How every night thereafter Trinidad had let her dance. How for weeks longer they had stayed. And something more! On their last afternoon she and Peña had walked through the bar on their way out. And there at a table beside the door was a group of people who recognized her. "Ah, our little dancer!" One of the men thrust a fresh white rose into her hand.

"Freddie!" The lady beside him jumped abruptly to her feet, one hand clasping the front of her gown whence he had plucked the rose. "You're drunk and you have torn my gown!"

Guadalupe stopped dismayed, flower in hand outstretched to the woman. "But the lady's flower . . ."

"Señorita," began Freddie, rising to his feet unsteadily and pushing it back, "the lady shall have a new gown, but the rose is for you. The rose of Spain, of purity . . ."

For an instant Guadalupe stood still, Peña's hand pulling at her arm. Then the lady with a curt wave of her hand acknowledged the girl's childish mixture of hesitation and eagerness, smiled and motioned her away.

"Freddie, you beast! Little you know of Spain or purity either! And a new gown—listen to the man! He wouldn't have bought me a flower if he hadn't been drunk."

The laugh that went up followed Peña and Guadalupe out the door. It meant nothing to the girl. Only the fresh white rose held in her hand all the way through the dusty, squalid border town to the train that was to take her home to another ten times worse. And for a hundred miles as she sat in her coach looking out upon the ragged sunburnt hills and dense chaparral, she held it wrapped in her handkerchief. Occasionally she wet it with water in the ladies' toilet, finally pinned it to her own dress. And still a week later after it had wilted, shriveled, changed color and died, it hung over a water glass dropping petals on the cómoda like a fading tribute from that resplendent world she had never known before.

Barby let her talk on, without asking questions. And day by day, like a phonograph, her voice began to run down. Still he forbade questioning her, fearful of her sullen silence. But carefully cataloguing all he heard, he began to feel she was leaving something out.

She was like a religious who had been granted a peep into paradise and was thus consecrated to a world more real to her than this one. Yet there was more to it than mere singing and dancing.

Barby knew. That small deep voice within him now shouted it was so every time he touched her.

CHAPTER EIGHT

TAI LING'S single hour of daily pleasure—that sunrise interlude between his morning meditation and morning work when he delighted in watching his fish—was ruined completely.

For one thing Chugoku was not sending him any more specimens. For another El Sol de Mayo's trade was falling off. Why? Barby openly, and Cheon confidentially, both had posed the question. Reluctantly the old man had agreed to squint into the matter and offer a suggestion.

But Barby's books for the cantina were no better kept than they had been for the shop years ago. They told Tai Ling, as did Cheon, that Barby merely paid bills out of the cash drawer and stuffed the rest in his pocket. There was another discrepancy. Barby always seemed to have money for fancy clothes and trinkets for Guadalupe even lately when the place was empty.

How distasteful all this was to Tai Ling, who had believed himself free from this balancing of worldly profit and loss!

He dismissed all bookkeeping; the boy would have to learn to conduct his own business.

Yet undoubtedly trade had fallen off. The crowds of summer workers and the harvest hands of fall had departed. With winter Chino Juan was pushing his rivals to the wall. Not only did he have a shop wherein he peddled marihuana, and the Casino Chino, a gambling house. He had opened his new bar, the Chinesca, with a crib of girls behind it expressly to combat El Sol de Mayo. It was markedly successful. So much so that Cheon was privately in favor of getting in some prostitutes themselves to stave off disaster.

Tai Ling was shocked. "You know me better than that," he said sternly. "To imagine that I would countenance such a thing! It is well that you have imposed on my friendship instead of mentioning it to the owner of the cantina, your employer. Have you forgotten it is no longer your establishment? Now be gone. I will try to think of something that can be done for his respectable place of business."

So he had, and vainly, till this early morning interlude when he played absent-mindedly with his remaining fish.

The big bowl before him was filled with hungry snappers. Into it he thrust a pickle jar of tiny minnows. For moments now he watched the excited fish swarming round it, mouths pressed against the glass. From time to time he jerked it out, emptied one of its bait, and inserted the jar again before the heaving, frothy water had subsided.

Meanwhile he ruminated on the practical application of wisdom which might be derived from watching his fish. These fish symbolic of all sentient beings immersed in a sea of illusion.

He had it! Suddenly it had come to him—the remedy for El Sol de Mayo's dwindling trade. He put away his fish and settled back on his stool. The more he thought of it the better he liked it. Wholly in accord with his principles, it would benefit many with a minimum of harm. . . .

2

A few weeks later Tai Ling bestirred himself. Perhaps he ought to go to the cantina and observe how his suggestion was working out. Chinese New Year also was approaching, the traditional time for paying debts. He thought it proper also to repay Chino Juan's brief summer call to El Sol de Mayo, his only debt.

So now on a cold January night Tai Ling rose carefully, for his patched trousers were a little tight, and let out a sigh of reluctance. From a nail he took down his worn, black sateen jacket, dusted off a slouch Stetson, and stepped outside.

It was the first night Tai Ling had been out in months, and he shuffled down the street as though seeing it for the first time. What interested him most was Chinese John's new cantina. He looked the Chinesca over carefully before entering. Its weather-beaten adobe face was covered with a new cosmetic mask of gaudy pink; it was brilliantly lit. But the cantina was almost empty.

Tai Ling restrained a smile of worldly satisfaction and inquired of Chino Juan. Swift fright leapt into the bartender's eyes. His master was at the Casino Chino. Tai Ling nodded gravely and walked on up the street—slowly enough, he knew, for a messenger to precede him.

A few moments later he reached the gambling rooms of his rival. Nodding courteously to a rurale who stood at the door to keep out all Mexicans, whites and Negroes, he stepped inside. Not a corner nor a person escaped his first glance. Chino Juan was standing in the shadow of a curtain in back.

Tai Ling shuffled down the room, speaking quietly only

when addressed. At the last table he stopped. He got into a chair, smoothing out his patched trousers in the seat, and opened a new pack of cigarettes. When one was smoked he made his bet—an American ten dollar gold piece which he laid down gingerly as if it might be soiled by the greasy oil-cloth. Within a moment it had drawn its mate. Tai Ling rose slowly and took up both coins, giving the newcomer a rub on his worn sleeve before putting it into his pocket. Then laying down the pack of cigarettes besides the dealer, he stepped back against the wall.

This was the moment, had Chino Juan chosen. But nothing happened. He simply stood there at the back curtain locking glances with his rival.

Tai Ling turned and went out. He had made his first call.

From the Casino Chino he went to El Sol de Mayo. As he had known, the cantina was filling. Around the stove near the edge of the dance floor sat Sal and a group of other percentage girls wrangling among themselves at their cursed luck in Las Quince Letras and keeping a sharp eye on the door for any spender who might happen in. Several couples were dancing. Cheon was busy at the bar. The cosy air of intimacy, compared to the Chinesca's bright emptiness, instantly warmed Tai Ling's heart. He settled down on a chair at the end of the bar, and leaned back to watch his biggest aquarium. His little human fish!

Like Sal, once she had been invited by both Guadalupe and Barby at Tai Ling's insistence, they had started coming to loaf away the dull winter evenings after their work at the cabaret. They still kept coming when there was no work at all. No one checked them in; no one checked them out. A chair beside the stove in good company was a comfortable port that invariably ended the day's monotonous voyage. Here they could dance with whoever pleased them. Their company cost a man nothing; there were no rules and no percentage due the house. If any of them wanted to meet a gentleman friend, receive a love letter, or hold a rendezvous with a likely lad, the place was El Sol de Mayo. And the joke of it all was that each night they were given a peso for their presence.

Both Barby and Cheon begrudged the money, they knew. But like Sal the girls believed them tightfisted no-accounts under the domination of an old codger's infatuation for Guadalupe. Not for a minute could they have believed themselves helpless specimens viewed through glass.

But to Tai Ling they were not girls; they were fish. He delighted in their antics as he delighted in the antics of their inspiring prototypes. His little human fish! Independent, lazy, drinking up beer and soaking up the warmth of the stove, they were the most foolish and helpless of all minnows.

Against the windowpanes, like hungry pouting snappers, pressed faces eagerly eyeing them inside. Tai Ling knew he would not have to jerk them away. He was content that they believed themselves free, and allowed life to catch them at their own pleasure. They were stubborn and capricious. No one could anticipate with certainty a kick or a kiss. This lent zest to the chase and brought customers back night after night. What men knew they could get they didn't want. So that while the Chinesca with an ample supply of prostitutes was almost empty, El Sol de Mayo with no cribs in back prospered nightly. It had the liveliest and surest bait of all.

The piano in back had begun to play; a half-drunk nigger was at the keys. Occasionally a man or two came in to lounge at the bar and eye the girls in the mirror. One of them ambled up to the circle around the stove, bent over a girl. She went on talking.

"Why not, honey?" he asked again.

"God Almighty! You here again? What for now?"

He patted his coat pocket clumsily, gave a foolish grin. Still talking, the girl got up and pushed back her chair. They had a drink at the bar. A moment later they were out on the floor. To the nigger's crazy tune on the piano he was trying to feel her breasts, and she was trying to coax a hand inside his coat pocket.

The girls around the stove went on talking. "I wouldn't dance with nobody," said Sal lazily stretching out her legs. "God, but my feet's killin' me!"

"Dyin from lack of use, I reckon," answered a scrawny little youngster from Arizona. "You don't do nothin' all day!"

"Nothin' but worry where in God's name I'm goin' to get my next meal. If you little bastards would give me a chance, the Big Fella might lay off me. Him and his crabbin'! I can't bring summer no faster."

"Give you a chance! My deah!" spoke up a tall blond Texan named Cutie, rolling her blue eyes around. "Aren't you at the first table? But heah! Don't say we don't give you every chance."

Sal glanced lazily over her shoulder, then got up with alacrity to meet a flush-looking rancher coming in the door. She was not aware of Cutie who innocently followed her to the bar for a match and stood nearby in her most provocative pose. The rancher talked with Sal easily enough while downing his drink, but kept looking over her shoulder. At last with a grin he spun a dime across the bar to buy her a beer, slapped her good-naturedly across the bottom, and walked past her to Cutie. Sal spun around. As if coyly surprised by his invitation, the girl was leading him out upon the floor.

"The little bitch!" murmured Sal, and flung herself down in her chair.

"What you'spose the old Chino's here tonight for?" inquired a voice in a lower tone. "You don't reckon he's goin' to make Cheon quit givin' us our dollar?"

"Naw," answered another. "Can't you see he don't expect nothin' from us? Or we'd be workin' our tails off like for Gonzales. On our feet for nothin' all day long. This old boy's just screwy. Chinesey."

"Don't kid me. This dump ain't goin' broke. It ain't so hot on looks, but you ever stop to notice the people comin' in? More'n in The Fifteen Letters if you ask me. Looks like he'd wake up to business."

Tai Ling was not asleep. He was appraising his bait. Cheon had whispered there were two missing.

The first one came in like a lioness. Redheaded, freckled and half drunk, she let out a roar at everybody and started singing her way across the dance floor. Her cub followed meekly behind—a slim dapper Filipino with a penchant for all white girls and this very white-skinned girl in particular. He stopped at the bar, counting out his money for the cheapest pint. It was obvious that if it held out—she could take so much! . . . He wet his lips and followed her to the piano in the dark corner. There she slumped down on the platform at the nigger's feet, with the Filipino impatiently trying to empty the bottle down her throat between notes.

Tai Ling saw Cheon smile; she had brought him business. Still he waited for the second.

She came in shortly, very docile, with a mean twist to her mouth and small, bitter, almond eyes.

Cheon nodded to Tai Ling, and got out his canvas sack. It was time to pay off the girls.

Cutie stopped dancing long enough to drop her dollar down her stocking. The first young lady and her partner were still playing for higher stakes at the far end of the hall, but did not resent the discreet intrusion. To the redhead slumped against the piano Cheon offered the coin, and let the Filipino take it. It meant another pint. Under Tai Ling's watchful eyes he paid off all the girls around the stove but one.

"Come on. Where's mine?" demanded the last to enter.

"No. None."

"Why? Ain't I been gettin' it ever' night same as the rest?"

"No money. No more." Cheon was obstinate.

The girl began to rave.

When she paused for breath, Cheon answered. "I saw you in the Chinesca. You take man there for drink. Now you go get money there. No more here."

"Why? Ain't that a public place? I didn't see no Indian sign on it!" As there was still no money forthcoming, she turned to Tai Ling and began to whine, "It ain't fair! The fellow took me. I ain't done nothin'! Make him give me my money too."

Tai Ling was helpless. "I have no quarrel against the Chinesca," he murmured sadly, "but this is not my cantina. I am but a visitor."

Cheon abruptly took her by the shoulders and spun her around. Before she could collect her wits, he had sent her flying through the half-doors. She did not come back.

The room was still. Only the nigger in back went on playing. The girls settled back in their chairs. "Jesus Christ!" whispered one. "I guess I ain't goin' inside *that* place. A warm fire and a dollar for grub ain't much till you ain't got it."

Tai Ling got up. This was business, ugly always. Even with all the good he could do, there invariably remained a modicum of harm.

When he got outside, the girl was still leaning dejectedly against the wall. He reached inside his jacket pocket and gave her his ill-begotten gold piece. Without waiting for her amazed thanks he shuffled back to The Lamp Awake.

It was just ten o'clock, and from upstairs came the voice of a phonograph faintly screeching:

"Ah ain't crazy; you bet Ah ain't no fool!
But from now on, Daddy, it's fifty-fifty;
I'se tired of all yo' rule . . ."

Tai Ling did not look up. But again adjusting his tight trousers to the stool behind his counter, he turned down the lamp a bit. Perhaps now, both his calls completed, he would be left in peace.

3

By day, by year, The Lamp Awake never changed. The boxes and bales, the sacks and cans, the matting, hardware and sundries forever cluttered the place in a hopeless confusion that never improved. New canaries came, sang their songs and were replaced by others whose voices seemed quite as sweet— just like poets who as unknowingly take up the one song of all the others who have gone before. So too its fish shimmered in the morning sun, faded and died, like rainbows that come and come again.

Yet subtly Tai Ling's cluttered shop did mark the passing seasons. With fresh hearts of mezcal and a stack of sugar cane; with strings of green, yellow or red chile—chile colorado, pasilla, sol seco, pequeno, poblano; fresh corn husks for wrapping tamales; a single poinsettia, la Flor de Noche Buena—the Flower of Christmas Night; and then a bowl of water lily bulbs blooming in the window; by such successive signs did The Lamp Awake mark time.

But now Chugoku had stopped sending him fish either for sale or pleasure. Reluctantly the old man emptied his last dead specimen in the alley. Likewise he stopped ordering fruits and vegetables; no customers came in to buy them. And for the first time in years Chan Foo had not sent him a poinsettia for Christmas, and Chewlee Singkee a lily bulb for New Year.

With this disappearance of variable matter, the phenomena of time vanished also. Day and night the yogi of Cockroach Court sat in his dusky shop unaware of the difference. The lamp on his counter was always lit. By its feeble glow he polished more assiduously that lamp of self-knowledge flickering deep within him.

That was his way, as opposed to the man of action.

For both, the road of evolutionary progress was an ascending spiral stairway. But each saw it from a different angle.

Seen by the worldly active from his horizontal plane it was always a broad and level highway that obscured the spirals above and below. So slight was its incline he never saw it lift. So long was it he measured it by time, which he could subdivide, rather than eternity.

Hence he restricted his attention to the relation between the individual and the society of fellow travelers around him. His life was concerned with action that bore directly on purely social ends. He had achieved an ascendancy of reason over spirit, matter over mind.

Tai Ling heard the yowling in Cockroach Court and knew it was repeated everywhere on man's horizontal plane. He saw in his mind's eye the jungles of vast cities; watched the beasts of nations creep upon others with the soft padded feet of diplomacy; heard the doctors of science wreaking death on the battlefields with the tools they had conceived to cure man of his ills; saw the tyranny of the Church give way to the divine right of kings, and it to the almighty power of the sacred dollar. All in the name of evolutionary progress. While mankind crept round and round, bound as if to a wheel, without knowing where it was going.

No! The horizontal was too limited a view.

But for the passive yogi on his vertical plane the illusion of this broad level highway was dispelled. He could see the spiral staircase for what it was—slowly ascending from the first spark of life in primeval muck, up through plant and animal kingdoms to man, and thence upward to the higher consciousness that finally knows itself a part of the one macrocosmic mind of all.

This was the Path. All else was an illusion. But each man had to tread it alone. And his progress depended, not on the ease, the pleasant companions or material encumbrances with which he traveled, but solely on self-realization.

Hence the yogi fixed his attention on the relation between the individual and the universe. He shunned society, ignored power, abhorred violent action. His life was concerned with mind, time, space and causality. He sought by meditation to achieve ascendency of mind over matter, and to combine reason and spirit in light of the transcendental true knowledge.

So Tai Ling tightened his belt and meditated alone in his empty shop. Life was his teacher, intuition his guide, his own self his textbook, and obliteration of this self his goal. What a wonderful winter!

4

Winter! To Guadalupe it was something else. It seemed the prolongation of an already interminable night. The cold with the quick-coming dusk made it more unbearable than ever. With darkness she could feel the life receding slowly from her thinking mind, draining her nerves, sinking down into the pit of her subconscious. And the cold, the bitter, dry, desert cold, seemed then to seal her nerve tips, coagulate deep within her that serpentine blood-life which never melted until the coming of the sun. A strange mindlessness, a black negation, held her in a spell nothing could loosen. It was not a period of gestation, but of stagnation.

"Why don't it come—my letter from Trinidad?" she would ask Sal each morning. "He promise sure that I dance again. They love me, Sal!"

"And gave you a rose. A purty rose!"

"Yes! Una rosa—la flor . . ."

"Hell! Go down the hall there and do your dancin' by yourself. It'll do you as much good as dancin' for Mr. Five-Cents'-Worth-of-Sugar. That cripple and his wife ain't worth worryin' about. Even if they did show you the sights of Rome."

The girl flung herself on her knees beside the bed. "They will write, Sal. It won't be long!" Only an entrancing vision of light and sound, colors and people, seemed to keep her alive. Like the summer sun, it too must come again.

"No, it won't be long," the woman's voice came more quietly. "He'll get you another swell place to dance. And then, God Almighty! With that baby face and figure you sure got all the luck. A finger in every pie, and you stewin' because the plums ain't jumpin' out at yeh!" She flopped over in bed; an empty bottle dropped on the floor. "What you raisin' a rumpus for? Look at me!" her voice broke out suddenly. "They wasn't ten people come in The Fifteen Letters all yesterday afternoon. And me with no pay tryin' to eat on four checks a day. And that damned bouncer—after me all the time. Jesus God! What have I got to last through the winter for? There's always another comin' ten times worse."

"Don' you get a dollar from Cheon every night? Don' I

give you money from Barby and Tai Ling? But Sal. You only buy whiskey and beer, beer, all the time."

"Hell! Ain't it bad enough to lie around with cold feet without havin' a dry mouth? Wouldn't hurt you none if you took a swiggle. Might take that letter off your mind. Or a good cry would do you a heap of good, honey. But Lord God! How long it's been since I forgot how!" She stared dully across the room.

Still every night Guadalupe returned to the upstairs room of The Lamp Awake. Barby was waiting. The girl unwound her rebozo like a nun discarding her somber wrapping. She stood forth more slender, more beautiful to him than ever. He got up, put his arms around her with an intimacy that to him never grew casual. He loved her so!

The girl stood still and unresponsive. Her passive acquiescence repulsed him quicker than any word. He dropped his arms and turned away. She gave him a quick look from a face which for all its blankness did not hide a peculiarly female contempt because he gave up so easily, and switched on the phonograph.

Barby had learned not to demur. He lay belly downward on the bed, smoking, propped up by his arms so that he might stare his full at the girl. Half undressed she sat on a chair between a rusty kerosene stove and the phonograph. Her stockings were rolled down to her ankles; she kept stroking her slim, bare, brown legs. Occasionally, to change records, she turned about. Then the light from the lamp on the cómoda lit up her dark oval face. A face that in all the boy's life would never lose its first promise, its enduring mystery, its ineffable charm.

And yet to him it had become a face like granite. To the day and its casual strangers it flickered alive, showed its changing moods, reflected a Guadalupe he himself had known once.

But to him and to the night it closed up like a book. He owned her; she had returned to be his again. And his eyes, his will, his hands closed only upon a silence that gave him nothing.

He knew that Trinidad and his small troupe had gone on to Juarez, and that Guadalupe was expecting him to find her another fine place to dance. For hours, for days, he had heard her prattle. Of course she wanted to go away again! To the bright lights, to the rich gringo pigs! Cristo Rey, wasn't she a woman?

Yet the letter had never come, and the imminent danger of losing her again had worn away. Once more he felt secure in her possession. If only she would forget that tantalizing vision of beauty, of wealth and splendor, which seemed to hang before her. Or was it entirely that? He had begun to wonder if there weren't something else still hidden behind this.

"Mother of God!" he wanted to cry aloud, "what is there in her that seems so strange? Why now is she so different? Why she come back to me?"

And now again, in winter cold as in summer heat, he took up his merciless, casual and persistent questioning. It was a game they both played warily. In his casual questions, her casual answers, they both now showed an intense awareness of the gulf between them.

What struck him, as once again he went over her early life on the Reservation and at the Lascelles, was the appalling difference in her now. He had learned to piece the incidents together, to brood over their continuity. They formed for him a picture of a girl whose tragic freshness had arrested him that first evening on the floor of Las Quince Letras.

But now—he looked at her in the lamplight as if seeing someone completely different. The outline, the form, the little telltale marks and loved mannerisms were there as before. But the substance was changed. Something wrapped unseen within that freshness and astounding innocence of her girlhood had begun to eat its way outside. Something inherent in her very nature. He swore it was so! Hadn't he known her every moment, spied on her, watched her even as she slept?

He went back over her life with a mind that had learned to retain and piece together every little scrap of information she gave him. One night he asked her casually, "You ever hear about Lascelles hunting for you?"

"No," she answered dully. "I run away and never go back even for my clothes. They never know where I go. Never!"

"I guess running away on the cold desert you were very afraid. You had no place to go." When she nodded, he added simply, "Was it so very cold that night?"

"Frio. Frio. At night it was very cold. My feet almost freeze when I take my shoes off to rest."

The boy's face set in a scowl. "The fight that night when I saw you was for the Cinco de Mayo fiesta. You were here only a week before. That is early summer—very hot. What you mean telling me about coming here with Sal right away?"

Guadalupe sat without blinking an eye, waiting for a string of freight cars to rumble by outside. "Maybe it was hot; maybe it was cold. What is the difference? I tell you I run away from Lascelles and I never go back. Never!"

"That ain't what I asked!" he shouted. "You said Sal took you away from the old woman and you came here. It was cold when you left and hot when you got here. Not two days the stage takes. Two days! Hell! It was close to a month. Where were you? What were you doing?"

The girl jumped to her feet. It was the first time in weeks she had shown a spark of life. "Questions, questions! All the time silly questions till my head ache. I tell you to shut up.

What business is it of yours what I do, where I go? Now I am here. And when Trinidad send me a letter I go!"

She slammed open the lid of the phonograph, jerked the switch. With the raucous blast and her own sudden outburst, Barby was stilled. She blew out the lamp and went to bed. The record ran down; he turned off the stove also and crawled in beside her. Feigning sleep, the girl lay watching him smoke a cigarette. Long after he had crushed it out on the iron railing of the bed, cursing the sparks that dropped on his bare shoulder, and had gone to sleep, Guadalupe did not move.

Mi Madre! Had he found out too?

The boy rolled over in sleep, his hand falling limply on her thigh. Guadalupe did not dare to shake it off. Like the old woman, he too had the power to hold her transfixed. She was frightened and repulsed by them both, yet this very fear and repulsion contained the germ of attraction which held her prisoner. Only Peña—Guadalupe bit her lip as if to stifle the thought as surely as she stifled the merest mention of the woman's name. If darkness and winter would only end! If only a letter would come to take her far away!

5

Even the most casual thoughts carry fertile seeds. They take root; in the most barren soil they grow; and suddenly, as if from nothing at all, there appears the strange progeny of a vagrant notion, hardy, full-formed, too tenacious to be uprooted.

So it was with Barby's tantalizing suspicion of Guadalupe. All her past life he had made his. Only an enigmatic month— a single month of all her life!—remained wholly hers; a priceless and secret possession which she kept inviolate. With his most adroit questioning he could not approach it without arousing in her an antagonistic repudiation of everything else she had told him.

Yet in the fearful and doubting soil of his mind a tiny seed was implanted; an obscure grain of suspicion which suddenly grew into an overwhelming conviction of reality.

It was an early winter dusk not quite five o'clock when slouching homeward from El Sol de Mayo Barby noticed Sal across the road. Something furtive in her manner held his gaze. All the percentage girls were due at Las Quince Letras, he knew, yet Sal seemed strangely hesitant, peering forward and dodging back to light a cigarette before lounging on. Barby slowed up to watch her.

The passage into which they turned, both walking slowly as if on a casual paseo, was a narrow hard-beaten alley running tangent from the Callejon de los Chinos to the cribs and patios of Cockroach Court. Abreast of old Chan Foo's cellar cafe, Barby caught up opposite Sal. Lazily he slumped down on a lower step and peered out at the woman.

Sal stood across from him, bending forward to discern in the crepuscular light whomever she was evidently following. She was too engrossed to look around, and with an impatient fling of her arm tossed away her cigarette.

Barby turned his head. He was at first not sure of what he saw. Then the quick step, the nervous left hand which fluttered up to draw the rebozo closer about her face, verified the sudden jump of his heart. Guadalupe paused, standing at the edge of the gutter. Both her hands drew up to her chin, gripping the edges of her rebozo as if its dark blue cotton folds might enshroud her completely. Barby could almost see her tremble. He flashed a quick look back at Sal. The woman had stepped inside a doorway where she stood almost invisible in the thickening dusk.

Suddenly he heard a chuckle, saw Guadalupe flinch and

then step out into the street slowly, reluctantly, as if drawn by a rope.

There was another chuckle; Barby turned around in time to see old Oakie step out from an adobe two doors to his left. One skinny finger was still beckoning to Guadalupe. The girl approached her, stopped at the gutter. For a moment neither moved. Then Oakie reached out and drew the girl up beside her. Guadalupe did not resist. Shrunken in her loose cotton shawl she seemed powerless to flee the old woman's low-voiced entreaty.

Before Guadalupe could answer, a whistle sounded across the street. The girl spun about. Sal, still whistling, had stepped out from the opposite doorway and was strolling down the alley. Casually she seemed to glance around.

"Jesus Christ!" her deep voice boomed out in the deep dusk. "What a hell of a place to run across you in! The Big Fella will be comin' after you as well as me—unless you're comin' my way."

The girl ran out into the road, grasped Sal's arm. The old woman stood cursing them in a low mumble. It wasn't the first time that that pasty-face Sal had interfered, or that the brat . . . Her loose body shook with rage as she watched them walk swiftly up the alley. Then suddenly, even as Barby watched, she dissolved, rusty coat and all, into the thick dusk.

Somebody came up the cafe steps, nudged him in the ribs with a boot tip, and walked on. Still Barby did not stir. He sat asprawl on the steps, gazing up the dark alley. He had it now; the single secret month the girl had thought to keep from him!

He lunged downstairs and sprawled out at a dark corner table. Enlivened by a bottle of rice brandy, his mind became excited as a dog which has treed its quarry. It raced back along the trail of the girl's life; filled in the missing gap; retraced it to the night he had met her—here down the hall, in this very place! Her awkwardness then, her strangely compliant frigidity ever since, and her flinching repugnance of late: it all focused perfectly in the confirming incident he had just seen.

He rose and lurched upstairs. There was nothing he could do; Guadalupe would be at the cabaret till nine-thirty. Roaming up and down the cobbled alley, the dark runways of beaten earth, he fought for the time when she would be through.

It came; he saw the lamp awake in the upstairs window of Tai Ling's shop. Slowly he walked inside and climbed the stairs. The door was ajar. Through the crack came the raucous blast of the phonograph:

"I'se broke foolin' with you—and lost a good man too!
You ain't goin' to get away, makin' a fool outa me;
I ain't through with you—till the Doctah say you has passed
   away . . ."

Guadalupe looked up and down again without a word. Even in the quick and casual glance he noticed that her eyes were clear and untroubled, her face innocent of expression. As if he did not know! Barby pushed back his hat and walked across the room to stand looking down at her.

She was sitting on the floor between the bed and the window, her slim bare legs outstretched to the stove. On the chair beside her, where she could reach it without rising, the phonograph came to the end of its tune. Guadalupe switched off the key and turned over the record. In the momentary silence the water in a rusty pan on the stove simmered faintly. Then the phonograph began, and Guadalupe bent down again to the floor.

She was playing like a child with a dozen small clay

mice. Barby remembered with what foolish delight she had bought the first one from the old blind beggar. With a lump of clay and a tin can of water balanced on a piece of board across his knees, he had molded it before her eyes. So tiny, hardly bigger than her thumb, and so real it almost squeaked between his fingers! The girl could hardly wait for him to give the last turn to its tail before carrying it off, still wet, to set on the cómoda. For days thereafter she sought him out in sunny corners, followed him down into the arroyo where he slept in a half-fallen, deserted adobe hut. Each time she brought home another clay mouse. They were all small, some no larger than her finger tip and never more than life-size; in all postures; turning greyish as the clay hardened. They were the only things he made; as though during the perpetual darkness of his days he recreated his only companions of the night, the only things he really knew and felt. And they gave back with every touch of the fingers an extraordinary sense of aliveness that aroused in Guadalupe a mingled feeling of repugnance and admiration. She often played with them for hours.

They were all spread out before her on the carpet: little grey creatures sitting upright with their tiny ears open for every sound; leaning forward, noses out, tails curving over their backs; or on all four feet, muscles bunched for instant flight should a miracle greater than the blind man's fancy give them life. Guadalupe bent over them, completely absorbed like a child with its toys.

This childish posture inflamed the boy still more. Her dress, drawn up above her bare knees, revealed the riper curves of her upper legs; whenever she leaned forward arm outstretched, he could see the outline of her small firm breast. But her face, half hidden from the lamplight, suggested a woman playing at being a child. She did not look up all the time he stood there.

Deliberately Barby stepped forward into the cluster of little clay mice and ground them into the floor. Guadalupe slid half around on her haunches, her back against the bed, to look up at him. She did not speak. In the lamplight shining full upon her face he did not detect a single change of expression. Only the bottoms of her black eyes seemed to open, revealing a fathomless pit of unutterable contempt. The phonograph record, played out, ran round and round with a noisy scratching. Barby flung back his hand and knocked the needle out of its circuit.

"Why didn't you go with the old woman?" he demanded abruptly.

The girl's body stiffened perceptibly.

"Yeah, old Oakie. This afternoon. I saw you."

He had caught her unaware; watched her squirm about, hunting up another lie to tell him. "Afraid you be caught by Sal, hey? Think she don't know, too?"

Guadalupe opened her mouth, tried to get up. He thrust her down again and stood back a step to taunt her further, brushing the hair back from his eyes. They were wild and just a little bloodshot, for the first time revealing to her that he had been drinking. He ran his hand across his dry lips. "If Sal hadn't been there! Yeah, if she hadn't! You'd of gone like you did before—like all the other times!"

"It is a lie!" she screamed. "It is not true! Only once I see her, many days ago. She tell me if I do not come to hear what she tell me something bad will happen. Then today when she pass me and touch me on the arm to come after her, I cannot but go. By Our Guadalupana I swear it is so!"

Barby paused, well pleased he had got this much out of

her already. "Like all the other times," he repeated. "Like you been sneakin' to her right along."

The girl struggled up, crawled upon the bed where she crouched before him.

"I know," he went on in his thick voice. "God damn yeh, I know. Running to that old bitch all the time." The thought, now that he had finally expressed it, almost drove him mad. All this time that he had thought her only his! "Why not? Because you were with her a whole month. Tellin' me you come here right away with Sal! Cristo!"

Her eyes came alive with an intense awareness of a terrible fear. Then slowly she slumped down on the bed under his condemnation.

"Barby, I swear! It was not a month. Only two weeks! No more. . . . What was I to do? She take my money—me. I know nobody. I could not run away. Then one day Sal come like I tell you and take me away. Here. And never have I been with the old woman since. Verdad! I swear!"

Her voice rang out with a courageous sincerity that almost swerved him from his conviction; a childish voice he hated because it always had the power to move him. But still a lie. The unalterable memory of her going to Oakie convinced him it was so. He stood before her, his face covered with a thin veneer of sweat that began to glisten faintly in the lamplight. He had her now. Nothing in her words or voice could alleviate his mounting passion.

Then suddenly she raised her face. It was tense but curiously calm; her eyes had lost their frantic fear and regained their steady black glitter. It reflected the transformation which had taken place within her; like a child who at last had stepped across the threshold of her youth with a mature courage to dismiss all the specters of her past. She opened her mouth to reveal, in Peña's words, the conviction of her new creed—"I am what I am!" The words would not come; and her jaw, unhung, revealed only her thin white row of teeth.

Still he stood there, the muscles in his face twitching, the rank smell of mezcal on his heavy breathing. Suddenly he spewed out a vile epithet in the idioma. Guadalupe jumped to her feet. Her face froze solid; she closed to him forever.

Barby saw it. If he had been wholly white or Indian he would have killed her coldly and forgotten her. Or being Spanish, done the thing in heat and turning sentimental carried roses to her grave. But being what he was, a half-breed, he merely did the brutal thing. He struck her viciously with his fist. The blow caught her on the head and knocked her to the floor. As she struggled up he kicked her in the side and tore off his rawhide belt. A dozen lashes he gave her before she sank down before him, her arms weakly entwined about his leg. He kicked them off and for a minute gazed down on her. The sight of her passive, prostrate body was too much for him. He took advantage of a noisy switch engine passing outside to vent upon her the full force of his long pent up anger. Then panting hoarsely, he grabbed up his hat and clumped downstairs.

6

Guadalupe dragged herself up on the bed. An hour or two later she rose and blew out the light shining in her glazed open eyes. Still later she undressed in bed, pushing her clothes outside the covers to drop on the floor. Gradually she became herself. The tenseness went out of her bruised body. Her thoughts began to untangle.

Like Barby she went back in her earliest memory, retracing the events which slowly and inexorably had built up into their climax of self-realization. Sister Teresa, Lascelles, old

Oakie, Barby—what had they wanted, what had she wanted of them, that she had succumbed so helplessly to a nameless ache and longing rooted in fear and revulsion? She had not known, had never guessed. Never! until that night with Peña.

Not even during those first days they all had spent together at the big casino had she been aware of Peña other than as a loyal friend who comforted her after Trinidad's sarcastic lectures. Then the night had come when Trinidad went away to town.

"I'm going to be lonesome. Come in before you go to bed," Peña said casually. "We're always doubling up on these tours. You'll have to get used to it."

Guadalupe should have known then by the look in Peña's eyes, the sudden flutter of her own heart. Nervously she kept delaying, then finally, timidly, opened the door. Peña was waiting, dressed in an old pair of red slippers and a faded blue robe. Without a word she stood up, put her arms around the girl, and kissed her slowly, fully, on the mouth.

Only then did she speak. "Why, child, you're trembling!" Smiling gently she held Guadalupe away from her. "You are what you are. Don't you know that yet?"

Her hand reached out and switched off the light; the girl heard her drop her robe and sink down on the bed. With frantic slowness and trembling hands Guadalupe undressed and lay down beside her. The woman did not move. At first it was dark. Then a thread of light from a crack in the door fell across the bed. Minutes passed before Guadalupe turned her head. Peña's body was so startlingly white and voluptuous she caught her breath.

The woman reached out and placed the girl's hand on her body. A sudden ripple of excitement passed through Guadalupe. She turned over, arm around Peña, and sank her head in the woman's arm.

Gently Peña kissed her, the fullness of her lips lingering, tantalizing, with a heavy sweetness. More firmly she began to caress her. Guadalupe could feel the fingers on her breast, running down her thighs; they were like tiny flames, like trickles of warm water. There was a catch in her throat, a pounding in her ears.

Suddenly an overpowering tide of passion caught her. She flung over on Peña, threw both arms about her, gripped her closer and ever closer, wanting her but not knowing how. She had never known such a longing, such pain.

Abruptly the woman touched her; a terrible, exquisite and convulsing pleasure possessed her. There was no darkness, no thought, nothing but this mounting wave of ecstatic pleasure that bore her swiftly to a crest. She screamed out—a great sigh, fell back down into a trough of glorious lethargy, and closed her eyes.

When she awakened in the morning Peña was already up. "Come, child; time for your morning practice,". she said with a smile, brushing back the girl's hair. "How do you feel after such a long sleep?"

How does one feel when overnight the world has changed? And lying now in the dreary darkness of Tai Ling's upper room, Guadalupe could still evoke the feeling of that exquisite touch, of that glorious mouth.

In that mouth the cloying nullity of dark night had been vanished; it became instead a prolongation of her intense and living day. And with that touch she felt erased forever all the others upon her: the fearful cold white hands of Sister Teresa; the rough demanding hold of Lascelles; the slimy clawing of old Oakie; the passionate brutality of Barby. And at the same time Peña's companionship nullified the friendship of Sal; it was warmer, more intimate, closer. For the first time Guadalupe had known what she was without fear, shame or revulsion.

"You must take me with you!" she had begged Peña, alone, the night before she left.

"Of course. But we must have patience," replied Peña. "I will see that Trinidad makes a place for you first. Then we will be together again, no?"

So lying now, swathed in darkness and silence, Guadalupe felt creep over her the comforting assurance of that promise. All fear had gone. She was at last wholly herself.

7

Near three o'clock Barby found himself in front of The Lamp Awake. He spread his legs, threw back his head and shouted. No one answered. He sat down. The upstairs window was dark. But overhead was something bright, fixed and enduring—a single star. It reminded him vaguely of another light he had seen somewhere, sometime, in the depths of a woman's eyes.

Getting to his feet he wobbled across the road and crawled up the steps to his room. He opened the door and stepped inside.

The room was dark. A faint stir on the bed broke the silence. It seemed to recall something to his mind. For a minute he stood wrestling with its meaning which just wriggled from his grasp. Then he dropped to his knees, stared at the bed's uneven horizon outlined against the window. Gradually his eyes began to distinguish the girl's sleeping form smothered in blankets. It seemed important; why, he could not think. He began to crawl toward her. A movement at a time, and very warily lest both she and the bed take instant flight. In a quarter of an hour he had reached the edge of the bed. Quietly he slumped down on the floor, turned around, and leaned back his head.

At daybreak when the girl awoke he had not moved. He was still sitting on the floor, legs outspread, his head thrown back against the bed. His hat had fallen over his face. Beneath its wide brim he was puffing stertorously in a heavy drunken stupor.

CHAPTER NINE

TAI LING for the tenth successive evening was meditating upon "The Ten Best Things" when he was suddenly interrupted.

Curses, a scream, another rumpus upstairs. The boy was giving his girl a beating. Tai Ling restrained a sigh. It did not concern him; and just or unjust, a beating was sure to clear the air. For involved were not personalities, but principles of nature. The male principle must assert its dominance over the female or, thwarted, run rampant in the bitterness of its inadequacy. The female principle must accept final subjugation without rancor, or else, victorious, find itself perversely distorted. There was no escape. Denying the existence of a greater reality beyond their common humanness they were forced to obey the laws of their lower nature.

The rumpus upstairs illustrated the need for the first of his ten precepts: "For one of little intellect, the best thing is to live in strict conformity with the law of cause and effect."

Barby refused to understand. Weeks ago after he had

given the girl her first beating, he had ambled downstairs to shamefacedly confront Tai Ling with his dilemma.

"That girl!" he muttered, thumbing overhead. "I suppose you heard me last night. I had to give her a few licks. . . . What the hell's wrong with her anyway?"

The yogi stared at him calmly. "Is it she or you who is now complaining to me?"

"I am! I don't like to beat her. But—"

"Then let us talk about you, not her."

"There's nothing to say about me. I want—"

The yogi stopped him with an upraised forefinger. "That is the whole trouble as usual. We have discussed it many times. You want."

"Cut out the preachin'! It's always the same!"

"The falsity of desire. Yes, it is always the same," said the yogi gently. "You desire, and at the same time you desire to escape its consequences. Now you desire to inflict pain on another. Can you escape resentment? You desire to possess. Can you escape the responsibility of your possession?"

"Yes, but she wants—"

"Yes, you desire. Do you not expect her to have desires also? No, I cannot judge between your desires. They are both illusionary, being temporary. I would only say to you as I have said before, banish your own desires if you would be a master. Then you would be impervious to its consequences."

Barby stormed out in a rage of indignation. Thereafter he stalked by Tai Ling without further words on the subject of his noisy quarrels.

Guadalupe also crept past next morning, sleepless, her bare legs covered with welts, as if ashamed to face the old man behind his counter. Tai Ling did not embarrass her, and watched her return again without comment that night.

One evening she stopped before him and demanded trucu-

lently, "What do I come here for anyway? You hear him beating me, don't you?"

The yogi looked up from behind his lamp and smiled.
"Cease hating him and then you will be free."

The girl's expression of belligerent anxiety gave way to
a perplexed frown.

The yogi continued in his soft voice. "You come here to
be beaten, no? First you came here out of fleshly desire, love.
This fleshly desire expressed itself in the physical action of
love. Now there is no more love. . . . There is its opposite
pole, hate. So now hate expresses itself in the physical action
of crying, cursing, beating. What is the difference? The pendulum swings to both extremes. And both are illusionary. Has
not love vanished? Now you must banish hate. That is what
brings you here. Then you will be free to leave or stay."

"Never did I love him! I didn't know," protested Guadalupe. "I don't hate him either. He just—"

"He is not concerned," answered the yogi blandly. "You
come here of your own free will, do you not? Yet you cannot
stay away. Be truthful. Realize that you hate and then hate
will vanish. Then you will be free."

"I don't hate him, I don't love him, I tell you! You are
trying to mix me up. It's just—" She fled miserably out the
door and thereafter excluded him from her confidences.

Tai Ling sighed with regret. Yes, the second precept justi-
fied his own objective view of the quarreling participants:
"For one of ordinary intellect, the best thing is to recognize,
both within and without oneself, the workings of the law of
opposites."

But Tai Ling still aspired to the third: "For one of superior intellect, the best meditation is to remain in mental quiescence, the mind devoid of all thought processes, knowing

that the meditator, the object of meditation, and the act of meditating constitute an inseparable unity."

Lately it had seemed to him that he was making better progress along his chosen noble path. It had been difficult, surrounded as he was by the most adverse influences. But he had arranged his worldly life, and persevered. His shop was now almost perpetually deserted. His frugal diet had shrunk to a meager subsistence. His power of concentration had increased.

And all this had borne fruit. He had transcended his environment; Cockroach Court no longer existed; even Barby and Guadalupe he saw as images of worldly illusion. He had escaped the desires of his body. With unbroken concentration of his mind he had been able to obtain momentary freedom from the tyranny of his thoughts. They were all steps which he had won in this lifetime over the pitfalls of self-hypnotism and the barriers of false pride.

It was not enough! He could analyze his thoughts, and reflect upon the deductions derived from the analysis. But the last stage of profound meditation he could never achieve. He was but able to reach the boundary of that state of non-thought which was the other extreme of the state of thought. But only when with perfected tranquillity could he realize both extremes of this duality as inseparably one, would his mundane consciousness recognize its oneness with the supramundane consciousness and the goal be attained.

Yes, thought the yogi, everything outside had stood in his way. Now he was his own barrier. It was one thing to recognize Barby and Guadalupe upstairs as merely quarreling principles. But it was another thing to realize that he himself was just as nonexistent. How could he impute ignorance to them without indicting himself? How could he know anyone, anything, unless he knew himself? And what was he—this consciousness partially self-conscious of its own questioning nature? He had reached as always the limit of rational thought.

All noise upstairs had ceased. Cockroach Court outside was dark and still. Alone again in silence, he prepared to enter that state of mental quiescence wherein he might sometime achieve this transcendental realization in meditative abstraction by the unmodified primordial mind.

2

To each of them the other's presence had now grown almost unbearable. And still he loved her. He loved her so! The very sight of her filled him with an intolerable anguish nothing could dispel. And still she kept returning to him: an everlasting and reoccurring mystery that was his final despair.

"God damn it!" He jumped up from the bed on which he had been sprawled and stood above her. "What you hanging around here for?"

Barby could taunt her thus because he had no fear of losing her now. He had beaten her, seen with triumph how the woman in her cowered before his mere physical strength. Then he had become weak and abjectly contrite, humbled himself again. And this, not the beatings, had marked the end. The unutterable contempt in her eyes had removed her forever beyond his further violence. He could have beaten her unconscious before she moved an inch away.

He prodded her with his foot. Guadalupe did not answer. She merely reached up to the phonograph and watched him grab up his hat and flee.

No! Not a moment of her life was free from the stupefying sense of imprisonment that bound her within herself, followed her every step. Each morning she still went to Sal's hotel to look for a letter. Invariably the woman refused to leave her bed till noon. Worn out from sitting and talking to a mummy swathed in blankets, the girl was glad to leave her. She had given up dancing, practicing new steps or keeping her wrists and fingers limber with the castanets. She seemed cut off, stagnated, abandoned to decay. Only during the short evening hours at Las Quince Letras was there any life at all. And it was dreary too. A few stragglers from across the Line and a handful of laborers in for an hour's warmth at the price of a drink were her only audience. Halfheartedly she sang a song or two and did a turn with the few percentage girls sticking out the winter. It was even more dull at El Sol de Mayo. She returned to The Lamp Awake.

Late one afternoon on the tail of winter the spell seemed broken. The very air had changed. Guadalupe got up from the floor, stretching like a cat, and peered out the window. The sky overhead was thick and grey as wool with still more clouds unraveling from the horizon.

The blessed rain! It would soften the cold, temper the surly days and bring out the sun again. Then spring would rush in behind it, touching its torch to the yucca, the Candles of Our Lord, to the ocotillo, the desert primrose and the verbena.

It was midnight before it came. At the first splatter on the pane, Guadalupe jumped out of bed and ran downstairs. Bareheaded, without her shawl, she stood in the street on naked feet, with face and breast lifted to the sky.

The storm was but a short squall blown up from the gulf. A quick lash of cold rain that drenched the town in sudden fury and whirled away before an hour. Drenched and shivering, Guadalupe crawled back upstairs.

In the morning things were ten times worse. The streets

were soggy, the wooden walks covered with slimy glue which
was tracked into every cantina until dancing was impossible.
The sullen cold held on. For days the thick adobe mud made
the roads and alleys so impassable she had to forego even her
shortest walks. Everything conspired to increase the girl's
misery and to drive her back within the shop to listen to
Barby's taunts.

"How was the old woman, eh?"—she had been gone fifteen minutes; or "You come back to me so soon?" after she
had spent the morning with Sal.

Guadalupe did not answer. Unwinding her rebozo she
slumped down on the floor in front of the stove and took off
her shoes and stockings.

Barby, swinging his leg back and forth along the side
of the bed, nudged her with his foot. "You get the letter from
the cripple today, eh?" he inquired maliciously. "And tomorrow you go to the big hotel to dance in fine clothes before all
the rich Americans? Guadalupe, la artista! 'La Alma de
Mexico!" He let out a laugh.

Guadalupe stared into the hole in the stove. "When the
letter come, I go," she said quietly. "I go and never come
back!"

It was their only conversation all day.

She wound up the phonograph, put on a fresh record.
Barby did not demur; he was willing to accept anything, however trivial, that broke the unbearable tension. He lit a cigarette. With it dangling from his lips, he lay watching her from
under the brim of his hat, pulled low to shield his eyes from
the lamplight. She sat on the floor, passive and inert, listening
to the music. His gaze moved from her around the room.

He had bought a carpet for her, red with blue roses; replaced the cracked windowpane; added a new chair and a
gaudy silk coverlet for the bed. Yet everywhere, under the

cómoda, on all the bric-a-brac with which he once had pleased her, the dust lay thick or stirred gently in coagulated wisps. The new window curtains were getting grimy and needed shaking free of cinders. The bed was never made. Guadalupe did not even hang up her clothes. Everywhere they littered the place. And the stockings, the worn-out stockings she let fall on the floor whenever the heels broke out! He was always throwing them angrily out the back door. She cared now for nothing but shoes; and these, a long row of colored slippers, stood neatly lined up against the far wall where she could step into any green, pink or yellow pair that happened to strike her fancy.

Outside a freight went by, rumbling and shaking the room. The vibration jarred off the washstand a small bottle of hand lotion. In the passing clank and the hiss of steam the bottle tinkled into pieces on the floor. Guadalupe looked around vacant-eyed. With a stray stocking she sopped up the mess in one sweep and threw the silk into a far corner, then bent back to her usual posture.

What good could a beating do with such a woman? And yet to this disarray, this room in which she always seemed to encamp just for the night, she returned again and again. A la casa! Home! She had no home, would never have a home, save the inside of a phonograph. It still played on; and she was ready with another record before it ran down.

Roses from the South; Wine, Women and Song; Tales from the Vienna Woods; The Beautiful Blue Danube—how she loved those waltzes which over and over again broke the deep stillness of the upstairs room of an old Chinaman's shop and sounded a faint and incomprehensible music to a belated passer-by shuffling warily down the alley. Always they reiterated a melodic freshness, a limpid cheerfulness which nothing could gainsay. A Strauss waltz! It had become to her the only expression of that world deep inside her and its reflection outside and faraway—their only connecting link. Immersed in its spell, she could always forget the cruder world about her. It was her only escape. Sister Teresa's beads she wore around her throat. But those waltzes! They were entwined about her heart.

Over and over she turned the records, sat staring into the stove. Barby sleepily undressed without getting off the bed, hurling his clothes to a chair. Only his surprised curse aroused her when he lay down and discovered he still had on his hat. Wearily, a half-hour later, she too got in beside him.

They lay together in darkness. The stove grew cold. The chimney lamp crackled slightly, contracted, crackled again. And then the silence—dead, oppressive, unendurable even in sleep.

Barby turned suddenly on his side, flung his arms about her. Always her presence intimate and close beside him at night refuted the day's suspicions and hates, obliterated his thoughts and freed his senses. Only the dark silence, the peculiar dull deadness of it, remained between them, restraining the words that he could never speak. He loved her so!

Guadalupe did not respond, nor did she shrink from him. She simply did not move. Not a finger, not an eyelash. She lay on her back, arms down along her sides, inert, unresisting, almost lifeless. Barby raised up on his elbows, looked down at her smooth oval face palely illumined by moonlight. She was staring straight before her, and did not raise her eyes. For a long time the boy sought in them what he had always sought—a light shining like a star to guide his faltering way— the first thing in her he had ever seen. It must be there for him to find again. But it was not. He flopped down wearily beside her, lay also staring before him.

Both children of darkness and of silence.

3

The long monochromatic winter did end. Each day the sun washed earlier over the sand dunes upon the town, and ebbed later on the chaparral slopes of the sierras. The air seemed lighter, warmer, drier. Life quickened about her. Yet Guadalupe was still stagnant.

It was an hour before she was due at the cabaret for the first floor show, and wearily she plodded through the harmonic half-tones of evening to Sal's hotel. The place was empty. All the girls, dealers and bartenders already had left for work. Guadalupe dropped into a chair in the dusky lobby, staring out the door at the brilliant cantina signs which no longer had the power to arouse her.

For minutes she ignored the Chinese proprietor who had emerged from his cubbyhole underneath the stairs and stood beckoning to her. Even when he nodded toward the rack overhead the thing seemed unbelievable: a grimy envelope impaled on a nail.

The girl drew it off carefully, stood for a moment with it upheld to the light, then carried it back to her chair. It was the first letter she had ever received.

Over and over she turned it in her lap. Every crease and thumbprint, her penciled name, the postmark, its smudges and the nail hole through its center were impressed upon her memory with an indelibleness that would never fade.

A clock struck seven. Guadalupe stuck the letter down her stocking and went out. At first she walked as if stunned. Then gradually she began to awake. The letter had come! After all these months of waiting Peña had sent her letter! She could feel its caress just above the knee, on the inside, creating an ecstatic tingle like her lover's hand. Her heels began a quick tattoo upon the walk.

All at once the hard knot melted inside her. All her fear and misery, the clotted hopes and foolish fancies frozen within her became fluid. The sluggish serpent-blood warmed and raced through her veins, seemed to melt the film across her eyes. The gaudy cantina signs, the big mug of beer raised up into the night, the great green owl with its blinking eyes leaped forth with a meaning almost forgotten. She could smell the deep dusk with its faint and peculiar odor of dust and urine; could hear the clatter of a piano, the whine of a guitar—she, who had been so deaf and blind, so insulated by loneliness.

She kept it down her stocking even as she danced, the manifestation of a mighty miracle that had brought her back to life at last. Even Gonzales, so long disappointed, sat up on the mezzanine rubbing his hands together with renewed delight. The little morena had come alive again!

Leaving him after the last revue, and bidding Sal to wait for her in the hotel, Guadalupe went swiftly to The Lamp Awake. Barby was already there, as usual, sprawled upon the bed. He was lying profile toward her, the lamp shining upon his broad brutal face with its crescent shadows and high cheekbones. His mouth was slightly open, accentuating his full lips, powerful jaws and flat chin. He lighted a cigarette. The movement of his arm opened his unbuttoned shirt, revealed his strong corded throat and the swell of his chest. So strong and brutal and yet so inutile! Like a powerful frame eaten within by an insidious weakness; a man rendered forever harmless by a woman's eyes. He lay smoking, oblivious of her steady stare. Still she looked at him as if seeing him clearly for the first time. His fancy pleated trousers with their three-inch rawhide belt, the pointed patent leather shoes restlessly chipping the last vestige of paint from the iron bedstead, his soiled silk shirt and imitation ruby ring. They all brought out, with their proud vulgarity and unkempt indifference, the inmost texture of his mind.

A gesture, a look from him, and she would have told him freely. Instead, staring at his boots, he asked derisively, "Pues, the letter come from the cripple today, eh? To the great artista to come and dance again! For the rich American pigs who love her!" It was his favorite taunt; a private and perpetual joke never worn out with the months.

It was the tone of his voice more than the words that brought the girl to herself. She could feel herself close up like a turtle, knew a moment of deathly coldness that cleared her mind and stopped instantly the tremble of her knees. She stooped and pulled up her stocking; the letter was there to fortify her still further. Raising her head she said calmly, "Verdad. The letter come. Now I go away."

Her astounding impudence struck him queerly. He reared up on one elbow and twisted his head around to stare at her steady black eyes and resolute face. So she had learned to mock him, eh? Bah! He slumped down again and lit another cigarette.

He was aroused a moment later by a clatter on the top of the cómoda and flung over on his belly to watch her. Guadalupe had taken off her rebozo and spread it across the dresser. Upon it she was heaping her comb and brush, a couple of unbroken clay mice, a pair of fancy lace garters, a half-empty bottle of hand lotion, and a heap of stockings and colored handkerchiefs. Still fogged with unbelief he watched her gather from the floor her painted slippers. Deliberately and carefully she piled them one upon the other, toe to heel. The boy lay quietly watching her without a word.

Guadalupe moved more swiftly. She gathered up the ends of the long scarf, knotted the corners, tucked in the sides, and slung the bundle under one arm. For a minute she looked around the room. Her clothes lay strewn everywhere. One at a time she lifted up the worn soiled gowns, threw them into the far corner. Only a dress or two and an old coat hanging from a row of nails along the wall she took down, with a small packet of folded underclothes lying on the shelf above. This done, she turned around to face him.

For a long moment she stood holding his glance with an inexpressive calm that never wavered in the full glare of the lamp. Abruptly she spun about, flung open the door, and ran quickly down the steps.

Barby jumped off the bed and ran to the head of the steps. "God damn yeh!—where you goin'?" he shouted. There was no answer. "Sorda hija de tal!" he muttered to himself, backing into the room and standing with a perplexed frown on his face. Going to move in with Sal for a change, eh? Well, she'd be moving back soon enough; she always did. He kicked the door shut with a slam that shook the walls. Then swiftly he crossed the room to the window, got down on his knees, and stared across the tracks. The girl's laden figure, just discernible under an arc light, passed from him into darkness without a backward glance.

4

Quickly she fled across the tracks from that face whose sullen uncomprehending stare was more terrifying than any impassioned pleading. Reaching the hotel, she ran up the steps and breathlessly flung open Sal's door.

The woman was sitting cross-legged on the bed in her stockings and a soiled lavender slip. An old purse lay open at her side; she was laying out rows of coins on the wrinkled sheet. As the girl dropped bundle and clothes into a chair, Sal gathered up her silver and moved over so Guadalupe could sit down. "So you got your letter, huh? Is that it? And now you're going? You wouldn't be here with your duds for nuthin'. So spill the beans."

Guadalupe raised a tense face. "I tell Gonzales. Then Barby. And he"—she sat upright, looking back at the door— "perhaps he does not believe me, and when he find out . . ."

Sal rose from the bed and locked the door. At the dresser she lit a cigarette, and stood looking down at Guadalupe. "Yep. I seen the letter when it came yesterday morning. Right then I made up my mind it'd stay there till you come after it. And if you was too afraid to leave that damned half-breed you could stay till hell froze over without any sympathy from me. But now you've made up your mind, fer Christ's sake quit starin' at that door. What's the cripple say he's goin' to do for you? And what strings is tied on it?"

The girl rolled down her stocking, took out the letter.

"God Almighty!" Sal roared. "You ain't opened it yet!" A look of unutterable amazement spread over her face. She grabbed the letter, slit it open with her thumb, and read through the single page. The amazement on her face changed to incredulous astonishment touched by an unholy awe. The implicit trust of the little fool! She could only stare at the girl's upraised, expectant face. Then she tossed the page to Guadalupe and sat down beside her. "Well by God!" she kept muttering to herself.

Guadalupe crouched over the letter held in both hands, spelled through the words. Then suddenly she jumped to her feet. "Sal! She say for me to come. Trinidad, he want me to come right away! I knew! I knew!"

"Yeah. Reckon you did," drawled Sal. "God Almighty! You sure must have!"

They stared at each other without speaking. The woman

sitting limp and amazed on the bed; the girl standing before
her tense and wide-eyed. She had waited so vainly, had en-
dured disappointment so long that the commonplace words
of Peña's letter seemed yet too miraculous to be true. Even
their brevity stunned her. Warm and irrevocable, they were an
epitaph which spelled the end of a misery she had thought
endless.

Sal took her hand, drew the girl down on the bed beside
her. "Jesus, girl! Cry or swear or somethin'! Ain't you been
bellyachin' all winter for this chance to leave?"

"Sal! I can't do nothing. I can't think!"

"Rats! Let's have another look at that letter. Where'd he
say he was goin' to take you, across the Line?"

"No, not yet." The girl sat up without releasing the letter.
"See, I stay with Peña in Nogales and dance in the big new
casino, The Cave, for Trinidad. A big fiesta to celebrate the
new railroad to Mexico, that is why! Then maybe I go along
the Border with them. What you think now!"

Sal answered quietly. "The cripple's goin' to make money
out of you; you can bet your bottom dollar on that! If he has
to keep you in one-horse Border dumps till the last possible
minute. But the woman sounds friendly all right. Well, that's
good. No more old Oakies." She took the letter again. "He
didn't send no money. Christ! If you were so sure of goin'
why ain't you been savin' up a bit right along? Well, I got
the fare. And you better be gettin' off on the early mornin'
stage. Just in case."

"You are so good to me always, amiga mia! I will never
forget. If it is a big new cantina I shall tell Peña and Trinidad
about you. Maybe you get a job, too. Anyway we will all come
back soon like last year." Her voice dwindled away into its
anticlimax.

Sal shrugged. "You're not kiddin' me, honey!" she said

resolutely. "Just remember this. Everyone you stay with, me, the half-breed, the cripple and his woman, too, is all right for a time. But the time always comes when you're through. Cut it clean, kid. No excuses. Don't raise a howl when it's time for either one of you to move on."

She had known it was coming, certain as sin. And now, all doubts removed, she quieted with stolid resignation. It would never enter the girl's head to try and get her a job once she got there. The knowledge was without bitterness, born of her own irrevocable loneliness. She lit a cigarette, scratching the match on Guadalupe's shoe, and lay back on the bed. Hands under her head, she expelled the smoke in a long sigh and lay motionless, the cigarette drooping from her lips.

Guadalupe stared out the window. "What you do when I go?" she asked as if reading the woman's thoughts, but without any conviction of real concern.

"Me? Why I'm goin' to show the Big Fella a little flamin' purgatory and lead him by his lily-whites right through the fiery furnace if it comes to a showdown. Then I'm goin' to take care of myself like I always done." She put her arm for the moment across Guadalupe's shoulders and then slapped her on the back. "Guadalupe, you're still a kid. But you're goin' to get on; somehow I always could feel it. And if you don't get hung up again with somebody like that Barby— here, put up your arms and I'll yank this dress off you."

For a moment her eyes played over the small ripe figure of the girl: the laughing knees, the full thighs swelling the stocking rims, her slim supple waist and gentle curve of breast. Then she eased her own heavy body down upon the bed and lay quiet.

"Come on. Sleep it off." Again, hoarsely, she laughed down deep in her throat. "We both got some interestin' days

comin', and a full night's sleep that's paid for already ain't to
be missed from now on."

Turning down the lamp, she seemed almost instantly to
fall asleep.

Guadalupe did not stir for several minutes. Every tick of
the alarm clock on the dresser clanged out tinnishly in the
silence. She drew off her stockings, splashed at the washstand
across the room, rearranged her few belongings to stuff in a
suitcase upon arising. Then she blew out the light and lay
down beside Sal.

In the darkness the clock ticked on. But faster, as if time
were hurrying on again. Barby, Tai Ling, Gonzales, old Oakie,
even Sal—all these already had loosed their hold upon her.
Soon they would be as remote as Sister Teresa and Ma Lascelles. It made her feel a little sad and a little superior too.
The power we have over our friends by being able to leave
them! The illusion that they will always be waiting, unchanged, for us to pick up again!

Sal began to snore. Guadalupe lay alone at last, hugging
the thought of Peña. Never had Barby known. Not once had
Sal guessed. This was the final victory of that quick touch
which in an instant had fused her whole life and set the course
of her future—that secret light of longing which had banished
forever the cloying nullity of dark night. At peace, she let the
ticking clock sweep her off to sleep.

5

Turning from the window, Barby got up and flung himself across the bed. For an hour he lay there rolling brown
paper cigarettes, puffing at each a moment or two, then raising up to fling it into a tin pail. It gave him another opportunity to peep out the window at Sal's hotel across the tracks.

The lamp in her room was lit; as long as it remained so he could restrain the suspicion gnawing at his unbelief.

Past midnight the light went out. With it was extinguished the mean temper that served him for courage. He rose and prowled around the room, jerking out the drawers from the cómoda, kicking at Guadalupe's clothes strewn across the floor, taking inventory of everything she had ever used. The much remaining gave him no assurance; it was the little she had taken that plagued him. Again he flung himself in bed after blowing out the lamp.

With darkness came silence. A donkey engine went up the yards; an hour later it rumbled back with a string of flats. Then silence again. The intolerable, cloying, noiseless night. It was so thick it seemed to clot in his throat. He got up to wash out his mouth, changed his mind the minute he was on his feet, and slunk down the steps and out the door.

Crossing the tracks, he stood awhile under Sal's dark window. The voice hid in his heart told him that Guadalupe was inside, within reach of his will. With this comforting assurance, he had a drink at the corner cantina, leaning back against the bar to keep his eyes on the dark brick wall across the street. He even kept glancing backward on the way home across the tracks as if, like a ship, that gaunt hotel might slip its moorings and be lost in night. Again upstairs, he crawled into bed and lay tossing in restless sleep.

In the morning he rose and did his work at the cantina, sharpening taunts with which to greet Guadalupe. When by noon she had not come back he began to stew and fret again. It had been weeks since she had left him to sleep with Sal. Nor did he miss her, their relationship had grown so unbearable; it was only that she had dared to deprive him of the only unresisting object of his taunts.

That afternoon he stopped in the hotel again. Guadalupe

was not there. Neither was Sal. The door was locked and the proprietor downstairs could give him no news of their whereabouts. Aroused now, he made the rounds of the bars where they were most likely to be loafing. As he walked he took off his belt, swinging it viciously along his side. Another beating was what she needed. And in a public bar! She wouldn't be leaving him again!

She wasn't there: at the Owl, the Mague   El Molino Rojo, the Tivoli, or La Gloria. Nor the Cantina Shanghai, El Palacio, Las Tres Luces, nor even the Xochimilco. The sudden thought of old Oakie stung him into a red rage. He could hardly imagine what he would do if he found them together. When finally he had roamed through Cockroach Court without seeing either, he desperately returned to Sal's.

It was just after three, and in the mellow warmth of the afternoon the hotel dozed sleepily. Barby went up the stairs and strode through the empty hall to Sal's door. For a moment he knelt and listened at the keyhole. Silence; the same mocking silence that followed him like a shadow. He rose and pounded on the door with both fists.

The bed squeaked; he could hear the woman awakening and grumbling inside. He did not answer her call, but pounded on the door again. This time he heard her steps and the catch being unfastened. Watching for the first narrow crack as the door opened an inch, he suddenly gave it a shove backward.

"Christ! I might of known it'd be you!" Sal spit out, blocking his entrance.

Barby did not attempt to step inside; his first swift glance revealed that Guadalupe was not there. It stunned him for a moment. He could not imagine where else she might be.

"Guadalupe? Yeah. What about her?" asked Sal.

The boy could hardly restrain himself from striking her

in the face, it looked back at him so emptily and sleepily from its frame of disheveled tawny hair.

"Where'd she go? After she left here?" He kept his voice down with effort, yet had to clench his fists at seeing her head cock to one side and the familiar look—blank and yet a little sly—spread across her face. He had been asking his questions in Spanish. This sudden realization, and worse, the knowledge that she always understood it and refused to let on, just to irritate him, inflamed him still further.

"Where is she?" he shouted in English.

Sal pushed back her hair, dug out an ear. Deliberately she yawned in his face and wiped the sleep from one eye, the other watching him sharply enough.

"Hum," she drawled in a meek and mocking tone, "well now where is she about this time of day?"

Then suddenly, before he could stick out a foot, the door slammed loudly in his face.

Barby stared at it a moment with a livid face, then turned and hurried across the tracks to The Lamp Awake. Perhaps Sal had not lied; her contemptuous look and utter unconcern almost convinced him she had not. Guadalupe, as usual, might have been at Tai Ling's all afternoon.

She wasn't, nor had she been there all day.

Now it began in earnest: a slow nauseous commotion in the pit of his stomach, like a fermentation coming to a boil. With all his will he kept it down by dwelling on the obvious: that Guadalupe had not been away a full day, had indeed no means of leaving nor a place to go. He tried to convince himself that she would be at the cabaret tonight. And the instant his mind wavered from this reasonable assumption, the churning within him began again. It sputtered, boiled over and spread through his insides like a fiery poison he could not vomit up, try as he might.

He stood it for an hour. Then the sun beginning to settle behind the sierras and bringing on a langorous twilight, recalled to him Guadalupe's evening walks. The tardecita, the little afternoon, when she loved best to take her daily walk before going to work. He went out and began to retrace her steps along a route that never changed.

From The Lamp Awake he went up the avenida to La Casa Blanca where she always turned and followed the railroad tracks to the crossing at the Line. Often he had seen her standing at the big wire gates watching the horde of returning Mexicans emptying their bundles and baskets for inspection upon the walk. He turned and crossed the street to the shop where she might have stopped to listen to new phonograph records. Thence he turned south, his glance sweeping from side to side to catch the familiar jaunty meneo of her hips. At the Hong-Kong, suddenly remindful of the old blind peon and his clay mice, he turned and walked rapidly across the wooden bridge, climbed down into the arroyo. In five minutes he had clambered back, and stood leaning over the bridge railing.

The sun had set; and the darkness slowly rising from the arroyo like an exudation from deep inside the earth seemed to fuse with the shadows draining from the sierras. It was the crepusculo vespertino, the dusk of the evening star, when for an instant the world stood still. Yet its perpetual revolution seemed to continue inside him, churning in that nauseous commotion which obliterated for him the faint sound of a bell across the campo.

The ecstatic calm was broken by the muffled patter of a burro, loaded with firewood, crossing the wooden planks. With it the world took up its march. The street lights and cantina signs blazed forth across the barranca. Barby trudged back across the bridge and continued down the avenida. It was the end of Guadalupe's circuit, and nowhere had he seen her.

Worn out, he slipped down a side street to a lonchería, but could not eat. The beans stuck in his throat, the tortillas seemed dry and unpalatable as leather, and the faint odor of chile and onions stewing in a pot over the coals increased the sickness within him. He gave it up in disgust and pushed back the tin plate. Arms outspread on the oilcloth, he sat staring across the counter. Routed from his seat by a group of noisy paisanos, he slouched away and sat down on the gutter.

At seven o'clock he came alive again, rushing to Las Quince Letras and hiding himself in a far corner to wait for the first revue. At sound of the first bar of music he stood up and clung with staring eyes at the "entrada para las artistas" across the dance floor. His knees trembled; he was wet with sweat and too nervous to decide what to do when Guadalupe did come out. Only to see her! It was as far as his mind could go.

The door opened. The line of percentage girls filed out and did their dance, Sal among them. And still he waited. The Big Fella yelped through his megaphone. Somebody sang a song. Somebody else did a shimmy. Then they all scampered back; the orchestra struck up a tune; the floor filled with dancers as before. That was all. All! Struck numb, he lumbered out again into the night.

And now it was as if his whole inside had become a seething cauldron whose fumes, rising as he walked, kept deadening his mind. He began to drink: a spot of rice-brandy here, a gulp of mezcal farther on. The cheap liquor had no effect upon him whatever. It only, for the moment, doused the fire inside him that it might break out afresh and more sickeningly than ever. But it helped to pass the time till nine o'clock. For then, after the last revue in the casino, he meant to wring the truth from the other members of the chorus.

A quarter after the hour the percentage girls began to straggle into El Sol de Mayo. He waited a while longer for Sal, and when she did not come went over to the group of girls with a swagger that could not conceal his feverish anxiety. At his approach they looked up with an habitual air of contempt mitigated by a wary politeness.

"Guadalupe," he blurted out with a hoarse voice. "She wasn't at the cabaret tonight!"

In the sudden silence this astounding statement sounded flat and stale, like a truth at once trite and meaningless. Every girl in the group turned upon him an amazed stare. He stood there before them with bold bravado but with hands that shook as he clumsily lit a cigarette. He tried to look unconcerned, and the wild beseeching stare of his black eyes betrayed the stony immobility of his drawn, tense face. Again he tried to speak, to draw them into a casual but revealing conversation. And the moment he opened his mouth, his unhung jaw began to quiver; he stood gasping out a faint eructation of alcoholic fumes. The only words that came forth resolved themselves into another hopeless assertion. "She ain't been around all day!" It too seemed to wither away in the silence. And then, as if suddenly conscious of his foolish statements, he attempted a knowing smile. "She tell you where she go? And that she come back tomorrow?"

For a moment not a girl said a word. Then from the back a voice rasped out resolutely, "No! We ain't her wet nurse!"

The forced, unsteady smile broke on his face, seemed to droop downward pulling his features into an expression of hopeless despondency. Gradually it set and hardened as still he stood there, irresolute, in the face of a collective and amused disinterest. Then he spun about and lurched violently out the swing doors on his way to The Lamp Awake.

Always with the coming of night, whatever the day had brought and despite their most violent quarrel of the night before, she returned. It was the one invariable consistency in both their lives that he could not possibly imagine changed. Even from the corner when he saw that the upstairs window was dark, he could not believe she was not there. He entered the shop from the alley entrance, ran up the steps, and flung his arms across the empty bed. He lit the lamp, even then expecting to find her squatting silently in the corner beside the phonograph. But she was not; and the room, derisively empty and silent in the lamplight, seemed now to shriek out the truth that had coagulated, caught fire, and was now raging unchecked within him.

He let out a groan and ran back down the steps into the alley. In a minute he reached the corner, took the gutter in a leap, and ran full speed across the railroad tracks to Sal's hotel —the one place besides The Lamp Awake where he felt she must be. His whole inside was now a conflagration that seemed to light up in his murky mind his last few moments with Guadalupe. He could no longer doubt the astounding, unbelievable truth of her single assertion that she was going away. But to get there before she left! It was now his only thought. With a groan at the day he had wasted, he flung open the hotel door, rushed up the steps, and hurled himself upon Sal's locked door with both fists.

When she did not answer, he drew back and kicked it, one foot at a time, till both were numb. Then he beat at it until his knuckles were chafed and bleeding. Breathing heavily, the sweat beginning to drip down his cheeks, he quit and looked around. The long musty hall was feebly lit by a jet at the far end. He got down on his knees to the lock and found it plugged by the key on the inside. Immediately he lay down on his belly upon the floor. A bright thread of light lay along the warped threshold. It roused him to another onslaught on the door. He got up and wrestled with the stubborn knob. Then worn out, he flung himself against the door, his cheek against the wood, pounding on it with upraised arms.

Between poundings he listened with a preternatural concentration of all his faculties to the faint squeak of the bed inside, the woman's bare feet tiptoeing across the carpet. The first real sound—that of a chair placed against the door— shattered his nerves completely. With a resurgence of energy he began to hurl himself, shoulder, head and hip, at the door. And this, at last, aroused the woman inside.

"Cut out the racket! You outside! What the Goddam hell is this, anyway?"

The voice was tangible, resistant and alive, a new objective that drew from him a fresh attack. This time a bombardment of expletive. He cursed her in fluent Spanish, damned her specifically in English slang, and then losing voice and breath, began to howl unintelligibly his vituperative demands.

"No, damn yeh! This door ain't goin' to open!" And after a pause, "What do yeh want?"

What did he want? Holy Mother, when all his mind and soul and body were shrieking out her name! His voice took up the refrain: "Guadalupe! Guadalupe, I tell you! She's there!"

"No, you damn fool. She ain't. She's gone."

"You lie, lie, lie!" He tore at the doorknob again, inflamed by the truth in her words. The woman did not answer, and her silence was more expressive than any effusive explanation. It seemed to seep under the door into the dusky hall like a cold and clammy mist. It enveloped him, began to stifle him like a shroud he could not tear asunder. And the woman was its cause, the instigator of his misery, the accomplice of an unbearable truth. He let out a howl and began to curse her again. He was going to break down the door. In the next breath he begged her to open it that he might wring her neck and beat her lying face into a pulp. Faithfully then he promised to wait for her downstairs a night, a week, and wreak his vengeance upon her, to follow her for days until he caught her. "Don' you come to El Sol de Mayo no more. You'll never get a dollar again!" he shouted, and then slyly, "Now you open the door and let me see if she there!"

"Take your dollar and stick it! I quit goin' there last night!"

He yelped at her derisive voice, like a coyote caught in a steel trap who could not budge from the source of his pain. Now he began to beg and promise her exorbitant rewards if she would open the door and let him see inside.

"You're drunk!" was her only answer. And this, unaccountably, convinced him Guadalupe was really inside. He started to pound again.

The rumpus finally had awakened everyone up and down the hall. Their one creed was to keep their noses out of anyone else's business, but now after a half-hour they began stepping out into the hall. Barby, weak but stubborn, was still kicking and beating at the door. Sal, now thoroughly aroused, was shrieking maledictions from inside. She had thrown open the outside window and her shouts, heard in the bar on the corner below, were attracting other nondescript loiterers. Followed by the old Chinese properietor they came running up the steps. With Barby they too began to pound noisily on the door.

There was a sudden bang and clatter overhead. Sal, with a happy thought, had stepped up on the chair and loosed the catch on the transom.

"What the Goddam hell!" she demanded, peering down

from above. "They ain't nobody murdered in here. Get that
drunken bastard out of here before he breaks the door down.
That's all!"

At sight of her face, the boy leapt up and clung to the
sill. They dragged him down, held him kicking and mouth-
ing, "She's in there! The little morena. . . ."

Sal looked down, but without budging. "There ain't nobody in here," she said quietly. Then, as if compelled by some
strange compassion, she stated flatly enough, "The poor fool
means Guadalupe, the little dancer at the cabaret. Well, she
ain't here. She left on the first stage early this mornin'." The
boy below seemed suddenly deflated. "If you wasn't so drunk
and dumb you wouldn't be so surprised," she rasped out at him
unmercifully. "She told you she got the letter she'd been
lookin' for all winter, didn't she? And that she was goin' away
to dance? Christ! you seen her pack her things. What more
do you need to get in your head the idea she's gone? Gone!
Get me? On the first stage early this mornin'. A thousand
miles away by now. Now, God Almighty, get the hell out of
here and all this racket. And this convention, too!"

She ducked back her head, slammed up the transom, and
they could hear the squeak of springs as she flung back in bed.

Barby stood staring fixedly at the door, limp and helpless
as if stunned. The people looked at him queerly, left him with
a backward glance to return to their rooms down the hall or
to go on down the stairs. A rurale, the last to arrive at the
rumpus and the last to remain, prodded him in the ribs to
move on.

Barby preceded him down the steps, went out slowly into
the night. Then gradually quickening his steps, he began to
make his way to the open road leading east from town. The
night was clear, the moon full. Jovially its fat face looked

down at the amusing spectacle of the boy weakly running across the desert, hat off, and stopping like a dog to vomit at last at every clump of cactus.

CHAPTER TEN

FEAR IS a peculiar thing.
Not the sudden fright that stabs out from the dark, the awesome hush that gathers heavy as a pall about Death's departing heels, nor all those momentary terrors with which we are most familiar. For mercifully they are too quick. Their very unexpected swiftness serves but to shock the nerves and numb the mind so that we stand paralyzed.

A really terrible fear is not an affair of the moment. It is a parasitic worm that sucks at every nerve and fattens upon the heart. By night and in the cheerful sun of day it fastens upon your thoughts, preys unceasingly upon your secret soul. Its coils thicken with monstrous growth until every little window of your mind has been closed to escape. But always the fear grows there, an insidious thing moving and twisting about within the pregnant womb of your mind. Fear of poverty and of slow hunger is like that, and the inevitableness of an approaching end. A fear that cannot be hurried any more than it can be escaped, like a cancerous growth that spreads at its own slow pace.

Thus it was with Sal.

Always inside her she had carried the fear of a certain end. It had grown with the passing years; for poverty and prostitution are a strange world that cannot be seen from the outside, and only those within know its true confines. Time and again during her hectic Border life Sal had stood at the brink of that chasm yawning at her feet. Immeasurably deeper than her own profound knowledge of all human frailties, its frightful profundity opened her eyes to the irremediable follies and the inexorable price of her misspent youth. But always before, by a turn of her luck, she had stood free again.

This time there was no turning. Intuitively she had sensed the change in Gonzales the moment Guadalupe left. Now she saw it in his eyes as he waddled down the mezzanine stairs of Las Quince Letras. It was a late Saturday night just after the last show. The Seven Sweet Seductive Señoritas—herself among them—were gathered in a group at the end of the bar waiting for their week's pay. Gonzales called his bouncer, the Big Fella, gave him the canvas sack and talked awhile.

Then the Big Fella came up. He paid five of the girls off in the customary silver and waved them away for the night. As he paid the other waiting beside Sal he began to talk. Señor Gonzales, now that the season was in swing, was making some changes. She wasn't going to be paid any longer, but if she wanted to she could stay for house-money as a percentage girl for the rest of the summer. Provided of course that she minded her own business and did as she was told and . . . The girl nodded eagerly and with a look backward went swiftly out the door before he could change his mind.

Sal alone now remained standing before him, gathering up the short stack of silver which the Big Fella deliberately slid down the bar toward her.

"That's all," he growled. "All, savvy? Can't use you no

more. You're no good. Don't bring a bit of business. Sorry, old girl, but you got to get out. And I won't have you hanging around here makin' trouble tonight or tomorrow or the next day either. Come on. Clear out."

Sal revolved slowly on her elbow resting on the bar. She had felt it coming for months. During the last night with Guadalupe she had planned her every move as she had a dozen times before. But now, somehow, the thing got home to her. It wasn't just losin' another stinkin' job. It—Christ! this was the end of everything.

"You ain't firin' me?" The question seemed not Sal's, so hollow her voice sounded to her own ears. Almost in the same breath she added, "Are yeh?" And then quickly, "Say, you're goin' to keep me too, ain't you? Not with pay. I don't expect to be on the floor no more. But on whatever house-money I can get. I been a good percentage girl for years. I'll make you a better one, Big Fella."

"The hell you will!" he snarled. "You ain't been doin' it and there ain't goin' to be no argument about it. We been watchin' you too long. And what's more we ain't goin' to have no trouble with you in here at all, old girl. Not a damn bit. Drink up now, you're goin' out peaceful and you're not comin' back!"

Before she could remonstrate, he spun her around by the shoulder; then grabbing and twisting her arm, led her to the side door. Kicking open the door, he shoved her out.

The step caught her heel, tripped her and sent her sprawling across the narrow walk. But it was the fear which had eaten within her through the years, undermining her completely, that kept her down on hands and knees, staring piteously at the door slammed behind her. Gone was her vindictiveness, the quick rebound with which she was wont to meet rebuff, the courage to fight again. She rose slowly from the gutter, and as though ashamed to face the cantina lights slunk home to her room.

That night she got hopelessly drunk. She did not leave her room the next day and after dark she finished the last bottle.

On the evening of the second day she went out for food. Within an hour she was back with more gin.

Her actions of the days following formed an old, familiar pattern. But first, with a desperation strange to her, she advanced all the money she dared on her room. Each day thereafter was the same. She awoke at daybreak and lay for hours in thoughtless, timeless dread. With a dull surfeited look she washed out her mouth and squirted the water in the bowl. She wiped her eyes with wet fingers, dressed, and went down the stairs. All day she roamed the streets. Every bar, every cantina, all the cabarets knew her repeated efforts to find work. She tried tortillerías, grimy little cafes, a cigar-maker's shop around the corner. She made the rounds of the cotton gins and went to the brewery at the edge of town. Twice she crossed the Line to meet with the same ill success. On the second trip she encountered difficulty getting back across to her room, and this threw her into such a panic that she dared not try again. With no more than a week left her in the hotel the prospect faced her squarely. There was no work to be had. Sal was at the end of her rope and she knew it.

Her life that week would have driven a sane person mad, but obsessed wholly by fear Sal was hardly sane. A nameless dread, now terribly real, held her so that she could not move. All day she lay silent on the bed. At night she sat on her broken chair before the window watching the freight cars rumble past.

She had exchanged her few American dollars for Mexican pesos and rechanged these until there was now only a heap of small coins. These she arranged in rows of tiny stacks on top of the newspaper-covered dresser. The newspaper was an old one from Nogales. It was a fiesta edition containing on the front page a photograph of the Cave, the new cabaret made out of the former jail and utilizing the rock-hewn cells as private dining rooms. In the foreground stood all the entertainers, Guadalupe and Peña among them, arms around each other. As Sal had known, it had never occurred to Guadalupe to return the fare Sal had given her, nor had the girl ever written—not even a postal.

Sal no longer looked at the faded, dusty paper. She was obsessed only with thought of the coins on top. Each day the rows were one stack shorter. Once a day when she went out for food, she again rechanged them for coins of still smaller denomination to make them appear to be lasting longer. Yet with appalling persistence they kept shrinking. In a mad fury she would arise and bring the silver back with her to the bed. Lying on her belly, brooding, she would rearrange them until her anger passed. Sometimes at night, as though she had forgotten something, she would leave her chair and lighting the lamp take out the coins from the empty drawer. And then chin in hand she would stare out the window into the darkness.

On the day when more money for her room was due, Sal awoke in a strange cold calm. At daybreak she rose and opened the dresser drawer. In a corner were her last two tencentavo pieces. Sal took them back with her to the bed. She could think quite clearly. At eight o'clock she went to El Sol de Mayo and asked for Barby.

Cheon looked up from his bar, taking in her shapeless sagging body, the wrinkled clothes, her bleary eyes and tangled tawny hair. He shook his head.

"Come on. Sure you know me. Sal! Guadalupe and Barby's pal. I come here the first night to open up the joint. Don't you remember me workin' here ever' night all winter? I want to come back, Cheon. I'll stay all day too for that dollar and bring you lots of business!" She essayed a wink; instead, her whole face twitched nervously.

"No more dollars. No more girls. We stop long time ago," Cheon stated blandly.

Sal continued hurriedly. "But what I really come for is to find out where Barby is. I ain't seen him for a week. I got news for him about Guadalupe. He wants to see me."

"Not here. He gone."

The cold finality of his tone was a simple answer to every other question she could think to ask. Sal slumped down in her clothes and left.

That afternoon she went to The Lamp Awake. For a long time she idled outside, screwing up courage to tackle the old Chink. Desperation drove her inside. The place was empty; even Tai Ling was nowhere to be seen. But suddenly at the back of the shop she caught a glimpse of something that choked the scream rising in her throat and froze her on the spot. A horrible, leering, heathen idol with a staring eye in the middle of his forehead, and arms and hands sticking out all over him like a monstrous spider; squatting on a bunch of cabbage leaves with his feet turned soles up and crossed in his lap like a monkey's; and with a goldfish and a human skull beneath him.

It was Tai Ling's effigy of his favorite Bodhisattva, "The Great Pitier," the embodiment of mercy and compassion.

At the back door where he had been sunning himself on the step, Tai Ling got up and turned inside. Seeing the immobility of fear in his visitor's posture, he raised his hand. He wanted to assure her of the comforting meaning of the conventional symbolism so frightening to her Occidental mind:

the fish, symbolic of herself in a sea of fearful illusion; the skull filled with blood, symbolical of the Bodhisattva's renunciation of worldly life; his third eye of spiritual insight ever on the outlook to perceive distress; his thousand arms ever ready to succour the troubled; the lotus petals of his throne representing the same peace that palm leaves bore in association with her own people's Bodhisattva known as Jesus. Mere symbols, all of them, for the one great truth of all peoples, all faiths, separated as they were by ignorance and prejudice.

Sal saw his yellow claw reached out to grab her. She turned and fled.

Tai Ling ran to the door shouting, "Come back! It is nothing. Wood, paint! Meaningless, unnecessary! Come back, girl!"

Sal continued to flee from his shouts. That old, wrinkled, heathen Chink and the horrible idol he worshipped! God Almighty! Who could expect any help from him? Why, there was no tellin' what he'd do once he got you alone. Anything was better'n that. Anything!

She lay sweating with fear on her bed. But again that evening hunger drove her out. This time with her most valuable possession, a hand mirror, stuck down the breast of her dress. At a little back-street cantina she offered it to the man behind the bar.

"No. No money," he answered her without hesitation, and then added on second thought, "but I'll give you a quart of Hennessy for it. I'll take it home to the wife."

Sal took the bottle back to her hotel. On her way up the stairs she was met by the Chinese proprietor who was waiting to insist on the rent. Sal muttered something and went inside her room.

That night and for two days following she did not leave the room. Half-drunk she lay on the bed listening to the old

Chinaman who each morning, afternoon, and evening came up to try the door and to retreat mumbling down the hall.

Then, on the late afternoon of the third day, she went out for an hour. She had done up in a newspaper her brush and comb, a whole pair of stockings and an extra dress. This small packet she hid on the fire escape when the hall was clear before going down the steps. When she returned, the old Chinese proprietor followed her upstairs and stood in the doorway lest she throw the catch inside.

Sal flung herself on the bed, staring around with wide eyes at this, her last private retreat from this life but one. There was no need to say a word. At the end of ten minutes, the perplexed proprietor told her to get up and out. Without protest, Sal rose and flung a glance at the suitcase between his legs, hers no longer, and went out the door. Gathering up the newspaper packet left on the steps outside, she walked away.

It was twilight in the streets. On every corner glowed lights from doors and dusty windows. Acherontic figures lounged by lazily or sat against the walls. Sal walked on, her eyes upon the ground. In Cockroach Court she entered a dirty cantina. Passing through it she entered an open court. A terrible stench arising from the bagnio drove the faint essence of alcohol from the air. In the pale glow of two lights at opposite ends of the courtyard, a dreary lane of opposite cribs with names rudely lettered above each door received her. A few women clad only in stockings and colored chemises were chatting from their open doorways. They called out to Sal but she did not answer. She walked swiftly down the lane to the crib assigned her.

2

Barby was in a mean mood.

He had come to that period of insufferable loss which follows the shock of sudden bereavement. That Guadalupe's desertion was already beginning to appear in the clear light of an inevitable truth he had long known but ignored, made little difference. Everything he saw, everything he touched, reminded him of her.

The last time she had worn this old dress; a discarded stocking found under the bed while he was hunting a dropped coin, and the feel of firm flesh it evoked; the memory of her emptying this bottle of hand lotion; all these trivial anniversaries he celebrated with new anguish day by day.

Still the battle between her absence and the substantial reminders of her presence continued. The only thing in all his life he had possessed fully, she seemed only half gone. And to find himself now disowned of her voice and touch, her physical compliance to his mood, swept him into a mad delirium. For hours he lay concentrating all his strength of will to recall Guadalupe in a certain time or place, racking his memory for every detail of the occasion as if by thus recreating every instance of their life together he might compel time to roll backward and nullify her absence.

Suddenly, as though the intense and prolonged effort had snapped something in his mind, he found he could no longer command his memory. He would lie propped up in bed staring at the dusty phonograph without being able to envision her sitting there changing records. He would grab up a discarded dress and hold it out before him, unable to materialize her within it. Often there came back to him the memory of her anger, sometimes a gesture, the echo of her voice, but they too refuted his efforts to feel her again a living whole. And gradually these too left him. She became no more than the indistinct image of his own thwarted desire.

But as he was no longer her master, he was also no longer her abject slave. He was again free and alone, tempered now to a bitter hardness. And slowly there built up within him a petty vindictiveness that vented itself on everything around him.

Stumbling over the mop with which Cheon was scrubbing the floor of the cantina, he grabbed and broke the stick across his knee. "God damn it! Now get down and scrub it with your hands. That'll teach you to be more careful!" To a beggar who insistently whined for alms he gave a kick in the ribs. Tai Ling's frugality incensed him still further. Passing the old man contentedly emptying a single bowl of rice on his counter, Barby stopped to shout, "What the hell! Makin' out you're too poor to buy a square meal!" and threw down ten pesos before stalking out. No; nothing pleased him; nothing filled the howling emptiness inside him.

To this mean mood Mendoza was a ready accomplice. Nearly every week he brought a few barrels to El Sol de Mayo. Barby found out what was in them. The knowledge increased the price paid for their brief storage.

"What the hell!" he sneered, flipping open a silver cigarette case Mendoza gave him. "Is this what I get for hiding your 'wet Chinese'? I can buy my own clothes and toys."

Mendoza mentally staggered back from this unexpected blow. Was this the same ignorant, craven cholo he had been duping with a few inconsequential presents? Swiftly, with new respect, his glance roved over the boy. With the coming of spring and new crowds of workers the cantina was always full. No longer were girls needed to draw trade. Barby indeed could afford his new, demanding role.

"Why no, compadre!" remonstrated Mendoza. "I just brought you this case to match your cigarette lighter as a present. We never have settled on the amount due you—but I think we ought to, no?"

After a half hour's bickering Mendoza paid up. Thereafter the payments were extraordinarily large and regular. The money enabled Barby to hire a helper for Cheon and released him to loaf at will. Flashily dressed, mean-tempered, he swaggered through the streets. With his pocket always full of pesos and El Sol de Mayo behind him, he lost his craven fear of the big cabarets filled with rich Americans, gambled showily, watched the Saturday night fights with supercilious detachment.

Gradually he gathered around him a small pack of cholos eager to pay homage for his drinks. They sat in the back room of El Sol de Mayo admiring his clothes, listening to his authoritative discourses on boxing, praising his business management of the cantina. Barby despised them. But their praises fed his starved vanity, as his imagined power over them masked his inward inadequacy.

One day after an absence of two weeks Mendoza appeared with a new proposition. He had been up north talking to his employers. Business was so good that probably he would be needed more across the Line. Why didn't Barby take over his work here? In fact, he already had recommended it to Certain Gentlemen and they had agreed. "You've ridden down with me," he added. "And Chugoku and Tony Wong know all the answers. Easy money!"

"How much?" Barby asked curtly. The prospect of a truck to ride in around the country, a chance to trick the officious authorities, and more money all appealed to him.

"Why, I can't say how much," Mendoza answered cautiously. "You see, you'll be a partner in an important secret business. You'll be the boss of your own part of it. Why don't you name the amount, Jéfe?"

For the first time in weeks Barby smiled. "Have a cigarette, compadre?" he asked insolently, flipping open his silver cigarette case.

So every week or ten days now he rode off with Tony Wong who taught him to drive the old, deep-bottomed truck. At the head of the gulf they would load a few cases of imported Carta Blanca beer and a few aliens hidden in the false bottom or crouched in empty barrels. The aliens were no longer solely Chinese laborers, but "wet Mexicans" and stray whites who could not get a passport, as well.

Outside of the village they slowed up for inspection, waved and went on. Barby grinned. "Mendoza paid him off— too much. I'll make him holler a long time." But on top of the sierras the truck was stopped by two new rurales, armed and booted, Barby had not seen before. They made Barby and Wong crawl out of their seats and draw off the tarpaulin while they prodded about the truck.

"This is the second time they've stopped us," said Tony Wong as they drove off. "Looks like they're getting suspicious. You better make a deal with them or see somebody in town. Mendoza would."

"The hell with what Mendoza would do! I'm running this now!" shouted Barby. "Why hand out money to those ignorant bastards? They'll never find out what we've got."

He began to swear with unaccountable vituperation. Not even the new power over the inanimate wood and steel which hurled him through space, nor the greater power over its hidden occupants, could fill that old howling emptiness within him.

3

Tai Ling watched him stalk past the counter without a word, and waited with expectant curiosity as he ascended the stairs.

What was there to say? It all had happened as he feared. Denying the existence of a reality beyond their desire-created illusions, both of his upstairs protogees had been forced to obey the laws of their lower nature. The girl, unresolved between the two poles of her baser self, submitting finally to a perverted and permanent distortion. The boy, hopelessly frustrated, running rampant in the bitterness of his impotency of spirit. His poor little human fish!

Guadalupe was gone; Tai Ling dismissed her from mind completely. But Barby still remained to trouble him with his arrogance, greed and lust for power. The former slave of material circumstance, he was now the master of material circumstance without seeing that they were sides of the same mirror. Of such, mused Tai Ling, are made the petty tyrants and world dictators of mankind. Yet the very forces that created them were certain to destroy them; and this, he knew, was another law none could escape.

Nevertheless Tai Ling worried.

Barby was still the boy he had raised, and still plagued by the gross physical need his nature demanded. Tai Ling was not above trying to give him even this.

So, on learning a half-hour ago that the boy had returned, the old man had opened his cash box and taken out two silver dollars. Halfway to the door he stopped, came back and got two more. Clinking these in his long fingers, Tai Ling slipped out the back door into Cockroach Court. Shortly he was back; and now waiting hopefully as Barby clumped upstairs. . . .

No; all the way home Barby had been unable to free himself from the bondage that even the thought of Guadalupe evoked anew. And with the memory of her waiting in bed vivid in his mind, he opened the door.

The unexpected shine of the lighted lamp, and on the bed a figure of a woman in long stockings and a green chemise—this was all he saw. He stopped, one foot over the threshold, as if blinded and struck dumb.

"'Ullo swit'art!" she called, lazily unhooking her high heels from the foot railing and turning around. "Where you been all this time, boy?"

The strange throaty voice brought him to. He stood staring at her while his thumping heart calmed down. Gradually his mind cleared of the specter of a dark oval face and substituted for it the coarse, white features of the woman on the bed.

"You ain't bringin' nothin' to drink, are yeh honey? I'm dry enough to . . ." Her voice broke off into a muffled cry as Barby leaped toward the bed and grabbed for her throat.

With a powerful spring the woman tore herself free, and catapulting from the opposite side of the bed fetched up with a clatter against the wall. The sudden jar set off the phonograph standing against the window. It broke out with a sudden feminine wail, "An' so, fo' evah good woman . . ."

Barby's face went livid. Forgetting the woman for a moment, he dived across the bed and swept the phonograph off the table. It went to the floor with a crash, followed by a rain of splintering records from the stack beside it. In the midst of this slate-grey mound the boy jumped and thrashed about with both feet.

This lucky diversion from Barby's astounding welcome gave the woman a chance to scramble up off the floor and out of the corner. When Barby looked up she was standing against

the comoda, wide-eyed with fear and beginning to holler,
"Keep yer hands off me, you crazy bastard! I'll get ever'body
off the street up here!

"I ain't done nothin'! Honest to God, I ain't. It was the
old bird downstairs. He said you were lonesome for a girl.
Give me four dollars to come up here and wait for you." Beginning to edge backward toward the door, she mumbled,
"Christ! Is he crazy or you?"

At his first move, she turned and dived for the doorknob.
Barby caught her by the shoulder as she flung open the door,
and sent her spinning toward the stairs. Turning on a high
heel, she spun against the wall and tumbled down the steps.
With one last shriek the woman grabbed at the scarf which
tied up her four dollars, and fled out of the back door into the
alley.

Tai Ling, upraised and bent over his counter to watch her
go, settled back down in his seat. He heard Barby turn back
into the room, sweep a last phonograph record to the floor,
and then fling himself on the bed so forcefully that even Tai
Ling flinched from its squeak and groan.

A sudden premonition gripped the old man. The boy
was now completely mastered by the illusion of a vanished
desire. Unable to free himself of it by right thinking, release
of his pent-up bitterness and frustration was no longer possible
even by wrongdoing. He was not responsible now even for his
own actions; a mad dog that would slash at everything in
sight. Who could help him now?

Tai Ling wept at his own inadequacy: his gesture of farewell.

4

Barby lay twisting and turning, clawing at his pillow. The
presence of the woman on the bed had recalled his physical

desire for Guadalupe so acutely that his senses screamed. It was almost unbelievable that she was not there beside him, her breast in his grasp, her strong lithe thigh clutched against his. And yet, strangely enough, he heard the faint echo of another truth: that once he had made her his, she was desirable no longer. But the craving and the pain still persisted.

The boy sat up sweating, worn out with the vain effort to seduce even sleep to lie with him. God damn it! What he needed to get her out of his mind was a woman. Why hadn't he thought of it before?

Barby got up and went out. It was not yet midnight. The cantinas and the cribs behind them were still awake. He entered one on the edge of Cockroach Court, stopping at the bar for a drink. A half-dozen disgruntled customers and a few prostitutes were fooling with a jammed slot machine. One of the women ambled up and patted him on the thigh.

"You like to come with me, amigo?"

"Come on, no soliciting out front, Pilar," growled the sleepy barkeep. "I told you before."

Barby flung down a coin to buy her a beer and lounged out the back door to the entrance of the long open court. Under a single unshaded globe suspended overhead and a piece of greasy moon, he leaned against the wall, lighting a cigarette. The piercing rancid odor of disinfectant cut sharply the other smells lurking in the hot night air.

At the opposite end of the court two cholos stood urinating at an open mingitorio, clumsily dodging pieces of thrown adobe. The girls who flung them sat in two opposite rows along the sides. Above their open doors were lettered the names they went by: Dollie, Molly, Joe, Maria, Loulou, Katie, Sue. From time to time one of the closed doors opened to spew forth a drunken lad, now a little sobered, who slouched quickly away. A moment later the woman emerged and emptied a tin bucket into the open drain. Then after a fresh beer and a try at one of the slot machines inside the bar, she took her place again on the chair outside the door.

Barby scowled. The ugly bitches! To have to come to one of these after a woman all his own!

Seeing him lounging against the wall, one of the girls called out, "What's the matter, Caballero? Don't you know how, or can't you unbutton your vest?" The rest set up a howl of laughter. Another hitched up her stockings and waddled to where he stood. Hunting for a fat wallet, she pinched his breast, slapped him on the buttocks, maintaining the while an easy flow of chatter. Barby shook off her hands, flipped away his cigarette, and slouched down past the row of doors.

"Turista!" . . . "Turista!" . . . "Caballero!"

Ignoring the taunts and kicking at the hands grabbing at his legs, Barby drifted along. Fat, haggard, ugly, sweaty, sloppy—bitches all of them! He could not stop for the tantalizing image of clean-cut flesh and iodine-tinted skin still hovering in his mind. And yet he was driven onward by the mocking fire within him.

At the far end, the least advantageous place, sat a tall tubercular girl in a limp, dirty chemise. Chin in hand, her great sad eyes acknowledging the appalling slimness of her shrinking limps, she did not even look up as he passed. Here he turned back upon the circuit, greeted with more noisy shouts. Raucous laughter rang across the courtyard. Frowsy heads popped out from every doorway.

Then suddenly as he passed the second crib from the end the closed door opened. A long arm reached out and grabbed his sleeve. A second hand gripped the collar of his shirt. Without protest he was jerked up the step and into the tiny room.

The hell! What was the difference? Without turning around he blew out the lamp and slammed the door, hearing the woman flop down on the bed. Carelessly he tossed two pesos on the dresser and heard them ring against a pint bottle standing half full upon a soiled, spread towel. He threw his hat truculently on the floor. Abruptly now, for the first time, a blind wave of passion engulfed him. He lunged to the bed with frantic haste.

Ten minutes later he rolled over with a curse, and began weakly buttoning his shirt. The woman got up immediately to secure the money on the dresser. She lit the lamp.

"What the hell's wrong with you? You don't expect more, for Christ's sake?" he growled, bending down for his hat.

There was no answer. Barby sat up. As he turned around, a horrible burst of laughter exploded in his face. His eyes climbed swiftly up the pale, bloated, sausagelike limbs to the distorted face framed in its frowsy snarl of taffy hair.

It was Sal. A terrible, leering mockery of the woman of a few months before, but still Sal. At his look of frantic surprise she flung back her head again, with its long uncombed hair, and let loose another blast of derisive, almost hysterical laughter.

Barby jumped to his feet, dived for the door; and with that ghastly laugh still ringing in his ears, fled out of the court.

5

An hour later, still sober, he returned to The Lamp Awake. The yogi of Cockroach Court was deep in meditation, sitting, hands in lap, in front of the turned down lamp. Barby stopped. For the first time in a year—perhaps the only time in his life—he saw the old man clearly.

His figure had shrunken in its greasy, black sateen jacket and patched trousers. The hair on his round, yellow, bony head was sparse and thin. The empty fingers of his hands, palm up, were long, thin and slightly curved. He looked exactly like a failing, inept, old shopkeeper who had dozed off into another nap.

A dim resentment arose in the boy against his benefactor. The old fool! Sending a girl upstairs. Letting his business go to pot, starving himself, being made a fool of! Barby was about to step forward and speak when he noticed that the old man's eyes were open. Sudden fear gripped him: Tai Ling was dead. Then the fingers moved slightly and were still.

Barby could not move. Like everything else in the room, objects, insects, everything that moved and did not move, he seemed held at the edge of that circle whose fixed center was Tai Ling's tranquil face. It was at once relaxed and strangely set, like yellowish wax pliable enough to accommodate the slightest change in its mass of wrinkles. Only the big domed forehead reflecting the glow of the lamp stood out hard and smooth. Occasionally his lips parted for his slow rhythmical breathing; and this, a miracle of life in a face so dead, only enhanced still more the greater mystery of the face itself.

Still Barby could not stir. That strange, tranquil face, so terrifying in its unconscious repose! Never before had it seemed so enigmatic, so subtle of expression. The unmoving features assumed their natural pattern, and thus composed lost all their individual meanings. This was Tai Ling as he was —voiceless, devoid of smile or frown, without the warmth or coldness of a look. And what was that? Mesmerized, Barby stared as if at something he had never seen before.

Suddenly the old man's narrow eyes gave a brief flicker. It was just a flutter of his eyelids, like dry leaves stirred by the wind; yet in that instant the windows to his soul seemed opened. The boy jerked back, then stood still again as if terrified by what he saw within.

All that he had known of Tai Ling was there: the intangible peace and mystery of The Lamp Awake, his generosity, his humor and forebearance—yes, all the poetry and the beauty of his life was there in the momentary gleam of his open black eyes. But something else showed there too. A vast profundity, a monstrous impersonality, an overwhelming empty wilderness. And this, whatever it was, was something Barby could not stand.

He backed away and retreated softly upstairs.

He could not sleep. Was the old man drunk, drugged or crazy? Whatever it was, all contact between them seemed forever broken. He could no longer recall Guadalupe clearly, no longer curse Sal. Something had happened to him; he had reached an end. Clutched by a nameless foreboding, he lay stiffly in bed.

6

Tai Ling, as Barby watched him, was peeling an onion and weeping. The onion he was unwrapping was his own ego. The tears were shame and humility at what he found—just another wrapping.

He had turned down the lamp to a tiny glow. Concentrating steadily upon it in the darkness, he knew it to be not only the one distinguishable spot in the room. In the universal darkness of mankind it became the one infinitesimal reflection of that clear, boundless and eternal light of the infinite mind.

As he quieted it focused upon himself: his outward shell.

And seated at the core of silence within the shop, within that quintessential silence he had now achieved, Tai Ling heard a faint ringing in his ears. Gradually in turn he heard his regular and rhythmical breathing, the beating of his heart, the circulation of blood through his veins, the functioning of his bodily organs. It was as if he sat in the engine room of a perfectly controlled plant. But knowing himself completely detached from it.

Immediately it fell away from his consciousness.

There lay his mind. As an organ of his body also, its shape and color and material substance were likewise immaterial and meaningless. Its physical aspect vanished immediately.

But as a cognizing faculty it still remained, ceaselessly spinning thoughts. With every change of breath there came a change of thought. Inhalation, retention, exhalation; he could not retain a single thought longer than this normal duration.

Tai Ling wavered in his concentration; his breathing increased slightly; he felt balked.

Was he then—this mortal onion in a dreary shop—no more than an ever-multiplying layer of helpless thoughts? What lay beneath the thoughts?

He tried cutting through them by stopping each thought as it arose. And still they kept arising, one after another, so numerous as to seem interminable and inexhaustible. Till he knew that thought-forming was as natural as breathing, and could no more be stopped than any other biological process of his mortal body.

Once he realized this, he was free of their hold upon him. It was as if he sat on a mountain top indifferently watching the clouds roll by. Tranquil and unperturbed, he let them stem forth, take shape, vanish and be replaced by others, with utter detachment.

He had reached the realm of non-thought; attained mental quiescence. Like a weary traveler he rested for awhile, allowing his mind to remain in its passive, tranquil state. How wonderful it was! The pervading calm, the deep peace and utter freedom.

The darkness held, and the silence; his mind continued to

watch with indifferent detachment the formation of his thoughts. But slowly he became aware of their warning: this was not his goal. It was not the core of the onion.

He took up the search again; began to be conscious of the cognizing faculty of his mind itself. That mind at first capable of external analysis, and now equal to introspective analysis.

What was it? He had perceived that it was not a visible, substantial thing. Nor was it a complex of various sensations, feelings, reasonings, memories; these were but the thoughts it created, from which he could detach himself.

And yet it existed. It was able to examine itself.

Almost instantly he was intuitively conscious that it was not his mind which was thus observing itself. The observer had now become the observed. There was something behind the mind.

From this sudden, blinding glimpse of reality, the yogi plunged into darkness and silence. They eddied slowly about him like familiar waves rippling on his consciousness. Like an arctic explorer lost in the perpetual darkness of an unmarked waste, he floundered back to the known.

Immediately the darkness lessened; a tiny light appeared. The silence vanished, broken by the sound of his rhythmical breathing. He saw the lamp burning before him, heard Barby tossing restlessly on his bed upstairs. His meditation for the night was over.

CHAPTER ELEVEN

E ARLY THAT Saturday night it happened.
Barby and Tony Wong, carrying three passengers hidden in the truck, were approaching the inspection stop outside
of town when Wong suddenly leaned over and gripped
Barby's arm.

"Look! Did you see them? Four rurales, not two. Quick,
put out the lights! Maybe we can turn back."

It was too late. The truck already had topped the rise,
and in the glare of its headlights they could see the officers
walking out into the middle of the road waving arms.

"Pues. They won't find anything on us," boasted Barby
in a tremulous voice.

"You fool! What do you suppose they brought two more
here for? I told you you ought to of paid off like Mendoza
done."

"Hell with 'em! We'll make a run for it then!" Sudden
bitterness, a vast dammed up animosity, flooded Barby. Grip-

ping the wheel with both hands, he stamped on the accelerator. The truck jumped forward.

The four figures ahead spread out swiftly, stretching a chain across the road and anchoring the ends to their parked cars. Farther ahead another figure ran down the road out of the beam of light.

"That'll never hold us!" shouted Barby with rage and exultation.

"Get down! Turn off the lights!"

Cars, men and chains leapt at them in moonlight. There was a metallic crash, a merry jingle of broken glass. Then receding shots and shouts. The truck had snapped the chain, breaking both headlights.

"Verdad! I told you!" shouted Barby triumphantly. "Stupid pigs!" Wild exultation filled him. For the first time he felt the joy of complete victory, the madness of unrestrained power.

Tony Wong still crouched on the floor of the swaying cab, face pressed against the windshield. "Slow up. Can't see in the dark. Remember the arroyo. . . . The arroyo!" he screamed.

Out of a vast expanse of cactus studded desert it seemed suddenly flung in their faces—a quick, engulfing shadow, an immense rocky cave.

Too late they saw what it held: a Border Patrol car that had been hurriedly turned crosswise in the road.

Barby gave a wild yell of frantic rage, threw over the wheel. With a splintering crash the truck rammed into the front end of the car, rose sideways, and keeled over into the rocky arroyo ten feet below.

2

Two hours later Tai Ling heard the news. In swift Cantonese it came from underground on slippered feet.

Barby and Tony Wong had been caught bringing three aliens from Chugoku's to slip across the Line. All five had been killed. But the officers had got a statement from Tony Wong before he died. Faithful to his employers, Wong had confessed to working for Chino Juan.

Gravely Tai Ling nodded, and waved his informant away.

"Come please. When Chino Juan—"

"Go!"

Tai Ling continued to sit quietly at his counter. Barby had betrayed him; now he knew where the boy had been getting his money, and why he drove so far after beer for the cantina.

The boy was dead, and he was bereft of his companion of nearly twenty years. It was a grievous shock; not till it subsided could he think clearly what it meant.

What immediately confronted him were the implications of Wong's confession. Even now Chino Juan likewise was hearing of the jest played upon him. It had been so long since Tai Ling had concerned himself with the one-sided feud between them, that he flinched with repugnance at recalling what it meant. Yet dutifully his mind summed up the inevitable.

The Border Patrol would immediately report Wong's confession. Chino Juan would be taken in custody, accused of transporting aliens for delivery across the international line. Meanwhile Chugoku would be arrested. Clearing Chino Juan, he would implicate Mendoza and the rest of the ring who would be quick to include Tai Ling. Thus inevitably do our own past misdeeds ensnare us.

But meanwhile, much faster, other wheels would be turning. Such a mammoth jest was Wong's that the whole quarter was no doubt laughing. Chino Juan had lost face. All of his friends would believe that Tai Ling had outwitted him, and would be in haste to revenge him. Who ever had believed that Tai Ling had given El Sol de Mayo to Barby? Such is the fruit of pride, that it inevitably identifies itself with the tree from which it sprang.

Here it was then; retribution from Chino Juan's friends, and from the authorities too. Yet inflexible in the belief that no man can alter the path of his fate, Tai Ling refused to flee. Instead he opened the front door and returned to his stool.

How annoying, really, after months of quiet contemplation, to be dragged into this maelstrom of empty motion! All such action was an illusion. An individual committed a crime at the instant of making up his mind to murder; the knife thrust was merely an anticlimax. So too was mass murder by nations but an anticlimax to economic bullying, political treachery, racial restrictions and the weakening poison of propaganda.

All an illusion by which men, with mere muscular activity, sought to escape the responsibility of clear thinking.

Tai Ling sat pat. As he had known, swift action followed his surmises. There came voices shouting in the door that El Sol de Mayo was ablaze.

The old man walked to the open door and looked out. Already pink shoots of flame were growing into the sky from the low, black horizon of flat topped adobes. Even as he watched, the conflagration burst into sudden bloom. El Sol de Mayo had attained at last the brilliance of its name.

To it, past the shop, a hundred figures raced from bars and casinos. Their feet beat up the cobbled alley like the throbbing of a drum. Tai Ling slipped out the door and let the crowd sweep him round the turn.

There, blazing in a wreath of gold and fire, stood the cantina. Over all the throng it cast the ripe halo of its passing. In this lively red jostled the black cardboard figures of the crowd, though here and there flitted a girl clad only in stockings, shoes and chemise, her pale silk and pink flesh turning rosier under the spreading flare. As the fire bit higher, sparks caroming into the sky, a row of railroad cars leaped closer. Against the lemon-tinted sheds across the tracks writhed like serpents the reflection of the leaping flames.

Tai Ling pushed through the crowd in time to see the whole front window cave in. An escaping burst of smoke drove them back. Somebody screamed. Instantly they surged up again.

Plainly outlined inside the burning cantina raved Cheon's helper caught behind the bar.

Tai Ling and all the crowd saw his frantic figure dancing with the flames. They saw him throwing beer about him as though he were feeding handfuls of grain to a screaming flock of wings. They watched him crawl upon the burning bar and then drop back again. He beat upon the mahogany with wild hands and wiped the fire upon his clothes. He ran backwards and frontwards with fearful, awkward and silly gestures as he tried to beat back the spreading flames. Then he stood and screamed, screamed, screamed. . . .

Now upon the heavy acrid air rose the screech of a siren which drowned his cries. Again and again it shrieked across the Line for the great wire gates to open. The fire grew. With the open draft it leapt up the door posts. Letters and symbol on the sign above the door wrinkled and vanished. Great pieces of clay peeled off from the adobe walls; bricks began to crumble or drop away. Inside, the flooring resembled a vat of burning oil. For a time the place continued its lively roar, smothered at last by clouds of blue and yellow smoke.

With the Mexican horse-cart hysterical at its heels, the water-tank car from across the Line thundered up to the cantina. They douched the shops on each side and wet the adobe walls up and down the street; but for a half-hour not a bucket could they spare for what once had been El Sol de Mayo.

In another hour it was over. Tai Ling trudged back to The Lamp Awake. Cheon was waiting for him with Chewlee Singkee. They had latched the back door, turned down the lamp still lower.

Earlier that evening, related Cheon, he had been sitting in the doorway of El Sol de Mayo for a breath of air while his helper was dozing at the bar. A man had walked in. There was a sudden crash of a bottle, the smell of kerosene, leaping flames. Cheon had run next door for a water bucket. When he got back the whole place was afire. The man was gone. His helper was nowhere to be seen: knocked out behind the bar, he knew now. There wasn't a doubt but what—

Tai Ling wearily lifted his hand. Of course! Words, all words, were superfluous.

His old friend, the prosperous butcher, Chewlee Singkee, was not so apologetic or easily intimidated. "There are things to be said," he protested. "Chino Juan has burned your cantina, killed your barkeeper. Time is short. Where do we strike?"

"Barby's cantina," corrected Tai Ling quietly. "And he is dead—dead by reason of his own unconsidered actions. I would not add more evil to that already done."

"Enough of such talk! We have indulged your philosophy too many years, my good friend, to banter principles now. The sticks are thrown. You have made Chino Juan lose face at last. Even now he is dodging the authorities. He and his friends have burned your cantina and your barkeeper. You must strike back before they reach you. Luckily you too have friends to help you, despite your neglect."

"We strike, they strike back, forcing us to strike again. Already there are six dead since nightfall. When will it end?"

Chewlee Singkee scowled. "This quarrel is long overdue.

If we fail to show our strength now that we are challenged, every one of us—your fine forgotten friends!—will soon be run out of business and knifed in the back. The Mercado, the Casino Chino, the Chinesca—he is too powerful already!"

"It is a business venture then?" smiled Tai Ling.

"I am thinking of my helper," accused Cheon. "You too saw him trapped and burning!"

"I am thinking of your own life!" refuted Tai Ling swiftly. "No. I will not jeopardize the safety of my fine and forgotten friends."

Chewlee Singkee took out a revolver, squinted through the barrel. "So your years of fancy thinking have made you too cowardly to act? Well, the rest of us aren't. Perhaps when it is over we will know better which side you're on. You've been hiding in here alone too long to tell."

"I see," said Tai Ling soberly. "Murder or blackmail. Either I get killed by my enemies or by my friends."

"Take your choice! It is not a joking matter," answered Chewlee Singkee surlily.

He rose, inspected both doors, and blew out the lamp. Cheon seated himself on a pile of matting where he could watch the window. Tai Ling settled back in his seat, and with folded hands awaited day.

3

It broke over the horizon in a golden flow, drenching the dark corners with sunlight. An hour later when the Sabbatical morning was all song, the three men stepped to the door.

"Here." Chewlee Singkee handed a loaded Colt to Tai Ling.

"No. I have said I will not kill."

Chewlee Singkee put it back into his pocket. A truant sunbeam flicked over his yellow bloodless face as he stepped out. Tai Ling followed him in his old slouch Stetson, black sateen coat and patched grey trousers. They waited for Cheon to close the door and step up beside them. Then three abreast they walked down the alley.

Save for the distant clang of a switch engine simulating the sound of a church bell, the street into which they turned was silent and deserted. Only the blear-eyed bars and cantinas watched their approach.

Tai Ling, in the middle, walked slowly, head down as though lost in dreamy thought. Decorously, as if in respect for his venerable years, the others kept apace: Chewlee Singkee, hands carried in his sleeves, walking warily on the outside. Cheon, on the inside, staring into the doorways. At the corner they turned out into the road.

Two boys, jabbering in Cantonese, had just stepped out of the Casino Chino opposite. Not till they reached the gutter did they happen to look up. A swift shadow of apprehension passed over their faces.

"Now!" murmured Chewlee Singkee. Simultaneously two pink flashes brighter than the sunlight leapt out from his sleeve and Cheon's pocket. The two boys dropped like empty sacks. The street resounded to the roars of the two Colts.

The three Sunday morning strollers jumped over the fallen bodies to the wooden walk. They raced to the front of the Casino Chino and looked inside. The place was empty. Then they ran down the walk to the little side street flanking the railroad tracks.

In front of the Chinesca they slowed down, walked quietly in the door. There was only the barkeep wiping his mirror, back toward them.

"Don't turn around! Where's Chino Juan?" demanded Cheon.

The barkeep neither moved nor spoke. Paralyzed by what he saw in the bright polished glass, instant comprehension sucked the blood from his face. Cheon shot him in the back.

Chewlee Singkee, gun out, ran to the back room, flung open the door. "He's gone. . . . The Mercado!" Cheon nodded. Together they leapt for the front door, stepped outside.

Cheon got no farther than the gutter. Tai Ling saw him hit it head first, doubled up and with both hands clutching his middle, and sprawl over on his back. Then he heard the shot. Neatly Chewlee Singkee scooped up the gun from Cheon's outflung hand and ducked back inside.

Tai Ling by now was swamped by a flood of girls pouring from the cribs in back. Like a swarm of maddened monkeys they were screaming with fright and excitement, clawing at the bar for a look at the dying barkeep, and stampeding to the front door.

Outside, the cantinas were emptying a frantic crowd into the avenida. Among them, dodging from door to door, came those intent upon swift revenge. Chewlee Singkee turned back, in his ears a rising, shrill cry, a sound that once heard will never be forgotten—a human pack in full cry.

Clubbing his way through the girls, he grabbed Tai Ling and hustled him through the back court. "We've started it now! Here! Meet me at the Black Cat. The others are waiting." Pressing Cheon's old Colt into Tai Ling's hand, he went over the adobe wall and vanished.

Tai Ling gingerly passed the revolver from hand to hand, then dropped it into the open drain. With surprising agility for an old man, he swung over the wall and made it to the tracks. Thence, dodging circuitously between strings of boxcars, he reached The Lamp Awake.

He was sick, horrified, utterly aghast at what he had witnessed. It all seemed too fantastic to be possible. As he sat there at his familiar post of refuge from the world's passion and pain everything about him contributed to his disbelief: the brilliant Sunday morning sunshine flowing over the threshold, the cool musty interior of the cluttered shop, a canary chirping overhead. Even his mind, so long accustomed to functioning in the vertical dimension of philosophic abstraction, was unable to gear itself to record the swift violent details of the horizontal action that had taken place. No! It was all an illusion, spumed forth by that monstrous grey brain of the quarter itself.

But now a new phantasmagoria of sound smote his ears. The police sirens and fire alarms on both sides of the Line began to wail. Advancing rurales blew their shrill whistles. Trucks from the Garrison careened into the quarter with a troop of dirty, unbuttoned soldiers. Every cantina and casino was in an uproar. He could hear the shouts of half-naked girls pouring from Cockroach Court, the crowds rioting in front of the Chinesca and Casino Chino. And above all this, the steady intermittent crack of rifle and revolver as the two rival factions kept sniping at each other down the alleys and back courts.

Still Tai Ling was reluctant to admit what all this betokened. "Just like an American movie," he thought, fighting for calm.

A stray shot shattered the front window. Pieces of glass flew almost to his feet. "Amazingly real," he said aloud. Deliberately he retreated to his own back room.

While he was still trying to marshal his thoughts, Chino Juan's cronies continued to play the game of hide-and-seek which Tai Ling's friends had abandoned. From the carnicería of Chewlee Singkee to old Chan Foo's and the Nuevo Paris cafe they raced hunting Tai Ling. Someone thought of looking for him in his own shop.

Tai Ling heard their steps on the cobblestones of the alley. A new strange feeling attacked him: that of the hunter who had become the hunted. With the crash of the latch on the back door, Tai Ling ignominiously dived into the dark cellar. He was too late to avoid detection; one of his pursuers heard the trap door slam.

The pack rushed in, headed by Chino Juan himself. "Pry it open. I'll go down after him myself. Keep watch out those doors!"

Tai Ling was waiting, crouched back in the corner. He had found a case full of firecrackers. As the door above slowly swung open, Tai Ling lit the fuse. In the wan light he watched a hand with a revolver enter, a long arm. Then he tossed the threeinch crackers. There was a sharp report, a fusillade of explosions.

Chino Juan was jerked back. "He's got guns! Keep out, Jéfe!" The door slammed shut. Into it Chino Juan emptied his revolver. Tai Ling heard the lead ripping through the wood and imbedding itself in the soft earth before him. Tentatively he lit another firecracker.

The cellar was but a dirty hole scooped out of the soft adobe. Here long ago he had dispensed canned dreams to nightly visitors, and later hidden Mendoza's aliens. A few squares of rotted matting, a moldy blanket and the stub of a candle still littered the floor beside the case of unsold firecrackers which he had stored for safety from the intense dry heat of summer. But long disused and without supporting walls, the earth was caving in. Only a few square yards of flooring separated him from his would-be assassins; it was inconceivable they did not realize it.

Chino Juan had other plans. Raging above him, he shouted, "Grab those axes! Hack away now—this partition. Shove in the counter, anything heavy. Pile it up here so he

can't get out. We'll burn up the old rat in his own trap! . . .
Hurry, you fools! And keep watch out those doors!"

The pounding and splintering went on above Tai Ling.
The thin flooring creaked and groaned, the trap door began to
sag. Suddenly he heard a shattering crash; something side-
swiped him on the head; his whole being, with excruciating,
crying pain, focussed on his left leg. One of the timbers supporting the stairway had collapsed with the flimsy wall and
broken through the rotted flooring, crushing his leg.

Chino Juan did not see what had happened; there was
not even time to toss a match in the cluttered back room. The
rurales had reached The Lamp Awake.

Tai Ling, in a paroxysm of pain, heard shots, screams, a
scuffle, without knowing what they meant. A few minutes
later a rurale called down the small open gap. "Hóla! We
want you, Tai Ling! Are you coming peacefully?"

The old man could not distinguish his words. Weakly he
fumbled around, set off another firecracker. Then there was
darkness and silence and aloneness at last.

4

Some time later the yogi of Cockroach Court awoke. His
leg was numb, his head was clear. There was no sound overhead. He lit the candle stub on the wooden case at his side.
Save that he was in the cellar and pinioned by a timber across
his leg, he might have been sitting peacefully in his shop as
on any afternoon. But he felt oppressed by a curious sense of
guilt.

Little wonder! To be caught up so precipitately in a
maelstrom of worldly action. To let his physical self give way
to the sensory stimuli of fear, horror and repugnance. He was
shamed at the hold the gross physical world still had upon

him. Where did the root of his fault lie? Of just what was he guilty?

Chronologically and dispassionately he recalled the incidents of the past twenty hours without shirking the details. At least ten men had been killed. Their deaths had been horrible, none of them isolate, accidental, causeless. But who could say what had really killed them? They were anticlimactic effects whose causal genesis lay deeply imbedded in the victims' own karmic lives and in the society to which they subscribed.

Tai Ling imagined saying this to the jury of society. Well, they were facts. Barby, Tony Wong, three helpless aliens and Cheon's helper had died nominally accidental deaths; Chino Juan's two boys and barkeep had been murdered by Cheon and Chewlee Singkee, who doubtlessly had been murdered in turn with several more. The score was evened, the feud was over. He himself was innocent.

But no! Society demanded retribution. Fuming at the mouth it would rant of motives, accomplices, accessories to the crime. And it would clamor to hang him by the neck till he was dead too.

What? Did murder then consist, not only of the factual action, but of the evil cause, the motive, the contributory accomplices and accessories? Then society straightway indicted its own malignant functions—its international restrictions against the natural passage of free human beings across an imaginary line, its national and political chicanery, the economic slavery of the poor, its racial prejudices, its lawful greed, unrestricted disease, legalized immorality, and the hypocrisy of its churches.

Never! society would howl again. Stick to specific facts, not irrelevant generalities.

By the facts, the isolate circumstantial facts, Tai Ling was innocent. He had been ignorant of Barby's activities, had been forced to accompany Cheon and Chewlee Singkee, had not fired a gun.

But still the sense of guilt persisted in Tai Ling.

And he knew it would persist in society despite the factual proofs of his legal innocence. For society is not composed of members united for the express purpose of enforcing their ever changing laws of horizontal, social behavior. Society is also humanity. And humanity is the great forward life-thrust of millenniums which are dimly perceived only by man's vertical thinking in terms of spiritual abstractions. By these laws humanity knew itself guilty of every crime and every neglect suffered by one of its constituent parts.

This then was the one perpetual conflict of man: whether he give his allegiance to society or to humanity.

That Tai Ling gave his to humanity was alone enough for society to convict him. For society classes as outcasts not only the criminal and ignorant beneath comprehension of its laws, but also those who have advanced to the laws far above its own. To society the yogi is as far beyond its pale as the savage.

"I might just as well be hanged for a saint as a sinner," thought Tai Ling complacently.

But still he felt a sense of guilt more specifically than just as a part of humanity.

5

After a short nap he awoke again, not knowing whether it was day or night. His worries were gone. He felt peaceful and relaxed.

Barby had been killed, setting off a chain of events in the world outside. Two groups of rival thugs, thieves and line-runners had started a street war in a little town on the American-Mexican border. It might just as well have been any place in the world.

Mendoza was apprehended, then a group of wealthy American-Chinese backers. Mendoza implicated the corrupt Mexican officials; These Gentlemen, the American. Rich American ranchers controlled by powerful monopolies of land and water rights in Mexico became involved. Rival corporations and the public press in Mexico appealed to their government also. Old racial prejudices between American Yanquis and Mexican Greasers were stirred up. The Chinese began to clamor against the Yellow Peril restrictions of the Asiatic Exclusion Act. There was a split between Protestant America and Catholic Mexico. Notes between governments. An overt act. War was declared. Latin America south of the Rio Grande versus Anglo-America north to the Arctic Rim. Then Europe and Asia taking opposite sides. A shooting war, a racial war, a religious war, a world war—total war. Oh, the possibilities were unlimited! A street war of national thugs and thieves on a universal scale.

Tai Ling sighed. A perfect one-dimensional American movie.

But suppose Barby had not been killed. Suppose, instead, that he had prospered in his scheme. His little group of cronies grew on both sides of the Line to a large and powerful band. Defying authorities it soon became authority itself. State and big business, using Barby for its ends, became used themselves.

What of Mendoza and These Gentlemen? They had been assassinated as obstructing nuisances. For Barby had grown with power. He fed on power. A bastard half-breed, an ignorant cholo who had groveled in the gutters, he knew the secret of success—the promise of the wealth, ease, respect, authority and power denied all those as he had been denied. So now, a monomaniacal leader distorted by a chronic self-inferiority and the failure to hold as mistress a cheap cafe entertainer, he could not stop. Millions flocked to his call. Who could resist the hope of more power? Even nations applauded —until their own power was threatened.

And then over the five continents and seven seas spread another debacle. A new world-master, a modern Alexander, fell, dragging down with him another civilization. And once more humanity took up its weary march.

No; not until there were no conditions anywhere that would make possible another Barby, would the world ever be secure. Win or lose, thought Tai Ling, humanity was the perpetual loser. What had he to do with such a monstrous illusion? His only concern was with the eternally groping spirit of mankind, not its social behavior.

6

But unknown to him the world outside had reached another conclusion. The newspapers he had always ignored with a smile of contempt for their distortion of truth were screaming it in bold black headlines:

TONG WAR BREAKS OUT
Border Town Scene of Street Fighting

TWELVE DEAD IN CHINESE BORDER RIOT
Rival Factions Menace Lives of Citizens
Repercussions Feared in Los Angeles and San Francisco Chinatowns

News from the scene reliably reported that:
The initial killing of two men in front of the Casino Chino and one inside the Chinesca was instigated by the

leader of a secret Chinese tong engaged in transporting aliens across the International Line.

This was confirmed by "Chino Juan," owner of the two business houses, arrested for participation in the ensuing street war. Chewlee Singkee, a butcher, seriously wounded, confessed to the slaying, admitting he had been forced to accompany the mysterious leader.

This "mystery man" is believed to be one Tai Ling. Little is known about him. An aged Chinaman posing as a retired shopkeeper, he was a virtual recluse. It is known, however, that he controlled El Sol de Mayo, a notorious bar in the quarter, and had previously engaged in the sale of opium. Police are working on the theory that he burned it last night, together with one of his own henchmen, to avoid detection by officers.

The quarter is one of the most lawless districts along the whole American-Mexican Border. Largely populated by Chinese, it is a refuge for petty criminals of both countries as well. Immediate steps to clear up conditions once and for all are indicated. The resourceful detection of the Tong's activities by the Border Patrol, resulting in the slaying of two of the leader's accomplices, precipitated the outbreak.

Later dispatches revealed:

BORDER DISTRICT UNDER CONTROL
International Line Closed

Promptly following this morning's outbreak, a troop of soldiers were rushed out of the military garrison to assist local police. The quarter is now under martial law. All cantinas and casinos are closed. The streets are effectively patrolled. Members of both rival factions are being ruthlessly hunted.

The International Line has been closed until further notice as a precaution against fleeing tong slayers. The forces of the U. S. Immigration Authorities have been doubled and are standing by.

Governors of both neighboring states, American and Mexican, have expressed their willingness to meet for a discussion of joint precautions to be taken against any future outbreaks of kind.

Flash:
TONG LEADER TRAPPED
MYSTERY MAN BARRICADED IN OPIUM DEN

The aged Chinese "mystery man," Tai Ling, instigator of the current tong war, has been trapped. Armed with a machine gun, he is defying capture in his pseudo shop long used as an opium den. Little hope is held that he will be taken alive. He is known to be a desperate man.

Chugoku, a fish dealer on the gulf coast, and Mendoza, a line-runner, have been apprehended by authorities. Both were in Tai Ling's employ. They positively identify him as the sponsor of Tony Wong and the mestizo Darby killed Saturday night. The latter, they say, was his chief lieutenant and lived with him.

His shop is located near the junction of Callejon de los Chinos (Chinese Alley) and Plaza de las Cucarachas (Cockroach Court), in the heart of the quarter. It is entirely surrounded by heavily armed guards and under constant watch. The aged, wily Tai Ling has no chance to avoid paying for his many years of undetected crime and recent ruthless slayings.

Col. Maria Trinidad de Eluria y Policarpio, director of the assaulting party, was reached by telephone in his spacious suite at the Governor's Palace. He stated: "Tai Ling will be taken by the troops under my orders by noon tomorrow (Monday). National honor demands it. No mercy will be shown him. This arch criminal has plied too long his evil crimes of an outmoded century in this resplendent decade of glorious civilized achievement."

7

Tai Ling was roused again near morning by the weight of an intolerable sadness.

Spasms of pain contracted his whole leg. He was cramped, stiff and sore. Only by the greatest effort could he twist his body enough to relieve his swollen kidneys. He craved water, hot tea. Days seemed to have passed; he could not imagine what was happening outside that he should be so ignored even by his enemies. None of this mattered. He could overcome it. But the heavy sadness overwhelmed him.

A half inch of candle remained. In its flicker he tried to compose his thoughts. They no longer speculated on effects. They explored causes. Doggedly they trudged back from Barby's betrayal of him to the boy's greed and lust for power; to his obsession for Guadalupe and his bitterness and coward- ice as a child; to his bastard birth and drunken father.

Fully now Tai Ling exonerated society for all blame. And more surely than ever before he knew that the effects of the boy's actions were largely predetermined by causes far beyond his conception and birth. For just as all mankind is the for- ward life-thrust of milleniums of evolution, so is each man the individual summation of his own extended past—his own individual karma.

But being the slave of his past, he is also the master of his future. At the choice of his free will he can at once expiate all his previous misdoings and so escape from his bondage by achieving complete realization of his at-one-ment with the infinite whole.

Progress, then, must be made only by each man's efforts toward that perfection which lies within himself. Separate and alone, he must be his own leader, his own judge, his own priest and savior—a lamp unto himself. Society, civilizations crumbled away. Man remained. A vast humanity forever groping toward the truth of its existence. A conglomeration of divergent life-principles slowly but inexorably tending to a fusion.

And suddenly his own sense of guilt and his intolerable sadness were made plain. How could he have separated life from the principles which guided it; ignored the fusion that already existed if one could only see it?

He forgot himself entirely, and all the precepts which had engrossed him: the Ten Things to Forget, the Ten things to be Done, the Ten Things to be Avoided and the Ten Things Not to be Avoided, the Ten Errors and Thirteen Grievous Failures, the Fifteen Weaknesses and Twelve Indispensible Things, the Ten Signs of a Superior Man, the Eight Worldly Ambitions, the Three Fires of Desire, the Ten Grievous Mistakes and the Ten Necessary Things.

He only remembered the tragic, human loneliness of Barby and Guadalupe, the crying fear of the white woman who had come to him and had been frightened away, the pathetic hungering of Cheon and Chewlee Singkee for help, the haunting insecurity of Chino Juan. He thought of all the poor little fish and human cucarachas, the blind beggar at the corner, all the men betrayed, the mothers who had lost their sons, all the misery and sadness, ignorance and loneliness throughout the world.

The old man wept. He wept because he no longer felt separate; because he too was a part of all the misery that ever had existed.

Strangely enough the realization brought joyful relief. Tai Ling no longer had friends to forgive him, or enemies to forgive. Cockroach Court no longer was a geographical reality, not even a vast grey brain. All seemed to have been created for this one purpose of teaching him, in this brief incarnate existence, the falsity of his human ego. He could have fallen to his knees and thanked these circumstantial manifestations for the excessive trouble to which a mere old shopkeeper had put them.

Yet at the same time the yogi was more preternaturally aware than ever of that lurking consciousness which still separated him from Tai Ling's contrite mind and humbled heart. If he had only been more pure and courageous, if he had been granted but a bit more time! Perhaps even now . . .

The candle stub was almost gone. He pulled himself upright and gazed steadily at it. What was it made him feel and know what he felt, and offered him the path of freedom if he were only strong enough to climb?

8

Upstairs in early morning the time had come.

"The street blocked off, Corporal, the alley clear and the plaza also?"

"Yes, Captain."

"Select your men. Recall your sentries from the doors and come with me."

"Yes, Captain."

In shiny boots and buttons, and with a drawn revolver, the Captain peeked in the cluttered area of Tai Ling's back room. Covered by the Corporal's rifle, he stepped closer to the small crack underneath the crashed timber.

"You down there! Tai Ling! Are you coming out peacefully? We will give you exactly one minute," he shouted, without wondering how Tai Ling could get through the narrow crack.

There was no answer.

"Corporal, is the charge ready?"

"Yes, Captain."

"Light the fuse. Withdraw your men from the field of explosion."

He shouted again.

Still there was no sound, not even a signal.

The yogi of Cockroach Court was deep in meditation.

9

There had been the cellar and the tiny glow of the guttering candle, and that which came to know itself freed from the illusion of this space that cramped it and this time that flickered around it.

This knowledge, knowing itself composed so largely of physical sensations and stimuli, then knew itself a knowledge which detached itself from all this sensory phenomena; knew now neither the darkness nor the silence into which it retreated.

Yet again this knowledge began to know itself known.

It knew itself known as another complex compound of perceptions, cognitions, reasonings, memory, reflections.

And gradually the knower separated from the known with another curious certainty of detachment. In a boundless, timeless void, the knower observed the known give birth to the knowledge. The knowledge that included, impenetrated and connected the known and the knower. All in a vast and aching void.

But now the observer began to be observevd. The knower itself became another known. And no sooner did the new knower know the known, than it too became observed by a new observer.

So through the immeasurable, timeless void the observer pursued the observed, and becoming the observed was itself pursued by the observer.

And now suddenly in the unfathomable darkness, the quintessential silence of the illimitable void, there exploded light. An explosion of silent, radiant light. An explosion of transcendental bliss.

There was no longer separation of observer and observed. The knower, the known and the knowledge merged together and knew itself one.

There was but one consciousness that in radiant light, in transcendental bliss, became identical with the immeasurable and timeless void. As it was identical with every microcosmic reflection of the void in its illusionary boundaries of space and time and matter.

So that this consciousness being aware of its nature of the void, was also aware of its nature in the illusion of space, of time, of matter. It was aware again of the cellar cluttered with debris and falling earth, of the pale morning light flooding it, and of the figures bent over it.

10

"That him, Corporal?"

"Yes, Captain."

"Is he dead?"

For answer the Corporal spread his fingers, smote his palms together with a loud clap, then looked up and grinned.

EPILOGUE

THE MIDAFTERNOON train pulled in to the decrepit, empty station, and two girls got off the coach carrying old, scuffed suitcases.

"It's just around the corner, but we ought to take a taxi," said the older one, a sturdily built morena.

"Why throw away four bits?" asked the redhead. "Besides, this scrubby little burg never saw a taxi."

"It looks better, Gloria. Look, they have hung flags to welcome me. Oh, they love me! You will see!"

Still arguing, they reached the corner and turned into a hotel hung with Mexican and American flags. Waiting for the desk clerk, Gloria winked at the shabby bellboy.

"What you celebrating, pal? Another Fourth of July?"

"Naw. The De Anza Fiesta."

"De Anza? Sounds phoney. Who's she in society?"

"It's a he, sister. Somebody who discovered the desert or something."

"Oh, *history!* . . . Well grab these bags. It's your turn now."

Once in their room she plopped down in a chair and truculently shook out her loose copper hair. Guadalupe ran to the window. There it was, just as she remembered it—the dusty avenida, the high wire gates at the Line, the signs of the Owl and Las Quince Letras. A queer feeling ran through her; the years telescoped like an accordion.

"So this is the dump where that fat, two-timing bitch picked you up, is it?" asked Gloria. "And it might have been where that bastard blue-eyed doll on the train—" She broke off suddenly as Guadalupe dropped to her knees beside her, playfully running her fingers through the unruly coppery hair so unlike her own smooth wings of black.

"Gloria, you're jealous! That is why you are to me so cold, so cruel. It is to laugh, amiga mia! Do you not remember taking me away from Peña? Was it not you who found Trinidad cheating me so dreadfully? Years, years, comadre!"

She stopped to kiss the scowling face—that peculiar dead-white skin often borne by the redheaded; that transparent, blue-veined, white flesh which had stirred her so at their first meeting and which still held the power to fascinate her.

"Pues. Are we not one? Gloria, the American Skylark, and Guadalupe, la Alma de Mexico! Where have we not been? To Hollywood even!"

Gloria began to laugh. "Oh you're so goddamned impractical, Guadalupe! One scrubby Border joint after another along the whole damned Line, and three weeks in a Los Angeles movie house."

Guadalupe rose. "But we *will* go to Hollywood, to Mexico! We *will* be rich, famous, happy!" she exclaimed with vehemence. "My heart tells me it is so!"

A more instinctive shrewdness told her that Gloria was

now mollified and she could go. "I must stretch my legs after riding so long, while you take your bath and rest." She added casually, "Why don't you call the newspaper man and ask him to print something nice about us? And querida, find but a moment, a momentito, to mend my dress. The 'Cielo Sonora'—the blue one. Please!"

"What the hell am I, anyway? Your partner or the Soul of Mexico's secretary, press agent, flunky and personal maid? Seems to me I do all the work to make us a living while you strut around with all the airs of a famous dancer."

"So what would I do without you, Sweet'art?" Guadalupe blew her a kiss and closed the door.

Outside the hotel she spat daintily into the gutter. She was getting tired of their relationship. Gloria's jealous rages and mounting possessiveness had aroused again the old, familiar sense of imprisonment she always felt. She must be free. Her art demanded it.

Really, she reflected, Gloria had not done as much for her career as Peña. True, she mended their clothes, hoarded their money, made business engagements with American practicality. But her voice was too harsh for the soft Spanish songs she shrieked while Guadalupe changed costumes. Yes! At the first opportunity she would eliminate Gloria's singing entirely; use the castanets more; devote herself unstintedly to the art of Spain as Trinidad always had implored. Often lately Guadalupe had studied herself in the mirror. There was no denying it; she was becoming really a bit hippy. It would be necessary to forego her flounced dresses, to appear more often in short dance skirts. Then her firm, iodine-tinted thighs and round, muscular legs showed to advantage. Pues! As one matured in one's art, one must know exactly how to offer it.

She had reached the high arched gate over the Line. Walking through it with a now greatly pronounced meneo of her hips, Guadalupe debated whether she would look up Sal, Barby and Tai Ling or wait and graciously receive them after the evening's performance. Unconsciously she gave herself up to habit, following the route of her old evening walks: down the avenida to the bridge over the arroyo, up the street to the railroad tracks, across the quarter to the Callejon de los Chinos and Plaza de las Cucarachas.

It all came back to her—the grimy shops and shrieking cantinas, the crowds, the sounds, the smells. But somehow everything seemed strangely muted, shabby, stale. The streets were half deserted. The stores were almost empty. The very air was stagnant. Even the flags hung as if at half-mast for a life that had died during her absence.

The hut where the old blind beggar had modeled her clay mice had been swept away. Hurriedly she walked to Sal's old hotel. It was abandoned and boarded up. With a slight apprehension she approached El Sol de Mayo only to find it a lump of rain-washed adobe. Distinctly annoyed, she crossed the tracks to The Lamp Awake. The building was almost unrecognizable; it had been transformed into a garage, and was locked up for the fiesta.

Guadalupe, convinced now that she had been pining for years to see Sal, Barby and Tai Ling, felt cheated and aggrieved. Why is it that those we have abandoned are not always waiting unchanged to welcome us? She fled swiftly back through the quarter. Maldito! what was this? Most of the bars were gone, the few remaining converted into curio shops selling huaraches, tawdry serapes, picture postcards and Aztec Calendar Stone ash trays.

But at least Gonzales was waiting to welcome her in Las Quince Letras. He came running, hands outstretched, his fat cheeks and paunch shaking with excitement. "Guadalupe!

Our little morena! La Alma de Mexico! . . . You have come home again. *A la casa.* It is yours, Señorita. Command me!"

Guadalupe felt better. At last she was receiving her due as a local idol just returned from fresh triumphs abroad. But as Gonzales led her upstairs she saw that even Las Quince Letras had shrunk. The big gambling room had gone; half the length of the bar had been removed. Save for two men scrubbing the dance floor, the cantina was empty. The whole place seemed sad. Guadalupe sat listening to Gonzales' wail of ill-fortune.

"Yes, times have changed. Quien sabe? Who knows why? The Americans repealed prohibition. Poof! There went our cantinas. The government recalled all our gold; they forbade écarté, then blackjack and roulette. There went our casinos. Our rancheros are no longer raising cotton. Lemons, grapefruit —imagine growing trees on the desert! So now we have no more labradores—the Chinese, the Hindus, the Negroes, our Mexican peons. Nobody!"

He took a swig of beer.

"To say nothing of what that awful street war did to us! Shooting, stabbing, killing—soldiers, police, rurales. Blood of Christ, what a mess! And afterward they cleaned out the plaza of cucarachas. I saw them myself and did not believe it. Ugly, pock-marked, diseased and half-naked. From every back courtyard and crib they poured. Yes, poured! The officers had big clubs.

" 'You there! Name? Nationality? Let's see your license. Passport now. . . . O.K. Off you go!' And they would be loaded in the police wagon, given clothes and shipped out of town. Imagine! Right in broad daylight for everyone to see.

"But worse. Yes, there were worse than these. Old wretched hags with matted hair, open sores, half blind from living in the cellars. That's where they came from, these unspeakably foul wretches. Right up from the cellars of Chinese Alley where they had lived God knows how long. Right in broad daylight too, for even the crowds of Americans to see. No wonder we have such a bad name. . . . Forgive me, Señorita! Such disgraceful talk."

Gonzales emptied another bottle.

"But listen to that!" He pointed down over the railing to a raucous radio on the end of the bar. "Mother of God, child. Radios. Radios. Night and day, radios. Where are our orchestras, our guitars, our singers? In those cursed boxes! . . . I am forced to advertise in them myself. Ay de mo. What has happened to the whole world, the good old times? It is as if everybody has changed his mind and the world no longer looks the same." He wept into his beer.

But there was this Fiesta. It would bring back memories and business. "No?" he smiled, rubbing his hands together. "Our Guadalupe, fresh from her triumph in Hollywood, is here to dance for us again. Yes! And after her appearance I, her discoverer, her old patrón, am giving a fiesta dinner for her. Fresh quail, old wine, all the important people. Santíssima! What a feast! Look, they are hanging the flags now."

"That old Chino, Tai Ling, and Barby," interposed Guadalupe at last. "Señor Gonzales, you—"

"Yes, terrible. Both killed. The old man put up a fight, it is true. Line-runners, opium peddlers, God knows what crimes they committed. All in that little shop. No one suspected. No one! How lucky you were, child, to escape their clutches. Your art, that is what saved you. Nothing can stand in its way. I knew it the moment I saw you—from this very spot. And now you have come back at the height of your success to bring pleasure and honor to an old man. You will tell everyone of the dinner he is giving you, no?"

Guadalupe trudged back to her hotel in the growing dusk.

What had happened to this world she had known? It bore no resemblance to the one she remembered.

The glittering signs of the gaudy cabarets and the life which flooded them, a Strauss waltz, Tai Ling's gentle smile, and Barby's hand gripping her knee, the fears and hopes that had made it all alive and joyous and poignantly sad—all of it was gone. Unreal, evanescent and insubstantial it had passed without a trace.

Perhaps, as Tai Ling had once said, it had not even existed: an illusion in her own mind that was bound to pass.

She had reached another end; also a new beginning.

2

That evening the De Anza Fiesta was formally opened with a radio address from the Gobernador. In one hour and ten minutes he was able to state conclusively that the northern Border district had been purged at last of all undesirable elements, and was now entering a new era of substantial growth and permanent prosperity long ago foretold by the intrepid Conquistadores.

With a blast of bugles the torchlight parade ushered it in. First came the Capitan himself, Juan Bautista de Anza, clad in new tin armor, astraddle a spavined white mare. Next a company of soldados carrying gilded wooden spears in one hand and furtively squashing out cigarette butts with the other. Then a brass band and the local fire brigade. Behind followed contingents from the American side: the Chamber of Commerce and the Rotary Club. On a hay wagon emblazoned with a banner marked "Pageant of Progress" stood the Queen of Cotton giving her crown to the Queen of Citrus Fruits. Behind these rode Guadalupe and Gloria with civic notables in a line of automobiles. The gates swung open to admit a straggling crowd; for visiting Americans the International Line would stay open till midnight.

At eight o'clock, in the Teatro Xochimilco, la artista Guadalupe, la Alma de Mexico, appeared in her repertoire of dances. Some of these were her own creations and, as she confided to the audience, named from the color of her specially designed gowns—Cielo Sonora (now neatly mended), La Luz Colorado and La Flor de Mezcal. Que buena! What a consummate artist! She was accompanied by the noted American Skylark.

Shortly before ten o'clock, the Gobernador, the Mayor, Captain Juan Bautista de Anza, las artistas, and all the officials from both sides of the Line were entertained at dinner in the renowned and historic old inn of Las Quince Letras. As speaker after speaker affirmed, it was a gorgeous affair. Never had there been such a gala occasion.

Guadalupe, near the head of the table, sat as if engrossed in the speeches. Across from her sat a distinguished-looking woman in a black lace mantilla through which gleamed palely a band of snow-white hair arching above each temple. Guadalupe could hardly keep her eyes off her; and a slight nervous tremble of her knees assured her that the woman was acutely conscious of her own presence.

"Who is she—the lady across from us?" she whispered to the man on her left.

"Señorita Burrell. Tourist Agent for the Inter-American Railway. Charming. You must meet her," he whispered back.

"Not now!" She was afraid that Gloria might overhear, and hastily lowered her gaze. The woman was looking at them.

"What the hell you whispering about—her?" muttered Gloria suspiciously behind a napkin.

Guadalupe affected a giggle. "That old white-haired

woman?" She kept her gaze lowered. But the eyes across from her she felt boring through her forehead, demanding, questioning, imploring. Uneasily she twisted in her chair. How much longer could she resist them?

The instant came when Gloria flung about in her seat to clap for the finished speaker. Guadalupe flicked up her glance. Miss Burrell's brown, sharp and discerning eyes were waiting for the rendezvous. It was short but complete. They tacitly recognized each other, accepted conditions, made and signed a pact of perfect understanding.

Now the speaker was sitting down. Gloria turned back with a truculent stare. Guadalupe affectionately put an arm about her shoulder and squeezed. Out of the corner of her eye she glimpsed Miss Burrell's slight nod of approval.

Now they kept waiting for a moment free of Gloria's jealous vigilance. A flood of champagne kept tearing couples loose from the horseshoe table; and to the blare of an orchestra this jetsam and flotsam eddied slowly about on Gonzales' scrubbed floor. With a Mexican's penchant for white skin, Captain De Anza carried away Gloria for a fox trot. Not to be outdone, two portly Chamber of Commerce guests ambled up hastily for the dark-skinned Spanish Señorita.

"Gentlemen, please! The Señorita has danced professionally all evening!" broke in Miss Burrell smoothly. "Won't you please excuse her? Besides, how could she choose between you? . . . Here. The Señorita and I will sit this one out."

Guadalupe hastily moved over beside her. Hidden from the glaring spotlights they talked quickly to the point. But with a cautious politeness that kept a door open for unembarrassed escape.

"Just call me Heloise," said Miss Burrell, immediately using the familiar "tu" and handing Guadalupe a card. "You know I'm on the lookout for entertainers for all the tourist hotels along our route to Mexico. You are so beautiful, so talented! It's a pity you can't come down with us."

"I am so busy. I work so very hard," said Guadalupe modestly. "But Mexico! Oh I would love so much Mexico. I have dreamed of the city, the cathedrals, the bullfights, no?"

"Your cultural background, dear. You belong to it," said Heloise decisively. "I could place you, I'm sure. Your dancing would be appreciated. But," she hesitated, then made the plunge, "I'm not so sure of your friend. Such a charming, sweet girl! But in Mexico—as you say, a land of cathedrals, of bullfights, of old traditions—her voice . . . no, I doubt it."

No, thought Guadalupe, she wasn't old at all. That premature streak of white hair only gave to her lush figure a distinctive mark of charm and dignity. Guadalupe imagined her with her hair down. The streak of white like a ray of moonlight falling across the pillow. And such perfect Spanish! Murmuring with its intimate "thou" in the darkness, while outside from the shadow of the cathedral sounded the accompaniment of a guitar. . . . Guadalupe's head began to spin. Impulsively she clutched Heloise's hands. But she controlled her voice.

"Pues. It is as you say. I impose on her so, making her sing these Spanish songs for which she has no voice or feeling. Perhaps it is my duty to let her stay in her own country where she too will be appreciated more. But, amiga mia, I have dreaded being alone and friendless, as I always am."

Heloise returned the pressure of her fingers. "Not so alone," she whispered quickly. "You will have one friend at least!"

The dance was coming to an end. Gloria in the middle of the floor was wriggling out of her partner's demanding clasp, her roving glance trying to locate Guadalupe.

Heloise stood up. She was a discreet, capable woman.

"Well, so it is! I am most happy. Tomorrow come see me, any time; you have my address. We will talk about it undisturbed, no?"

"When I go for my walk. Yes!"

Miss Burrell tactfully retreated into the shadows and thence into the crowd as Gloria came up.

It was midnight; the fiesta dinner dance was over; the Line would soon close to the few straggling celebrants. Gloria and Guadalupe, refusing escort, walked back to their hotel.

Gloria was grumbling. "Did you see that fool trying to date me up? He wanted to take me home, all two blocks, in a hired limousine. I don't know which is worse, a drunken Mexican Army 'Heneral' or a slap-happy Chamber of Commerce President spending a night away from his wife. These men! These damned two-bit fiestas! I'm so sick of guitars and fandangos I could belch!"

Guadalupe laughed. "A beautiful fiesta! They love me!"

Gloria looked at her curiously in the darkness; her soft voice, like her body, was tempered hard as steel.

"You like everything because you use everything!"

Guadalupe smiled. "Life is simple," she said sagely, "when you know exactly what you want."

They walked on in silence.

Acknowledgement:

The yogic precepts quoted and paraphrased throughout this book were compiled in the middle of the twelfth century by the Great *Guru* Gampopa, founder of the Tibetan Buddhist Monastery of Ts'ur-lka. They were translated in 1919 by the Lāma Kazi Dawa-Samdup, Lecturer in Tibetan to the University of Calcutta; edited and annotated by the scholarly W. Y. Evans-Wentz, his yogic disciple; and published in 1935 by the Oxford University Press, London. The collaborative work of these devout scholars, which has made available to the Western world these wisdom teachings of the East, is herewith gratefully acknowledged.—*F.W.*